DEATH OF A FLY

DEATH OF A FLY
A NOVEL
Russell Dobrzynski

DEATH OF A FLY

By Russell Dobrzynski

Published by Montana Dream Publishing,
Helena, Montana
© 2025 by Russell Dobrzynski

Cover Art: *Death of a Fly,* Michelle Ogle © 2025
Back Cover: *Sutton's House,* Photo Courtesy of Carroll Jenkins

Design: Wyatt Design, Helena, Montana

Paperback ISBN: 979-8-9998761-0-2
eBook ISBN: 979-8-9998761-1-9

10 9 8 7 6 5 4 3 2 1

MONTANA DREAM PUBLISHING
Helena, Montana

ACKNOWLEDGEMENTS

Julianne Burkhardt, for editing and legal feedback, which helped make this story more believable. Michelle Ogle, for her amazing gift as an artist, and for being OCD. I couldn't imagine a better cover for this story. Geoffrey Wyatt, for all the technical support and most of all, for being a friend.

A special thanks to the group of old guys who hang out at the Blackfoot River Brewing Company. Thanks for welcoming me into the group and for listening to my stories over the years. I hope you all buy this book so I can pay my tab.

To Ginny, one of the toughest women I know—a loving
mother who never gave up, not on her husband,
her family, and not on me.

PROLOGUE

In the mid-2000s, the Missouri River was considered one of fly-fishing's best-kept secrets, with Craig, Montana, becoming the epicenter of the fly-fishing world. Located roughly halfway between Great Falls, the third largest city in Montana at that time, and Helena, the capital of Montana, it was a 40-minute drive from any major town, making amenities a challenge for travelers. Bozeman, Missoula, and Kalispell were much more bougie destinations for folks who may have watched the movie "A River Runs Through It" and wanted the quintessential fly-fishing experience without having to give up the comfort of big city food, lodging, and entertainment. However, for the serious angler, there wasn't a river in the Lower Forty-Eight that boasted the quality or the number of fish as in the Missouri. The moniker of "The Mighty Mo" wasn't just indicative of the actual size of the river but also the fish it held.

The headwaters of the Mighty Mo form near Three Forks, Montana, where the Madison, Gallatin, and Jefferson Rivers converge. From there, it travels north through a series of dams creating large reservoirs, starting with Toston, then Canyon Ferry, Hauser, and Holter. Below Holter Dam, the water is pristine and remains cool throughout the summer, and flows are relatively consistent, making it a perfect habitat for trout that were introduced to the system in the late 1880s.

Before the dams and well before Montana became a state in 1889, Westslope cutthroats were the native fish in the Upper Missouri, along with Rocky Mountain whitefish, mountain suckers, sculpins, and even grayling. It was these fish that Lewis and Clark would have survived on as they explored the headwaters of the Missouri River in the early 1800s. With the introduction of brown trout and rainbows, the native cutties were outcompeted, and although a few might get washed into the mainstem of the river from tributaries where re-introduction efforts have been somewhat successful, catching a true cutthroat in the Missouri is now highly unlikely.

Beginning at Holter Dam, the river flows approximately 35 miles along the Big Belt Mountains to the East, cutting through the Adel Mountain Range, creating magnificent canyons with high cliff walls stretching up hundreds of feet above the riverbed before dumping out into the high plains and on to the small ranching town of Cascade. It is this stretch that the Missouri is considered a Blue-Ribbon fly-fishing destination with an extraordinary population of wild trout and exceptional access for anglers.

The population of Craig in 2007, named after its founder, Warren Craig, who settled there in 1886, was less than 45 people. Two fly shops were operating at that time in Craig, and on any given day in June or July, there were more drift boats in town than permanent residents. Guides and outfitters considerably outnumbered the locals during the season, which caused a great deal of resentment as the seasonal travelers grappled with the locals for fishing holes, parking spots, and bar stools.

Nobody knows exactly where the phrase, "A quaint little drinking town with a big fishing problem…" came to be, but Craig had two watering holes: one being the Craig Bar and the other, Izaak's. The Craig Bar was the local dive bar, whereas Izaak's was the only place to get food service in town, offering an upscale menu for clients of the fishing industry and a bar menu for the guides who weren't fortunate enough to have a wealthy angler picking up their tab. Both have become iconic landmarks for the guide community and their clients, and I'm guessing, if you've fished the Missouri, you have spent some time in each place.

At one time, Wolf Creek, which is seven miles south of Craig, competed for the reputation of being the fly-fishing mecca. Similar in size, Wolf Creek also had two bars, two churches, and a school. However, with two shops putting down roots in Craig and only one in Wolf Creek, most of the traffic to the river flowed through Craig. In hindsight, the Wolf Creek residents are now surely breathing a gigantic sigh of relief.

The Dearborn River is a tributary of the Missouri with its confluence roughly 12 miles downstream of the Holter Dam. A freestone, meaning it's a free-flowing river not regulated by dams and fed predominantly from snowpack and spring storms, it originates high up in the Scapegoat Mountains and cuts through canyons as it heads southeast for 70 miles before dumping into the Missouri. Access to the Dearborn is limited as most of the river is bordered by ranches and private lands except for a few bridge access sites and a trailhead that eventually runs along the river in the Lewis and Clark National Forest and Bob Marshal Wilderness area. A short window when high water from spring run-off offers some access to the lower portion of the river by way of rafting. Otherwise, hiking in and staying below the normal high-water mark is an angler's only way to fish this amazing stream, which is why it has become a favorite for locals wanting to get away from the burgeoning crowds.

Death of a Fly is told in these small communities in Central Montana. Although landmarks like the High Bridge on the Dearborn and even Izaak's Restaurant in

Craig are actual places, and some of the characters of the book may reflect the personalities of some of the community members, it should be noted that this is purely a fictional story. Yes, some of the anecdotes throughout the book are actual events that have happened; however, they are only stories used to illustrate points that weave together a fictional tapestry and should not be used for historical reference or assumptions about any real-life individuals or events.

One note of concern for the younger readers should be addressed: the language and subject matter illustrated in the book are consistent with how guides and outfitters actually speak. No punches were pulled with the attempt at offering a less offensive or more "PG" version of real life.

As for the fly shops in Craig depicted in the story, they are also fictional places created by the author. A reader familiar with Craig in 2007 might try to extrapolate some assumptions from the descriptions of the shops, but those assumptions would be unfounded and have no factual basis. A quick Google search for Missouri River Angler will bring you to Wolf Creek Angler in Wolf Creek, MT, which did not exist in 2007, and High Banks Fly Shop does not exist.

Now that we have eliminated the curiosity of trying to connect any dots that could be interpreted as disparaging to any one individual or business, I would encourage the reader to strap in, buckle up, and enjoy the ride.

THE DREAM

"Come on, Chase, load up!" That's all it took for the chocolate lab, if he thought he was going somewhere cool, like fishing or hunting.

He launched himself into the back door of the red Jeep Cherokee, took one bounce off the rear bench seat, flew over the center console between the bucket front seats, and found his spot in the shotgun position. At some point, Rose gave up trying to keep him in the back seat because he'd never even acknowledge her if she told him to get back. If Rose ever had a friend join her, they fought over that front seat, and although Chase never won, he always thought he would.

The Jeep was still in good shape--definitely showing its 190,000 miles, most of them highway miles from the many road trips over the years, but miles, nonetheless. Rose Marie Davidson loved her Jeep. It was built before Jeep decided to go super SUV with their wagons sporting leather and power everything and a price tag well beyond the means of a humble fishing guide. At that time, Jeeps were built for the real outdoorsy folk. They weren't fancy. They were tough. Rose liked to think they were a lot like her.

Her toughness was deceptive, however, hidden beneath sun-bleached locks of wavy hair that cascaded along her shoulders, down to the middle of her back, that she spent less time on than most of the guys she had dated spent on theirs. Her green eyes were forgiving, yet stern when challenged. Her well-defined arms draped from shoulders meant for carrying the weight of years of hard work and struggle, but she would never let her posture expose any of the pain she had endured over her first 26 years on this earth.

A Midwest girl, Rose was a transplant to the West. Montana was the world she was built for. She was the poster girl for every cowboy pin-up, either bathing in a cattle trough with her horse next to her or skinny dipping in a mountain stream, that every crusty ranch hand fantasized about randomly running into on the range.

Working in an industry epitomized by quick-drying Patagonia chinos and vented button-up shirts, Rose sported Carhart dungarees that hung perfectly on her hips and a form-fitting tee-shirt with an owl asking, "How many licks?" finished with Chacos that allowed the sun to burn tan lines on her feet that lasted longer than the sandals themselves.

Grabbing the "oh Jeezus handle," Rose lifts her 5-foot 10-inch, perfectly proportioned frame into the driver's seat, glances across to the chocolate lab, who was now staring straight ahead so as not to make eye contact, and shakes her head.

"Meat head," she declares as she slides the key into the ignition and the Jeep rumbles into action.

As they rolled on down the road, Rose couldn't help but think about the latest email exchanges from the ex, making her driving a little more erratic. She wasn't the one to end it and certainly didn't want it to go this way—the visceral attacks and the anger—but she understood that is what happens when intimate relationships end. Each party wants to protect themselves from the sting of blame, so they find every fault and every mistake to pile up against their partner to prove it was them and not me.

So, on this day, Rose decided to leave the world behind for a couple of hours and lose herself in a place she'd come to know well these last couple of months.

With her foot planted firmly on the floorboards of the Jeep, she and Chase make exceptional time heading up Highway 434 until crossing Highway 200, turning into County Road 435, where the paved stretch of road ends and changes to loose gravel.

This part of Montana isn't what one normally sees or expects when watching the movies that made places like the Blackfoot River on the west side of the Divide famous. The Eastern Slope is much different. Considered semi-arid grasslands by some and semi-arid desert by others, (often depending upon the time of year one is observing,) the slope provides for miles of rolling hills that stay green into July on average years, then browning in contrast with the evergreen lodgepoles as grass butts right up to the tree line of the foothills on the Rocky Mountain Front.

County Road 435 winds through coulees and breaks but stays relatively flat until it drops off the table, so to speak, into the canyon of the Dearborn River. With the drastic change in topography, you know you are getting close, and just a few hundred yards further brings the man-made landmark of the red "High-Bridge" and the parking area on the other side.

Rose opens the door, and Chase jumps out in a ball of fury to get a leg up on the new scents this place has to offer. It only takes a few seconds for him to find the markings of another dog, and like the pro he is, a leg is raised, and by all accounts, this parking area now belongs to him. By the time Rose puts her fly-rod together, he's staked claim on the fence, the bridge, a rock next to the road, and anything else that may have some lingering scent of another would-be canine homesteader.

Rose asks herself, "A dog does run out of pee at some point, don't they?"

It was early September, and the water in the Dearborn was running low. Air temperatures had been in the high nineties much of the summer, but were dropping to less damaging temperatures as the nights grew longer and cooler. She had been working at the High Banks Fly Shop earlier that day and by the time they ran their shuttles on the Missouri River and actually got to the Dearborn, the sun was already on its downward path and although there were still a few hours of daylight, the canyon would soon be supplying the welcoming shadows that would help to bring nervous trout up.

Rose took a job at High Banks earlier that Spring when things went south with her live-in boyfriend, Lyndsey Carter. She aspired to pursue guiding ever since the first trout she caught on a fly. Lyndsey was more into building his career and buying into stability. He bought a house in Townsend since he felt it was more economically prudent. It was right before the housing crisis, and the cost of a home in Helena was quickly becoming unattainable to the average wage earner. However, Townsend was forty minutes south of Helena and a good hour-twenty from the town of Craig, which in 2007 was quickly becoming the epicenter of the fly-fishing world. He planned to go at it alone regardless of what she thought, so with his purchase of the house, she bought a 1967, 15-foot Shasta camper and moved it up to the river.

Lyndsey didn't even tell Rose he was going to purchase the house in Townsend, and that hurt. She remembered vividly the conversation they had when he told her of the purchase, and she re-lives that conversation in her head over and over—how it hurt—how she felt betrayed. He knew she wanted to become a guide. He knew how important this dream was for her, and instead of trying to find a place where they could both get what they needed, he was only thinking of himself. The resentment didn't take long to burn down any foundation they had built in their relationship, and now they were engaging in a battle of wills over who could gaslight the other more.

Rose had talked to the owner of the fly shop into letting her park the camper behind the shop and plug into one of the power outlets. In return, she would work at the shop running shuttles and selling flies for minimum wage and hopefully, fill her off days with guiding. She realized quickly that boys in this industry didn't play well with girls, especially not attractive girls like Rose. They resented her. They only saw her for her looks and thought the only reason other outfitters and shops hired her was for eye-candy. It was a rarity that anyone would actually give her any credit for knowing how to fish.

To be fair, Rose was pretty green to fly-fishing. The first trout she ever caught on a fly was with a co-worker at Alternative Youth Adventures, only two years before taking on this new career path. She was working at AYA, a back-country rehab program for troubled youth, for about a year when she was asked to fill a spot in a drift boat. Mike Garrett was just getting into guiding and needed a guinea pig, so he took Rose and another co-worker out to the river for some R&D.

Although Rose had never fly-fished for trout, she had grown up in a family of outdoors people in Minnesota and lived for fishing and hunting. She was the quintessential 'Tom boy,' and did everything she could to make her dad proud. At three years old, she caught her first crappie on a lake called Miller Dam in western Wisconsin while visiting their grandparents. She could remember that fish and how excited she was. Screaming while reeling in her first fish, her dad shushed her, not to bring too much attention to them and their lucky fishing hole. She loved being on the water with her dad more than anything—so much so that he could rarely ever get out with other friends or family members without her. When he tried to leave her behind, she would throw a fit until he would eventually cave, and Rose would get her way.

When Rose was nine, the relationship with her dad changed drastically. She remembered waking up one morning to her neighbor fixing them breakfast.

"Where's mom and dad?" She asked Donna, the neighbor and one of her family's closest friends.

"Your dad is in the hospital," Donna replied. "I'm here to help you guys get to school."

"What?" She asked. "Why!?"

"They think he had a stroke," Donna explained.

"What the hell is a stroke?"

As Donna tried to explain, a heavy fog overtook Rose's thoughts. She didn't really listen as she was scared and confused and knew, somehow, life was going to be different from that day forward, and it was. All the things her dad was teaching her, everything she was becoming as that outdoorsy little girl, was now going to have to be learned on her own, which set the path for her life as an independent child and, to some degree, a loner.

That next summer, Rose was digging through her dad's fishing gear and came across his Fenwick fly-rod. Before the stroke, he had delved into fly-fishing a little with some of the other men in the neighborhood. They would all meet at a public access site on White Sand Lake and wade out into the reeds and bull rushes and cast for bass and sunfish. Rose never saw them catch anything, but she was intrigued by the process. The casting was so much different than what she was used to, where she would reel in all her line and fling a bobber or a lure out into the water. Power and distance were gained through rearing back and flinging the weight of the lure as hard as she could. This casting she was witnessing was very different. These men were carrying 9 to 12 feet of line into their back-cast, letting it extend behind them, and then throwing the rod tip forward, letting more line shoot out as they whipped it. Then they would strip the line they had shot from the rod back, letting it fall to their feet and start all over again. When done correctly, it was elegant and graceful. There wasn't much grace in flinging a bobber.

As Rose picked up the fly-rod and assembled it, she remembered studying the men of the neighborhood casting at the lake. She remembered how some of the men seemed to be much better at it than others. In fact, it felt like some of them spent way more time untangling lines than they did fishing, and she never understood why they would want to subject themselves to that. But there was something about it that fascinated Rose, and now, with the rod in hand, she was going to give it a go.

She pulled out line from the auto-retrieve reel and was set to thread the line through the guides of the rod when she noticed the trigger on the reel and tripped it. The line shot back into the reel, and before she knew it, she found herself disassembling the reel to get the spring inside to re-engage. There is a reason they don't make those reels anymore, and she learned quickly that playing around with the reel and the trigger would lead to more time disassembling and reassembling than casting.

Rose didn't get too frustrated and was still intrigued, and once the line was threaded, she walked out into the yard. Making sure she had plenty of room to work, without anything behind her, she tried emulating the men from the neighborhood. She threw about 10 feet of line up behind her, but before the line could extend out, she threw the rod tip forward. With a crack, the leader snapped back and piled to the ground. It sounded cool anyway, and Rose thought that was the intended outcome until she noticed one very important thing: the leader kept getting shorter and shorter with every crack.

It wasn't long before Rose realized that probably wasn't the intended outcome, and she worked at not making the leader snap. She also realized, somewhat intuitively, that what probably mattered most was getting the line to lay out in an almost perfectly straight line and having it settle softly to the ground, which would eventually become the water after she practiced a bit. That was a little harder than she first thought, but she kept working at it and working at it. She became obsessed and didn't realize what she was doing to her hand until it was too late.

Rose worked at laying that fly-line down perfectly all day long and even started picking out the bases of trees that she would have to try to hit without catching the line in the canopies, which meant compressing the loop she was throwing and shooting line into small spaces. In the end, she developed the ability to cast an incredibly tight loop, but also developed a blister on her hand the size of a silver dollar.

Rose worked on her casting all summer long. She rarely fished with the rod but loved casting. The few times she brought the rod to the lake, she never caught anything because she lacked the knowledge of the essential gear and flies needed, but she loved casting, much like target practicing with her BB gun or her recurve bow. It was a challenge for her, and it was fun.

When she did fish, she would mostly revert to her spinning gear and bait. Sometimes she and her brother would even use frogs and fish for bass. Catching frogs along the shore, they would put the amphibious critters in a bucket and wade out into the reeds and cast them into pockets where large-mouth bass would be cruising around hunting for a big meal. The explosions were epic.

When they fished for sunnies and bluegills, they would use worms or pieces of worms. Rose wasn't like other girls. She had no problem with breaking pieces of nightcrawlers apart and threading them onto a hook. To her, it was just part of the process. She just wanted to catch more fish than her brother and would do anything to make that happen.

One day after catching a few bluegills, Rose dug through a Styrofoam carton of black dirt and strips of newspapers to find another crawler and realized she was out. The dirt in the central part of Minnesota, where she grew up, was very sandy, which is not conducive to raising crawlers. The crawlers she and her brother used came from one of two places. One place was the bait shop a couple of miles away; the other was hunting for them in Wisconsin while visiting their grandparents, where the dirt was black and rich and perfect. Either way, she was out, and she wasn't going to get any more crawlers anytime soon.

Sitting on the shore, Rose thought for a while about how she was going to catch more bluegills. She knew her brother was probably catching fish. She had hooks and bobbers but no bait.

An epiphany came to her as she sat there looking

into the grass for either a grasshopper or a bug to thread onto her hook. If she took a piece of grass and wrapped it around the hook to make it look like a grasshopper, maybe she could trick those panfish into biting. It was a long shot, but what other choice did she have?

Rose spent the better part of an hour trying to figure out how to tie a blade of long grass onto the shank of the hook and make it look like food to a bluegill. When she was finished, she looked at the presentation with a good deal of skepticism but also a fair bit of pride.

"This might actually work," she thought as she shrugged her shoulders. "Only one way to find out…"

Rose cast the hopper imitation out into the lake. She was fishing in a little bay off White Sand they had named Turtle Bay. In the springtime, bluegills would spawn there and were easy to find. The bobber plunked into the bay with a splash, and the grass-tied imitation floated just a couple of feet away. In a few seconds, a bluegill slowly came to the surface and, curiously, much to Rose's amazement, sucked it down.

Rose set the hook and came tight on this bluegill and reeled it in. The success of tricking that fish was exciting, gratifying, and unbelievable, and although it was the only fish that ate her first fly she ever tied, it was something she would put in her metaphoric tackle box for later in life. She didn't know it yet, but she had done something she would auspiciously draw from in the future.

It was 14 years later that Mike asked Rose to take a spot in his drift boat. Rose had never fly-fished for trout, and since that summer of learning to cast, had only picked up a fly-rod a few times. She had graduated with a degree in Sociology from the University of Minnesota, Mankato, and then went on to graduate school at the University of Wisconsin, Milwaukee. While in grad school, she was introduced to Alternative Youth Adventures through the stepdad of one of the employees at AYA. That employee was Mike Garrett, who was now poised to profoundly change her life.

Mike had planned a short trip for them. Things at AYA had become incredibly stressful, and Mike had figured it would be good to get Rose away from the job for a few hours. She was a Team Leader and was responsible for 10 teenagers and 4 staff members at all times, while they lived and worked on their rehabilitation efforts in the back country of Montana. She was being called out as support for her backcountry staff numerous times a week to drop the hammer on what had become an incredibly difficult group. When groups were spinning out or individuals were having a hard time following rules, Rose had to send a message that those behaviors were not going to be tolerated. Sometimes, oftentimes, that message was harsh and not only taxing for the participants but was also grueling for the Team Leader.

All kids at AYA were court-ordered to be there. Most had some kind of chemical dependency issues, as well as various other problems like anger management and anxiety issues. Some of the kids were just bored and did stupid things like stealing cars and running them into the ground just for kicks. They were given a choice by the courts to either spend a year in juvenile detention or to spend 5 months at AYA—60 days of that in the back country doing intensive wilderness therapy.

The job was stressful and didn't pay much, but it was something that Rose could pad her resume with, and it was a great opportunity for personal and professional growth. The burnout was high, however, and she was just about to the end of her wick. Mike had sensed that.

The day was a cool, cloudy day in April. The three-some hit the Missouri River at around noon. The water was still in the upper thirties, so it took trout a little while to wake up and become active. There was no need to get out early. Mike rowed first while Rose fished out of the back of the boat, and Mike's good friend Dave fished out of the front. Dave hadn't fly-fished much either, and Mike was focused on getting him into fish first. Rose was ok with that as she was more the type to lie back in the weeds and try to figure things out for herself without having the spotlight on her. Plus, she just took a lot of pride in self-learning.

At one point, Mike looked back at Rose and said, "Wow, you've done this before."

"It's been a long time, but I've thrown a fly-rod a time or two," Rose admitted.

Rose was amazed by the Missouri River. Her only experience with it was as it meandered through the Midwest. It was big and brown when it reached the Mississippi, but here it was very different and totally out of the realm of what she had expected. In fact, when Mike asked her to go fly-fishing on what is often referred to as the Mighty Mo, she couldn't believe there would actually be trout living there. However, the water was pristine, clean, and cold, and although big, it was a gorgeous trout stream and completely took her by surprise.

An hour into the trip, they had yet to see a fish, let alone have one take one of their flies. Dave took to the oars, and Mike jumped into the pole position. Rose was still working on her casting out of the back of the boat. Mike wanted to try chucking a streamer rig with a little more speed and precision than what Dave or Rose could accomplish to see if he could put something in the net, assuring that what they were doing was going to produce.

Rose took note of what Mike was doing, throwing the streamer right up into the rocks along the bank as they floated along and stripping the fly quickly away from the structure, imitating a sculpin or a crayfish being chased by a toothy brown trout. He was hitting pockets the size of a coffee can as seams dumped past rocks, creating eddies where trout could take refuge from the main current of the river. He didn't waste time. The casting was a kind of rapid fire, and the stripping in of line, erratic but also beautiful, with a kind of frantic precision. Rose emulated Mike's casting and stripping.

It wasn't long before a yellowish, brown streak came rushing out from one of those eddies towards Mike's streamer. Rose caught a glimpse of the brown trout out of the corner of her eye.

"OH!! There he was!" Mike yelled with excitement. "Damnit! He didn't eat it."

Rose chucked her streamer to the spot where Mike's fly had just come from and started stripping.

"Got him!" She yelled.

Somehow, the excitement of hooking that brown didn't send Rose into a panic. Everything slowed down. As she lifted her rod tip and grabbed ahold of the line in her trigger finger of her casting hand while stripping line in with her left, she was able to get tight to the trout and kept tight on it; letting the trout run when it wanted and stripping in when it allowed her and in a couple minutes, she had the 20-inch brown next to the boat. Mike netted it. Her first trout on a fly was crazy, invigorating, and like nothing Rose had ever experienced.

They only landed two fish that day. Rose caught both,

and after the second one, Mike said, "Ok, you're done. Until someone else catches a fish, you are done."

"So, what am I going to do?" She asked.

"You're going to row the boat."

"What?" She asked with nervous excitement. "I get to row?!"

"No," Mike explained. "You have to row."

Rose finished off the day rowing under Mike's tutelage. She couldn't decide what was more fun, rowing or fishing. It was all so amazing. She would watch the bank and try as hard as she could to position the boat in a manner that both Dave and Mike could fish the "fishy" water. Rowing her two anglers into the optimal position to catch fish was a challenge, and by the time they reached the boat ramp in Craig, she knew how she wanted to spend the rest of her life.

But her dream was not Lyndsey's dream, and in fact, they couldn't have been any more misaligned. Rose wanted to explore. She wanted to chase the unknown. She wanted to share that with other people, while Lyndsey wanted the comfort of a stable job and a concrete foundation under a roof that was rock solid. He couldn't understand what created this passion for her, and she couldn't understand what he saw was so wrong with it. It led them to a fork in the road where Lyndsey followed his plan, and Rose followed her dream—to be a Montana fly-fishing guide.

FINDING PEACE

Being a first-year guide, it's easy to overthink trout. In early September, there are only two things that matter to them: eating and not being eaten. Casting shadows is bad, especially in a river as small and gin clear as the Dearborn. You may only get one chance, and although low light in the shadows and under clouds can help, fish are constantly aware of anything that might look like a predator, and predators cast shadows.

Just a few days before, Rose had visited this same stretch of the Dearborn with clients. It's not always a greatly accepted practice to bring clients to such pristine places, such as the Dearborn; however, the outfitter she was working for had wanted her to take the father/son duo there to get off the big water of the Missouri and work on the son's casting. There are some unwritten rules when you become a guide, one of them being to save these waters for yourself and your closest friends. In Rose's position, she learned quickly, when an outfitter "suggests" a certain stretch of water or river, it's not her place to question.

She spent all day working with James, the seventeen-year-old son, and although his casting was getting better and fishing was ok, the catching was a different story. They fished pool after pool after pool. At some point, he stopped slapping the water with his line, and fish started coming up to his fly. With her voice in his ear, they picked apart every pocket and every riffle. He worked the inside edges first and moved outward so as not to throw the line directly over any fish that might be waiting for the opportunity to ambush.

"Get 'em," Rose would say as another trout popped

his fly, and again, James would be a step too late.

Rose decided to give James a break from hearing her voice and let him have a go at it on his own. She walked upstream to where his dad had been fishing, leaving him alone. James Sr. thanked Rose for helping his son out and was grateful for the improvements he was making in his casting. Fly-fishing isn't the easiest thing to master and can be quite frustrating. It's a lot like golf in that if you let it, the frustration from poor technique starts to control you, and any little imperfections can manifest into habits; habits that can lead to nasty slices on the golf course and line piling up into tangled messes on the stream.

As she walked back to see how James was doing, Rose realized how much self-control and restraint he had displayed when someone else was watching and how little control he had over his frustration when he was by himself. He was hooked up on a log just a couple of feet from where he was standing, and instead of walking over and releasing the fly from the obstruction, he chose to flail the rod around, whipping it back and forth in an apparent attempt to break the rod thereby dismissing him from the seemingly impossible task of catching a fish. Just before the objective was met, James looked up and saw Rose coming downstream.

"What's up?" she asked with an inquisitive sort of shoulder-shrug and continued with, "It's ok to be frustrated. It's not easy, and it's definitely not something anyone picks up on their first try. I tell you what, I'll take the rod, and you take the net for a few minutes."

James didn't say much, but Rose could tell he was in need of a break and also in need of something encouraging that would confirm that yes, these fish could actually be caught. So, she took the rod from him and started fishing upstream.

Somewhere around Rose's fifth cast, a nice little rainbow trout about 14 inches came up out of some skinny water to suck down her fly.

James netted it, and after letting it go, she gave the rod back to James and said, "They're there. You just have to keep plugging away and be patient. It'll come."

It was around 4:30 in the afternoon, and the group was facing a good half-hour hike back to the Jeep. James still hadn't caught his first fish.

"This is it," Rose proclaimed as they put the stalk on this last hole. "This is our last chance. But hey, bud, you've been kicking some ass here, and I have a good feeling about this one."

Taking a step back, she let him begin working the pool just like they had meticulously worked the last twenty or so before. His first couple of casts landed just outside the mark and resulted in no looks from any trout. He then put a cast right on the seam, and as his fly dumped down through the riffle and collected in the frothy water on top of the deep hole, a monster rainbow rose from the depths like an emerging submarine and, with its white mouth wide open, gulped the hopper down. James never even saw it.

"Get 'em!" Echoed Rose's voice through the canyon, trying not to startle him, yet getting his attention. It was too late.

Before James could bury the hook into the trout's lip, the imitation was spit out, and once again, James' fly line came up limp. It was hard to tell who was more disappointed, Rose or James—not because of the failure but because she knew how hard James had worked and for him to come up empty seemed so unfair; especially since there were so many people Rose had taken out previously that didn't know what it was like to put the time in that James had. They caught fish despite all the mistakes, and in a weird way, she never thought they deserved the fish they caught. But James had worked hard. He had given it his best effort and had learned a ton in the process.

So now, just a few days later, this fish has already thrown down the gauntlet, and Rose is going after him. Her trip here has taken on two purposes: to clear her head of the frustration and hurt of the emails from Lyndsey, and redemption for James' sake.

As Rose finished rigging her rod, Chase continued to search for strategic spots to mark. The beauty of these freestone creeks in Montana, especially this time of year, is that big bugs often get blown into the water. Grasshoppers, beetles, flying ants, and other terrestrials find their way from bank to water and eventually into the gut of a trout. Once trout get the taste, they'll eat just about anything big and ugly that's presented well. She ties on a "Frankenhopper", partially because she likes the pattern, but more because it just sounds cool—Frankenhopper.

There's a path that cuts through a barbed-wire gate that surely has claimed a few pairs of waders over the years. However, because the water temperatures are still up in the low 60s, Rose left her waders back at the camper with her spring and fall gear. She follows the path along the bridge embankment and down a steep gradient to the bottom of the creek. As she reaches the first run, Rose pulls her fly free from the hook keeper next to the cork on the butt section of her rod. Adjusting the drag on her reel and then pulling a few feet of fly line off the spool, she whips the end of the rod, and the slack shoots out the tip. She continues to strip off line while feeding more and more out the end of the rod. Casting away from the pool so as not to spook the fish, she finally has enough line to hit her target.

The run tumbles down into a deep pool. At the bottom of the pool, boulders and the root ball of a Ponderosa pine have collected over the years, providing perfect cover for trout while still allowing a vantage point for them to ambush crippled bugs. Shooting line at about a 45-degree angle into the run, Rose drops the fly onto the riffle and lets it dump down into the pool. Nothing. She picks the fly up again and casts into the run a little further, and still nothing. She continues working the pool and the run until she's satisfied that she has either spooked the fish that were in there, or there weren't any in the first place, and now it's time to move on to the next hole. More than likely, there were fish there, but somehow, either by stumbling over rocks or casting a shadow, they knew Rose was there, and no matter what kind of fly or how good the presentation was, those fish weren't going to rise, or "come up" for a while now.

Cattle run all through the bottom of the Dearborn drainage. The recent fires and dry weather caused ranchers to bring them down to the river bottoms for grass and water. A few cows and a calf occupy the bank on the inside corner of the next run. Chase never did like cattle, and although he only weighs 54 pounds, he feels he's got a chance against a 1500-pound cow with a calf.

"Don't do it, Chase," Rose says in a low voice as he lets out a somewhat controlled woof.

Too late. Chase makes good on his name as he takes off, barking through the brush, hot on the pursuit of the not-so-aloof Black Angus cow. At some point, the cow realizes the size differential between her and this annoying little lab and turns to confront her attacker. To her, Chase is that annoying housefly, and just before she can step on him, Rose yells, "Leave it!" and Chase turns back to her side, his head down, huffing and puffing, giving the impression that the cow was lucky she called him back.

Working her way upstream, Rose hears some low growling. She's never heard this sound from cattle before. However, with all those cows in the drainage, she can't imagine it is anything else. Surveying the next run, she makes a few false casts, contemplating where to set the fly down. A bellow elicits a head-snapping response to see a huge Angus bull standing directly behind her. She knows it's a bull because she lets her eyes drift down to a pink shaft protruding from a tuft of hair under his belly. He stares directly at her. She's not sure what he sees in her, but the feelings are definitely not mutual.

As a kid, Rose remembered going to a funeral for her great-uncle with her grandmother. The story was that he had jumped over a fence into a bull's area of the pasture to get some water from the creek that ran through the property. Somehow, he pissed the bull off, and it came charging. The bull caught him as he was climbing the fence to get out of the pasture and dragged him down to the ground. It then proceeded to trample and stomp him until eventually he was dead. He was found, bludgeoned to death, a few hours later.

Now standing there face-to-face with this guy, a lot of things were going through Rose's head—catching fish was not the priority. Letting the rod tip down and the tensions on her fly-line release, she blindly drops the fly onto the water. Rose thinks about running or sneaking out of there. She even contemplates using her rod as a weapon. Instead, she freezes for a few seconds, not sure of any of the options on the table.

Rose soon realizes the fishing gods must have a sense of humor. While standing there, face-to-face with the affectionate bull, her rod was just about ripped out of her hands by a 16-inch rainbow as it gulped the Frankenhopper down and tried to bring it back to its lair.

Obviously, one's life would normally take precedence over a fish, but this was a good fish for the Dearborn. Instinctively, Rose turns her attention to putting tension on her line. She looks back over her shoulder to see the bull still holding. She has time so she fights the fish right up to the bank and, with one eye on the bull, shakes the rainbow free from her line.

As Rose scurries upstream, putting distance between her and the bull, she gains some perspective. Angus bulls are, by in large, quite docile, that is, until a bull rider grabs hold of a rope that's cutting off the circulation to their scrotum. The perception, however, when you're staring down a 2,000-pound bull in the backcountry, is that of the rodeo bulls—thrashing around, snot flying, cowboys getting gored, etc. Rose guessed anyone would be bucking like a son-of-a-bitch too if someone did that to them.

Standing at the next pool, Rose can't help but notice this constant gloom that's been hanging over her. It made her numb, and kept her brow furrowed for weeks, and hasn't let up one iota since the break-up. And now, when she thought her head was becoming clearer, her interactions with Lyndsey were becoming more volatile.

Rose just wanted to feel like she was a good person worthy of being loved by the person she loved. Instead, what she was getting from Lyndsey was example after example of how she came up short and how she was a horrible person, not deserving love. He recalled fights from months ago in a way that would confirm his decision to end it, even though her recollection of those events was very different. He collected those memories as ammo against her, storing them up for the time he could launch his assault, and now he was trying to destroy her.

In a way, she just wanted to know that he was hurting too, which to her would mean the relationship wasn't a total fiasco. Rose would have even accepted him saying he hated her because at least that would show some emotion, but now, Lyndsey couldn't even say that. The opposite of love is not hate. It's indifference. Had he said he hated Rose in these emails, she would have at least known he had feelings, or that he was hurting too, but Lyndsey didn't say that. He said he was indifferent towards her, and that hurt even worse.

And now standing over another pool, all she can see is a distorted view of herself. Like looking into a cracked mirror, all she can think about is how she might fix the image. She focuses on that image Lyndsey has projected, and not the many other positive images from other people in her life. Rose has become obsessed with the negative image Lyndsey has provided and can't rid herself of her thoughts.

Peace is what she needs, and she figures she knows how she will get it. She'll take a break from fishing, and she'll pray. She'll give God one more chance to prove he exists. And what better place to pray than in the backcountry, in this beautiful canyon?

Seeking out a boulder to sit on, Rose sets her rod down and takes off her backpack. She has picked the perfect seat in the most beautiful place, and she's about to talk to God. The water rushes by as the remaining sunlight glistens off the ripples. She has gotten far enough away from the cattle, so they are no longer a distraction. Chase is happily doing his own thing, and there isn't a sign of civilization for miles. Even the jets seem to have bypassed the airspace overhead, and as she takes a seat, Rose thinks to herself, "It's just you and me, God."

Suddenly, she hears the buzzing of insect wings as a dozen or so hornets ascend on her. Rose sat on a hornet's nest, and the hornets are not happy.

"This isn't it. This isn't peace. Is this a joke?"

Jumping to her feet, she grabs her rod and pack and escapes without a bite or sting. Rose isn't sure whether hornets bite at this point or sting, and she couldn't care less. Rose takes another seat on the bank of the river, and within seconds, she's covered in ants.

"Forget it," she says to herself. "You've made your point."

Once again, Rose collects her things and starts heading upstream to the hole with the monster rainbow that eluded James just the other day. She manages a few more fish, and all said, is having a decent day of fishing, but she just can't clear her head.

Before she knows it, she can see the fishing hole she has come for. The water is so clear; every boulder, every fold in the strata of rock formation, and every pebble is visible as if you were looking into an unopened bottle of Beefeater. What she wouldn't do right now for a drink. The pool is deceptively deep, and with the clear water, depth is hard to decipher. The left bank is comprised of a limestone cliff, smoothed by time, wind, and water; cold grey in color and standing strong like an Old Woodsman guarding the pool, protecting it from the elements and the few fishing souls who might venture up this far.

Above the hole is a run that shoots through a low point in the limestone bottom. The stream meanders over rocks, creating a riffle of hard water dumping over a ledge and into a bubbling pool as the water deflects off the bottom and churns over and over until it spills out of the tail end of the seam.

The upstream point of the pool in the turbulent water is where the bigger fish stage. They wait for nymphs and fry that have lost their hold on the rocks above the run to tumble down into the pool. The seam becomes a feeding trough as well as supplying much-needed oxygen, and as the shadows get longer, the fish start looking up for food on the surface.

On the right side of the fishing hole, there lies a somewhat steep gravel bank. The pebbles act like marbles when stepped on, and any uncalculated move might send Rose sliding right into the creek. It's the only vantage point to cast from, however, as standing in the creek is impossible because of the depth, and the Old Woodsman occupies the left.

It took Rose a good hour and a half to work her way up to this spot. The wind had lain down. The temperature was dropping. The cliffs were supplying the shadows she needed. Everything was perfect. Rose checks her leader for nicks or abrasions. If she hooks him, she wouldn't want anything to ruin her chances of landing him. She takes a moment and a breath and acknowledges the old man watching over the river and assures him she means no harm.

Working her way up the right side of the pool, Rose feels her Chacos slipping on the pebbles. She moves up the bank a little higher to make sure not to disturb the water. The problem is that the higher on the bank, the more visible she becomes, so she crouches as she sneaks. The closer she gets, the slower she moves as the last couple of yards seem to take an eternity. She positions herself to have the best shot at putting a 45-degree cast onto the riffle without casting a shadow over the fish.

Rose starts the meticulous process of picking apart this trout's home by first taking false casts behind the pool. She wants to get just enough line out to be able to set the fly down right at the end of the run, so she doesn't cover any more water than needed. A big mistake most beginners make is having too much line out, trying to cast too far. The problem is they throw line over the top of the water they want to be fishing, contaminating the fishing hole with a shadow from the line. It's also more difficult to manage the line the further the fly is out, which compromises the presentation and makes it difficult to come tight on a trout if they come up to eat. It's a lesson Rose learned a couple of years ago while fishing the Madison River near Ennis, MT.

It was the Mother's Day Caddis hatch and only a few weeks after Rose caught her first trout on the Missouri River. She had driven 2 hours to get to Ennis on her way to Bear Trap Canyon. She stopped at the Ennis fly shop to get the local flavor. The shop employee spent 40 minutes explaining the hatch that was going off, what size of bugs to use, how to rig a caddis with a dropper, how to throw a reach cast, a pile cast, etc. etc... He was the typical trout-bum; mid-twenties, long-hair, long-beard and what seemed to be a complete disrespect and/or lack of command for the English language.

Fly shops were always an intimidating venture for Rose during those first years of exploration. Just walking into a shop, she knew there was a spotlight on her. She was either going to get the cold shoulder for being an obvious novice or worse, she would get the dude that hovers over her and talks too much, trying to be too helpful. She hoped the reactions would be a result of her being a novice versus being a chick, but Rose knew better. She knew she was a rarity in the fly-fishing world, and she was a very attractive rarity at that.

On this particular day, Rose ran into the hoverer. Although he did give her a ton of great information and he was generally sweet, he also never shut up, and it was incredibly difficult for Rose to get a word in edgewise.

She remembered thinking, "Dude, if you'd just relax for a second and listen to what I'm asking, I could eventually get to the water…" which is what she was there for in the first place.

But guys in the fly-fishing world always seemed to want to take advantage of these encounters. They thought it was an open door they could somehow slip a foot into by showing off their extensive knowledge. They tried to impress Rose, but all it did was frustrate her.

"Just treat me like one of the guys," she often thought while drifting off into flight mode, struggling to find the words she could say to end the conversation without sounding like a bitch.

As Rose finally walked out the door, the bro yelled, "Oh yeah, and one more thing. If you don't catch anything, don't worry about it. I didn't catch a trout for 3 months when I first started fly-fishing."

"Wow, that was more than just a little discouraging," she thought to herself.

Rose headed out to the river anyway with some new ammo in her fly-box and a little more knowledge, even though she felt she had paid dearly for it—not necessarily in actual currency but in time and dignity. She hiked into the canyon about 2 miles before throwing a line. She fished for at least 3 hours without getting a single take. Feeling a bit defeated, Rose headed to the bank and sat down. She remembered what the bro-bra in the fly-shop told her. Then she looked back to see a fisherman a hundred yards downstream from her, fishing the exact same water she had just fished, hooking fish after fish after fish.

"God damnit," she grunted to herself.

Feeling completely defeated now, Rose had two options. She could collect her things and humbly head back down the trail to the Jeep, or she could try learning something. Rose chose the student role and spent the next 30 minutes watching her unwitting mentor catch fish.

What she noticed right off the bat was the amount of line he was throwing. Fifteen or twenty feet was all it took, and after letting the fly drift only about three or four feet through the seam or past the boulder he was fishing, he would immediately pick it up and put it right back in the zone. There was no time wasted. There were no unnecessary false casts. He didn't have any more line out than he needed to get the job done, allowing him to manage the slack in his line, make the necessary mends, and set the hook before the fish could spit the fly out.

After watching for a while, Rose regained some ambition and confidence and decided to have another go at it. She waded back into the current and emulated her teacher. In the next hour, she caught six fish and hooked several others. She was stoked to say the least, and like sinking that last par putt on the 18th hole, she left feeling victorious and knew she would be back on the water in the coming days.

So now, on the Dearborn after taking a few false casts well behind her target, Rose shifts her body slightly, making a single cast, setting the fly perfectly on the inside edge of the seam. Her foam hopper is easy to see and virtually unsinkable. Even in the hard water, it bounces down the riffle, rolling into the pool, only getting lost for a second before popping back up on the surface like it's a kayak, bouncing down a class four rapid.

The hopper floats through the zone, passing directly over where the monster rainbow should be, and nothing. Careful not to pop the fly off the water, Rose picks it up and again takes a couple quick false casts downstream of the riffle and then once again, sets the fly down on the water; this time a few inches further into the seam, and again, nothing. The third cast lands right on the outside edge of the seam, and as it drifts into the pool at the bottom of the run, the dark shadow of the rainbow reveals itself as it rises and turns to chase the hopper downstream. Rose sees the white mouth of the rainbow open as it chases the hopper, closing the distance much like an Orca in open water hunting seals. With a burst of speed, the trout makes its final run at it and, in an angry gulp, smacks at the hopper.

About the only thing Rose can liken to what happened next is a premature ejaculation. (She learned about those from her first "real" boyfriend her freshman year in college…poor guy.) It took everything she had to wait as long as she did to set the hook, but as soon as the mouth came up out of the water, Rose snapped the rod tip up and ripped the hopper from his closing mandibles.

She spent nearly two hours getting to that position, making that cast, coaxing that particular fish into taking her fly. It was almost painful how carefully she worked the pool. She had made the right choice of fly, and when the perfect cast was made and the drift was accomplished, she pulled the fly right out of the fish's mouth.

"No!" She utters to herself. "Fucking pathetic."

The feeling only lasted a couple of seconds as Rose thinks, "Maybe, just maybe I could get the trout to come up again."

Starting over, she takes her false casts and puts the fly right back where the rainbow was lying at the bottom of the pool. To her surprise, the trout showed himself again, but this time only coming up to about six inches from the surface of the water, then turning tail, and rolling back to the bottom of the pool and out of sight. One more cast and Rose was confident she had blown her chance.

There is a lesson here, however. After she finished kicking herself, Rose noticed something. For the past half an hour, all she thought about was the objective at hand. She was in one of the most beautiful places on the planet, participating in something she was truly passionate about, and for the first time in a long time, she was at peace. Nothing else mattered, and even though she hadn't actually caught the trout, her stomach wasn't churning, her brow was no longer furrowed, and she was relatively happy.

Wanting to document this special place, she turns to grab her camera and remembers she has left her pack about a hundred yards downstream. Deciding to retrieve the pack and the camera, she makes the short hike and returns to the pool and the Old Woodsman. She remembered a conversation she had with an ex-game warden who suggested fish have a memory of about seven seconds.

"Seven seconds?" Rose thinks. "That would mean

this fish should have forgotten her by now, right?"

Not fully buying it, she decides to at least change flies before trying it again.

Going in a totally different direction, Rose pulls out her box of ammo. In there, she had an assortment of hoppers, beetles, and other terrestrials. She also had the one go-to fly that everyone on every stream in the West should have: the Parachute Adams.

A little larger than the Adams she would normally use on the Missouri River, but much smaller than the hoppers she had been throwing, Rose adds some tippet to her leader and ties on the size 12 Adams. She coats the fly with flotant and then adds more of the flotant to the butt section of the leader. She drops the fly and watches the excess coating leach into the water. Standing in the exact same spot as just a few minutes before, she begins the ritual of taking false casts downstream from the run and working the hole guarded by the Old Woodsman.

The Adams is not nearly as buoyant as the foam hopper, and as she sets the fly on the inside edge of the seam, it only drifts two feet before tumbling down, submerging into the riffle, disappearing deep into the pool. Her initial thought was to jerk the fly up out of the water, take a couple false casts to dry it off, and then return it back to the seam. She snaps the rod tip up, and as the line straightens and tightens, her cast is halted abruptly.

When the weight of the fish stops the motion of your arm dead in its path, you know you've hooked something substantial. And when the headshakes jerked Rose's arm back and forth, she knew she was in for a battle. The trout ran through the pool and headed downstream, and all Rose could do was let him run. She knew he was in control seconds after accidentally setting the hook when he ran out all the access line getting to the reel before she even knew what had happened. He took a jump, disrupting the calm water at the end of the pool, landing with a "plat" on the surface, which only seemed to piss him off as he changed direction and charged back upstream.

Sometimes things don't work out the way they're supposed to. Sometimes we do everything right and we fail, and then sometimes we fall into success, happiness, and even peace. And sometimes the Gods—fishing or otherwise—wait for those moments when we are ready for peace, love, or catching fish to present those opportunities.

This doesn't mean we don't have some control over our happiness. We can choose to focus on things that make us happy, and we can choose to move on. But happiness or peace will only fall in our laps when we are ready for it, and the Gods seem to know when that time has come. Sometimes we get a glimpse of it. Sometimes it lasts for longer, but we only get the amount we are ready for, and if we choose to focus on the turmoil in our lives, we choose to hang onto turmoil and thereby choose to let go of peace.

Rose gave thanks to the trout, releasing him back to his pool, and as he disappeared, she was able to reflect on the profound lessons a day like this brings. Snipping off the fly, Rose buried it in the rocks, returning it to the earth, retiring it from its life as a fly and onto its new one, degrading back to the elements it was derived from. It was the death of a fly, but not a death from failure. It was a death manifested from triumph and now a chance at rebirth—an opportunity to move on to another life or maybe just another chapter in this life.

Breaking her rod down and placing the reel in her

backpack, the sun now fully hidden behind the mountains, Rose begins her hike back to the Jeep.

Trying to make better time, she follows a cattle trail that takes a straighter path, not following the bends and turns of the stream. Much of the path cut corners and ran through patches of alders and willows, and through some growth so thick, she had to crawl on her hands and knees to push through the entangled branches and stems.

Three-quarters of the way back to the High Bridge, Rose hears a sound she thought she had heard earlier. She had talked herself out of trusting her ears the first time she heard it and wrote it off to an active imagination for what she must have mistaken for a low growl. This time, she was sure that indeed, she was hearing the growl, and the hair on the back of her neck stood up.

"Chase!" she half whispers, half yells, hoping he was the source of this disconcerting sound, but he was not. Chase was on her heels and not at all close to where the sound was coming from.

The sun was well behind the canyon walls by this point, and a dull haze was settling into the river bottom, making objects hard to fully identify. As Rose pokes her head from the entangled alders and looks out into a clearing, she catches the movement of a large body making its way out of sight.

The animal was only there for a couple of seconds before disappearing, and Rose fought hard to replay what she thought she saw in her mind for some kind of proof of identification. It was large-bodied with long, brownish, grizzled hair, with the tips of its hair shimmering silverish in the low light. As it made its way out of the clearing, she noticed its muscular body rolling as it rambled off. Before it disappeared, the beast turned back to look at Rose, lifted her nose in the air, and curled her lips, throwing her head back before turning away and slipping quietly into the brush.

Rose's body trembled as she reached for her bear spray.

"Fuck me," Rose whispers out loud as she realizes she hadn't grabbed the bear spray out from under the back seat of the Jeep.

She was frozen mid-step and half bent over from working her way into the clearing. She didn't want to bring attention to herself. She just wanted to hunker down and let the bear create some distance before moving. She sank to her knees and hid in the brush.

"Fuck me," she whispers again. "Was that a griz? Fuck me."

Rose waited for what seemed to be an hour. It was really only about 30 seconds before she contemplated what she needed to do. She wanted to give the bear time, but time was running out. Darkness was quickly falling, and that seemed way worse than trying to sneak out while she still had light. She looked up the embankment to the road where she had parked the Jeep. The High Bridge was in sight but still a few hundred yards away.

Rose slowly stands up and decides to climb the embankment to the road, forgoing the walk through the alders to the bridge. As she works her way up, she calls out to Chase even though he is right by her side. She wants to make just enough noise to allow the bear to hear her without startling her. She knows most bears don't want to have anything to do with humans, and if you just give them their space, they will usually leave you alone.

Rose never knew where the bear went, but she was relieved when she crested the embankment and made the road. Her heart rate and breathing never came down to a normal pace until she had her rod put away, and she and Chase were on their way down the road, back to town. She was a bit shaken but also felt the awe of seeing the bruin.

FOOTBALL IS LIFE

Trick Patterson, whose given name was Patrick Patterson, was finishing up his senior year at the University of Montana. He learned to love Montana after transferring to the University in 2004 from Butte Community College in Oroville, California. Trick aspired to be a football player growing up in Chico, but was told he was too small to play at a major university, so he spent two years at Butte, and when the scouts didn't come knocking, he settled on Montana in hopes of a modest progression for his football career.

At the University of Montana, Trick stood out in the sense that he never really took on the look of any of the predominant groups that collected in the lounge in the Student Union. He towered above the tree-huggers and hippies and didn't sport the long hair or unkempt scruff on his chin that most of the guys wore in the Wildlife Biology or Recreational programs. Clean cut but dressed comfortably in plaids and flannel, Trick was unlike the jocks he was about to break in with. Undersized and between cliques, he was cautious in his interactions. He was a good-looking guy, muscular and well defined with just a hint of baby fat still hanging from his cheeks, but he was oblivious to any flirtations from the young women who secretly admired him. Trick wore a genuine modesty that was charming but also prevented him from realizing he might be a target. He was also incredibly focused on making a splash with the Grizzly Football team, so women were not in his purview.

Trick arrived on campus, six-feet-three-inches tall and weighing 224 pounds. He played tight end for Butte, but at that weight, defensive ends, even in the Big Sky

Conference, would eat him up. On the field, he played mean and never let his size be an obstacle. Off the field, he was a teddy bear. Regardless of his attitude or his fearless play, however, Trick knew he was going to have to put on some weight to compete.

That first year in Missoula, Trick took a part-time job at a Perkins Restaurant. His parents had some money, but they weren't rich by any means. Working for everything he got, he wasn't relying on them to pave his way—not so much out of defiance but more pride in being able to take care of himself. He was more of a giver than a taker and just liked the idea of being self-reliant.

While working at Perkins, Trick met Mike Morley, an ex-con and newly born-again Christian. Mike had gotten into bodybuilding while in prison in Deer Lodge, Montana. He was sent away for a combined burglary and aggravated assault conviction in Anaconda five years before Trick came to Montana.

Coming down from an opioid high, Mike was desperate for his next fix and didn't know the owner of the Georgetown Lake cabin would be home. He was a victim of the second wave of opioid abuse to hit the States, where doctors prescribed pain meds like OxyContin for non-surgical and non-cancer pain relief.

Mike was working on a home in Bozeman when he fell off the roof and cracked a vertebra in his lower lumbar. His doctor prescribed the pain meds and told Mike they would allow his body to heal naturally. A couple of doses a day turned into a dozen, and when the pills ran out, he had to find another way to relieve himself—not from the pain, but from the intense hangovers and withdrawals the drugs inflicted. Mike turned to heroin. He couldn't build houses anymore, so he started 'finding' ways to come up with the money to support his addiction.

To be fair, "cabin" doesn't represent the home Mike had targeted. The home was a 5200 square foot house on the lake that was probably worth more than the total of all the homes on the block in Anaconda, where Mike's parents lived and where he grew up, and now resided while trying to get back on his feet. The place was what one would expect from a multi-millionaire's second, or even third home, as he tries to profess a Montana homestead built with self-milled spruce logs carefully picked right from the standing timber that colored the ridges that lined Georgetown Lake. In reality, nearly all the materials that went into building the home, right down to the cedar shakes, di-cut metal rail panels for the deck, and even the decorative weathervane, were all imported from either Canada or China, or some other faraway land.

Mike entered the home in the afternoon of a brisk October day in 1999. He was looking for items he could flip quickly to make some money for his next fix. He knew the guy who owned the home was a collector of musical instruments and had a number of guitars displayed on stands throughout the home. Looking through the windows into the den, Mike could see an old Martin D-18 and an original American Fender Stratocaster. He had cased the house a few days ago and was doing the math in his head, figuring he could get at least three grand for the two.

What Mike didn't know was that the owner, an author, was actually there to do some writing on a historical non-fiction account of Jim Bridger and fur-trading companies of the mid-1800s, a common theme in this area. Georgetown Lake is gorgeous, and rich folk come from all over the country to be inspired. With the advent of the internet, a successful executive or author could work remotely at any time of the day or night and send their work off to their teams back in Silicon Valley or publishers in New York. It was quickly becoming a trend for out-of-staters to buy up properties like this on the lake to build lavish getaways and mountain retreats.

The owner of the home heard Mike break one of the windowpanes out of the French doors leading into the den. He was in the bathroom just off the master suite. Not the stoutest of weapons, he grabbed whatever he had available to him, which happened to be a guitar stand for another guitar he had on display in the bedroom. When the owner confronted Mike and swung the stand at him, Mike had no problem blocking the attack and turning the inferior weapon back on him.

Mike broke the stand over the owner's head and then proceeded to beat him to within an inch of his life. He was desperate and scared, and out of control. The beating only stopped once the man's body went limp and he could no longer defend himself or his property. Mike didn't even know if the man was alive when he fled the scene with the Fender Strat in hand.

Desperate people looking for a fix don't usually make very good decisions. Mike made the mistake of trying to sell the guitar on Craigslist a couple of days later and was arrested within a week. After pleading guilty, he was sent to the Montana State Prison in Deer Lodge, where he found rehab, then Jesus, then weightlifting.

That was five years ago, and Mike was trying to make amends. He had gone through the twelve steps. He had even apologized to the homeowner. When he met Trick, he saw a person who might have something he could give something to. Mike was in good shape, although not to the bodybuilding level he had gotten to while in prison, but he was still jacked and knew Trick needed help putting on weight. One day in the breakroom at Perkins, Mike confronted Trick.

"You play for the Griz," Mike asked, trying to open the door for a conversation.

"Well, 'play' is a little generous," answered Trick. "I transferred here this fall from a community college in California. I'm trying to make the team."

"Position?"

"Tight end," Trick answered with a slight hint of trepidation.

"It's your size, isn't it?" Mike asked, cocking his head to the side, and looking out of the bottom corners of his eyes.

Mike had this way about him. He was kind of eccentric, which one could imagine came from the drugs and maybe being institutionalized, but in reality, he was more childlike and enduring. His laugh was a bit over-the-top and often chortled out like a superhero's antagonist. He did that thing where he would cock his head and look out of the corners of his eyes. His teeth were perfectly straight, and when he smiled, his lips would open wide, so those teeth were on full display. Then he would let out a whiny little chuckle as sort of a bookend to his laugh, trailing off into that sideways look. His reddish afro, born out of the 70s, bounced with every chuckle as his shoulders thrusted, making his head bobble like a cheap baseball figurine. Right out of a comic book, he had the persona of the Joker or Penguin or a combination of the two, but without evil intent.

At first, Trick didn't know how to take Mike. What

was his game? What did he want? He was uncomfortable with the question and how Mike opened himself up almost playfully. Was he playing a game? Was he needling?

"I could help out with that," Mike said.

Thinking the worst, like maybe Mike was offering steroids or something, Trick replied with a, "nah, I'm good."

"It's all legit," Mike pushed. "No tricks, no gimmicks. Just a lot of ass-kicking weights and diet."

Mike was persistent, and the more Trick got to know him, the less uncomfortable the interactions with Mike became. In fact, Trick felt himself being drawn in—even seeking out those interactions. Mike was funny and had a good heart. He made everyone around him laugh. He was the opposite of the small child, who would take on adult traits, making parents' friends laugh. Mike was a full-on adult and a large one at that, but had the innocence of a child. With all he'd been through, Mike exuded a joyfulness that Trick just wanted to be around. He didn't drink or smoke. He just worked his ass off and spent much of the time laughing while he did.

That winter, Trick took Mike up on his offer. As a red-shirt transfer student, Trick flew under the radar of coaches and could pretty much train however he wanted and with whomever he wanted. It was up to him to take the necessary strides to make the team.

Mike was true to his word. He worked with Trick four days a week. They spent all their time in the weight room changing things up and tricking his body into building mass. Mike didn't believe in supplements. He believed in eating, which was perfect as they had endless supplies of protein and carbs working for the restaurant.

In 4 months, Trick put on 22 pounds and showed up to camp that spring weighing 246 pounds with a body-fat index of 4.7%. He was ripped.

In Trick's second year at Montana, he was taken off the red-shirt list and started seeing significant playing time. He was able to take on defensive ends in blocking assignments and had the hands to become a serious offensive weapon. In his final year at Montana, he was on track to set all the Big Sky Conference tight-end records for total yards and scoring until he was injured mid-season while playing their biggest in-state rival, the Montana State Bobcats.

The injury was far from career-ending. It was more of a tweak as his ankle was rolled up on by their half-back while Trick was sealing the edge on a sweep. It was a nuisance injury, but it lingered throughout the second half of the season until the Griz made the playoffs and Trick was able to contribute again.

Between the first seven games of the season and those final playoff games, Trick was able to turn the heads of a lot of scouts for the NFL. There was even talk that he might be drafted somewhere in the first three rounds, which is amazing when you consider all the talent coming out of the major Division I schools.

Trick was invited to the NFL Combine in the winter of 2008. He was still on the small side for tight ends in the NFL, but he showed he had the heart and the attitude to put the work in and be a leader. Coaches liked him. He had talent, and he had the right work ethic, and his draft status was on the rise. With the right training regimen, scouts and coaches believed Trick could put on a little more weight and become the tight end they needed.

As a break from the training that first year in

Missoula, Mike and Trick would go fly-fishing. Trick had never been, but Mike had learned from his grandpa when he was very young. It was a way to supplement the physical training with learning the life lessons that fly-fishing had to offer. Fishing kept Trick's mind in the right place when things got tough and helped Mike stay on his path to recovery. Mike would remember the lessons his grandpa would teach him through fly-fishing and felt like he could pass that along to Trick.

It was late that first winter that Trick and Mike started working out together when Mike brought up this idea of control and what we can control and what we should focus on. It was a particularly challenging time for Trick. All through high school and the first two years at Butte Community College as a Roadrunner, he was a starter. He never had to worry about being beaten out for a position. It's not as if he didn't work hard, but he just never had anyone really challenge him for his spot on the team. At the University of Montana, that all changed because the talent was so much better than where he came from. This wasn't something he was familiar with, and it caused a lot of stress and doubt for him.

One day, Mike and Trick were fishing on the Bitterroot near Missoula. Trick was still in the learning stage of getting his line out far enough to where trout wouldn't see his profile towering above them while rising towards his fly, which would result in a refusal of his presentation. But he was getting it. He was learning to be patient on his back cast, letting his rod load, and "painting the ceiling."

Trick couldn't remember how many times he heard Mike say, "It's not chopping wood, it's painting the ceiling."

The shape of the cast was a mystery to Trick. How

could Mike work so effortlessly, even into the wind, to lay out 30 or 40 feet of line like it was nothing?

"Paint the ceiling…." was always in Trick's head, even though he couldn't fully incorporate the motion into his cast.

Inevitably, Trick would get frustrated and try harder and harder with more might than finesse, and his cast would fall shorter and shorter in a bigger and bigger pile. The harder he would throw his line, the worse it got, and then he would hear Mike shout at him from across the river, "Paint the ceiling!"

The idea is that if you chop wood with your casting motion, you are creating an open loop with your fly-line where all the momentum is lost at the top of your cast. By painting the ceiling, you are using a motion that keeps the rod tip on plane right up until the end of the cast, building momentum as the rod tip moves forward. It compresses the loop and generates power, rolling the fly-line over, cutting through the air and wind.

It was skwala time on the Bitterroot when the casting finally started coming together for Trick. Skwalas are mid-sized stoneflies that hatch in late winter on the free-stones in Montana. The Bitterroot was known for its skwala hatch, bringing people from all over the country to fish it. The river can get pretty busy during this time because of how epic the hatches can be and how these bugs bring lethargic fish to the surface. With all the anglers coming to the river, finding open water to fish where a dozen boats haven't already gone through is just as much a part of the game as finding where these big bugs are hatching.

Mike had gotten word that the hatch was on from another buddy in Missoula. The weather for early April was going to be gorgeous with some sun and temps in the mid-50s, so he called up Trick to go out for an afternoon. The plan was to drive to Darby to a fishing access site and wade upstream. That would get them into water where boats had yet to float through, as most of the guides would be putting their rafts in at Darby and floating downstream. They would have a few hours to fish before the boats from the upstream access site would come through.

At about 1 o'clock, Mike and Trick saw their first skwala. The two were fishing a riffle with little to no success when a bug that resembled a helicopter came fluttering out of the sky to settle on the water. As the big bug touched the water, a small cutthroat rose with a vengeance, coming clear out of the water to smack it and hopefully drown it in the current. When it missed, another trout tried to crush the skwala and then another until finally, the big bug disappeared as a more tenacious trout snatched it down.

"Did you see that?" Mike yells to Trick while he laughs and does his 'Joker' little chuckle. "They're comin'!"

Trick was amazed. They had been fishing this riffle with Prince Nymphs and Royal Wulffs for the past hour and hadn't seen or touched a fish. Now this bug hits the water, and the entire riffle lights up with fish busting out, trying to beat their cohorts to the gulp. One bug, and the feeding frenzy exploded.

"Here! Throw this out there!" Mike says with the enthusiasm of a six-year-old as he ties a big dry-fly onto Trick's leader.

Trick takes a cast, but with all the excitement, he's too quick on his back cast, and the fly and line fall in a big mess, well short of the riffle.

"You knitting sweaters?" Mike asks. "Wait on your back-cast."

Mike untangles the mess and says, "Throw it again."

This time, Trick threw his line into his back-cast and, pausing for a moment, letting the line straighten out behind him, he then paints the ceiling with his rod tip and lays the fly-line out across the riffle, letting the big skwala imitation land softly on the water. As it drifted down through the riffle, the anticipation of a trout smashing it built in both of them. They watch as the fly tumbles down the riffle. Nothing.

As the fly drifts to the length of the line Trick had fed out and swings downstream, Mike says, "Throw it again."

Trick stripped in the excess line, picked up the fly, took two false-casts, and sent the bug back into the riffle. Again, the two watch the fly drifting through the riffle with the anticipation that one of those aggressive little cutties is going to crush it. That doesn't happen. What does happen is much more subtle as the nose of a trout slowly pokes through the surface of the water and gulps the fly down.

"Oh! Get 'em!" Mike yells, sounding as if he is coming unglued.

As Trick comes tight on this monster of a cutthroat, all hell breaks loose, and panic ensues. This fish was bigger than anything either of them was expecting. It rolled and shook its head and then took a run upstream, right through the riffle.

With the trout making its initial run, Trick put a death grip on the cork of his rod and the fly-line. His rod tip jerked down to the water, straightening out, putting all the pressure of that fish on the tippet material, and with a snap, his rod tip pops back up above his head, and his fly-line goes limp. There wasn't even a fly left; just the leader dangling in the water, getting swept back down through the riffle. The monster cutty was gone.

"Let 'em run!" Mike shouted, but it was too late.

"Fuckin A!" Trick blurts out. "Did you see that thing?"

"All right. So here's the deal." Mike cuts in. "There are only two things you can control while fighting a trout: the rod tip and your fly-line. You can't play tug-of-war with the fish because they're always going to win. Control what you can control. Get a hold of that fly-line and keep a bend in the rod. If your rod is up and it straightens out, you need to put more pressure on him. But if that rod tip comes down and it straightens out, you're holding way too tight. You just gotta let 'em run. Put just enough pressure on him to keep him tight, and eventually, you'll win the battle, but you can't force it. You can't make that trout do something before he's ready. Control what you can control and don't worry so much about what that trout is doing or how big that trout is…or was in your case."

Mike laughs and gives Trick a shove. "It's fishing, Tricky, Trick. Just fishing."

That was a profound lesson for Trick, and it set him up for the next couple of years at the University. He realized it wasn't just his battle with that trout where this idea of control applied; it was also on the playing field or in the locker room, or in the weight room. Trick needed to put on weight, which he did. What he shouldn't have done was to worry about what other players were doing or who was getting playing time or being moved off the red-shirt list. He just needed to work his ass off, and he did, and because of that, Trick had set himself up to make a career out of football. He was invited to the 2008 NFL Combine and was sure to be drafted. The world was in front of him.

Mike's life had turned around as well. He was engaged to a woman he met at the nondenominational church he attended in Missoula. Her name was Sara Rossi, a 28-year-old Italian girl from the Yaak Valley in Northwestern Montana. With her rich auburn hair and dark Mediterranean skin, she had no problem getting the attention from other graduate students and Teaching Assistants at the University. Graduating from Montana with a master's degree in psychology, she wanted to save the world and often spent her time volunteering with organizations like The Boys and Girls Club and Montana Food Share. She was initially interested in Mike for his persistence in his journey. Eventually, Sara fell in love with Mike's enduring childlike charm he exuded free of any guilt or condemnation.

Rehab for Mike had gone well, with no relapses and no missed appointments with his parole officer. He had gotten his life back on track and was set to get married in the fall of 2008. He was also back to building houses, which, between his job and Sara's position as a crisis counselor in the ER, they were able to scrape enough money together to put a down payment on an old miner's house up Rattlesnake Creek just outside Missoula.

Life got busy for both Mike and Trick, but they remained close friends. They fished together on occasion, although not nearly as much as they would like. They hung out almost every Sunday afternoon to watch football in the fall and shared lunches with Sara when there wasn't any football. As much as Sara hated the ego and bravado that usually came with the jocks she knew from the University, she saw Trick as being different than "those" guys. She respected Trick and valued the friendship he and Mike shared. She also saw that Mike benefited just as much from the lessons he was sharing as Trick. Mike was proud of Trick and proud of himself for being able to help. He felt valued, and that kept him on the road to recovery.

The end of the 2007 Grizzly football season came abruptly with a heartbreaking loss in the first round of the NCAA Division I, FCS tournament to the Wofford Terriers. Montana was undefeated up until that point, had won the Big Sky Championship, and was ranked 10th in the Football Championship Subdivision. Wofford had traveled to Missoula, spent Thanksgiving in their hotel in preparation for the Saturday game, and was a pretty significant underdog.

With 32 seconds left in the game, Wofford scored but failed on the two-point conversion, putting them up by only one point. Montana still had enough time to march down the field. With 4 seconds left, Montana attempted a 47-yard field goal. The Grizzly kicker pulled the ball wide left, ending their season in defeat to Wofford, 23-22.

For most of the Montana seniors, this would be the final game of their careers. That realization was obvious to some of Trick's friends he had grown close to over the years. Football was such a huge part of their lives, and now it would be gone—gone knowing they had come up short on their senior goals. Gone with the feeling that they could have done so much more. Gone, knowing they will never have the chance to redeem themselves.

For Trick, it was different. Although there were a lot of things that would have to happen for him to make an NFL team, he believed in his heart that this game would not be his last. He certainly was bummed about the loss. He wanted to win just as much as the next guy, and in fact, he really felt bad for his teammates and spent a good part of that evening and the next day consoling them. However, Trick didn't have a lot of time to think about the failure of this game. His mind was quickly shifting to the NFL Combine. Even while kneeling on the 30-yard line after watching the final kick hook wide-left, it was a bittersweet kind of feeling for Trick. A part of him was also excited to get on to the next chapter in his football career.

The 2008 NFL Combine was held in late February in Indianapolis. Three hundred and thirty potential draftees were expected to be at the Combine to be put to the test in front of NFL coaches, doctors, and scouts. Each had their own personal trainers, and although agents aren't allowed in the dome where the workouts are held, each player also had an agent present in the city.

Trick was a bit overwhelmed by the prospect of going pro. There weren't a lot of Grizzly players who had gone into the NFL, so there weren't a lot of players to take advice from. What was amazing was that so many people knew who he was and that he was on the radar of so many teams. Because of that, agents were crawling out of the woodwork to talk to Trick and, hopefully, be signed by him as his representative.

A few weeks before the Combine, Trick decided he would interview a few of these agents to have some representation in Indianapolis. A good agent will work with general managers from teams the player is interested in to get his name on their board if he isn't already. Mike Morley sat in on the interviews with Trick and acted as his trainer.

Mike knew fitness, and he knew Trick. He also had a sense for reading people and wouldn't let Trick fall to the charm of some of the sleezier solicitors. At this level, football is a business above all else. Some agents only care about their clients' well-being because they know that if their client is safe, healthy, and in a good place, they make money. Some agents actually care about their clients as humans. Mike was going to make sure Trick found the latter.

Bret Colter was one of those agents who reached out to Trick soon after the end of the Grizzly's season. He was relatively new to the industry, but as green as he was, he was also passionate about taking care of his clients and had the fire in his belly to prove himself on the big stage.

Mike and Trick agreed to meet with Bret via Skype a week before they headed to Indianapolis. As the screen popped up on Trick's laptop while sitting at Mike's kitchen table, Bret introduced himself. He wasn't a very large man and was obviously a bit nervous. Mike could see the beads of sweat forming on the peach fuzz that lined Bret's upper lip. He was well put together at first look, wearing a suit and tie that wasn't quite tailored to him but looked good enough. As Mike took a closer look, however, he could see the sweat stains on the almost white collar of Bret's shirt. Mike figured this was probably Bret's only suit, and he was doing the best he could to come off as a pro.

"Did you play?" Mike asks Bret with a bit of skepticism.

"Pardon me?" Bret returns.

"Football," Mike responds. "Did you play football?"

"Ah, no. No, I didn't after junior high." Bret admits. "I didn't have the size, and to be honest, I got tired of getting my ass kicked by dudes like your boy here. You are Trick Patterson, correct?" Bret makes a gesture towards the screen.

Trick pipes in, "Yeah. Good to meet you, Bret. I am Trick, and this is my trainer, Mike Morley."

"Well, it's good to meet both of you," Bret says. "And it's good you have someone like Mike looking out for you, Trick. This can be a pretty intimidating process. There are a lot of sharks out there. Trust me, I'm not one of them. However, this is a business, Trick, and I'm not going to bullshit you. You are a commodity and potentially, a very valuable one."

"How do we know you're not a shark?" Mike butts in.

"You don't. And I don't know, Trick won't be a bust, but that's what relationships are built on—a kind of leap of faith where we both take on some risk." Bret explains. "All I can say is that for me to be successful, we have to be successful as a team. I know that sounds cliché, but it is reality. We all have a role, and if we stay on top of our game and take care of what we have control over, we all prosper."

"Tight lines," Trick interjects a little under his breath.

"What's that?" Bret asks.

"Oh, it's just a fly-fishing thing," Mike answers for Trick. "Tight lines…basically just means control what you can control—keep the line tight and good things will follow."

"No, I know that," Bret proclaims emphatically. "You guys fish? Well, I guess you'd have to. You live in the middle of fly-fishing paradise, right?"

"Yeah, we get out from time to time," Trick says. "You?"

"Damn straight," Bret declares. "And I started before, 'A River Runs Through It'. My parents used to bring me out to Big Sky every summer, and I'd spend just about every minute of every day on the Gallatin fishing for Yellowstone cutties just downstream from the Park."

"No shit?" Mike hurls.

The three spent the better part of the next 1/2 hour or so talking fly-fishing before getting back to the business at hand, but that conversation did more to convince Mike and Trick that Bret was genuine and would become a valuable member of the team than any resume or client book Bret might produce ever could. The thing about talking fly-fishing with people that actually do fish is that you know when someone is bullshitting you, and Mike was convinced that Bret was a straight-up dude.

A week later, Mike and Trick were meeting Bret in Indianapolis the day before the Combine. They were all a bit nervous and spoke openly about it. Each had a role. Mike's was to provide support to Trick and to help him get to where he was supposed to be, when he was supposed to be there. Bret was meeting with general managers and doing everything he could to get Trick's name on teams' draft boards. Trick's job was to just be Trick and work his ass off, and he did.

The Combine is grueling with skills and agility tests, running obstacle courses, 40-yard dashes, and weight-lifting competitions, plus doctors' exams. Players also take aptitude tests and sit in on mock interviews with coaches, asking anything from who their favorite player is to what kind of animal they would be if they were reincarnated. It was all just a game to see how the players would do under pressure. The answers weren't really all that important. Being able to think on their feet and give concise answers with confidence was the goal

At the end of the week, the evidence was saying Trick absolutely crushed every opportunity he had to impress the coaches and scouts. Bret's job was made easier as he was hearing a lot of buzz from the general managers about Trick's performances. They were quickly moving up the draft boards of a lot of teams. Good tight ends are a huge commodity in the NFL, and finding one with the size and heart to block a defensive lineman, often out-weighing them by 50 pounds, while having the hands to catch passes downfield, isn't easy. The prospect of a player like Trick really gets the general managers excited, which was obvious with all the talk coming from the teams. Now all they had to do was wait for the draft and keep Trick safe and in shape.

The day after the Combine concluded, Bret drove Mike and Trick to the airport. They reflected on the week and spent a good part of the drive patting each other on their backs, sharing stories of some of the other ath-letes and what the teams were saying about Trick. They played the game of projecting who might select Trick in the draft, in what round, and from what quarterback he might catch his first NFL pass. It was all so surreal for Trick and for Bret; this could be the client that bolsters his resume, opening doors to other top prospects.

As the three walked through the airport, Mike decided to propose an idea to help keep them all grounded.

"You know what we ought to do?" He proclaims. "Let's go fishing. I feel like the wheels are starting to spin a little faster than we're ready for. I think a few days on the Missouri might help bring us back to center."

"What're you talking about, Mike?" Trick asks.

"No, I mean, I'm glad you're excited, but let's ground this plane for a minute and not get too far ahead of ourselves."

"You saw what happened out there, Mike." Trick

responds. "We crushed it!"

"Yeah, we did. Well, you did, Trick, and you should be proud, man." Mike continues, "But let's just dial it back for a minute. I don't mean to squash your excitement, but let's breathe—gain some perspective."

"Mike's right," Bret cuts in. "We should go fishing. This process can certainly catch up to you, and if you don't take some time to slow it down, you might find yourself getting trampled by it. Besides, I'd never give up an opportunity to fish with a real Montana angler."

"Who said you were invited?" Mike asks while cocking his head sideways and grinning ear-to-ear.

"Bullshit," Bret declares. "This sounds like a business trip to me, and I'm coming."

"Alright," Mike concedes. "But if you show up with brand-new Orvis waders, boots, and a vest, I'm not letting you in the boat."

As Mike and Trick boarded their plane, they looked back to say goodbye to Bret.

"Tight lines, boys," Bret shouted out.

"Tight lines," Mike and Trick answered back in unison.

It was almost 2 months before the NFL Draft, which gave the newly formed team plenty of time to plan a fishing trip. The weather can be a bit sketchy in the springtime in Montana, so pushing it back a few weeks was going to give them a better chance at hitting the weather right. They chose the weekend of April 12th and 13th, which fell two weeks before the draft. That would give them time to set some logistics for the trip, and the timing would give them a good break from all the anticipation for the draft and the strain from phone calls and pro-days with NFL teams.

Mike wanted to do something special for Trick. He wanted to take him somewhere he hadn't been yet. Living on the west side of the Divide, they had spent all their time fishing the Blackfoot, Bitterroot, and Clark Fork and their tributaries. Those rivers were amazing, and Trick had become a pretty respectable angler, but now Mike wanted to put him to the test. He wanted to take Trick to the Mighty Mo.

GUIDE POLITICS

Rose picked up her clients at High Banks one morning in early spring of 2008. Although this season, she had decided to focus all her time on guiding, she still remained somewhat friendly with the fly shop—purely as a business decision, as she was still doing some trips for them and couldn't afford not to be on as many of the shops and outfitters' guide lists.

She had traded in the camper for a small cottage in Wolf Creek, just seven miles upstream of Craig. The cottage was newly painted white and had a new roof. However, it was built in the late 1800s as a caretaker's residence for the Wolf Creek Hotel, and no matter how much paint and asphalt the owners applied, it was still showing years of weather, earthquakes, and neglect. It sat directly behind the hotel, nestled amongst the trees and alder bushes bordering the property. With no more than 350 square feet of living space, it was only a slight improvement over the camper. The inside of the cottage also showed its age with old shiplap and paneling walls. Although a modest residence for Rose and Chase, the cottage was convenient, and the price was right.

The landlords, Ross and Karren Ainsley, lived in the 17-bed hotel that was no longer serving paying guests. The cottage was named by the local guides, The White House, as numerous guides had squatted there over the years. The guides in the area were a resource to Ross and Karren as they provided an income supplement to the aging couple. Ross had retired years ago from the Air Force, and Karren was a retired teacher. They welcomed Rose in and soon became a surrogate mother and father to her. Rose often referred to them as her "Montana ma and pa."

Rose's clients were two gentlemen who had been coming to the Missouri for a few years, staying at a cabin just downstream from Craig in a group of cabins called The End of the Line. Ron and Buzz always rented a boat and guided themselves, which on the Mo can prove to be a challenge. After a couple of years of paying over $100 a day for a boat and catching nothing, they decided to take that money, only fish a couple of days, but spend it on a guide.

The two anglers contacted High Banks the night before the trip after much debate. They were proud anglers and wanted to be able to achieve their own success, but since it wasn't going well, the two decided it was time. Rose just happened to have the next day open, so High Banks booked the trip with her.

In Montana, every fishing guide is required to have a guide's license. That gives them the legal right to guide folks, but does not allow them to solicit their own business. Clients are required to book all trips through an outfitter with the appropriate outfitting license. Guides are independent contractors, much like a subcontractor in the construction world, where the outfitter acts like a general contractor. It gets a little sticky and a little political in some areas of Montana, where fly shops don't like the guides they hire working for competitors. However, the loyalty expected from the guides isn't always reciprocated by the shops.

Rose had done most of her guiding the previous year for High Banks, but things were not going well with that relationship. Josh Stanford, the owner of High Banks, hired Rose last year without realizing what a commodity she would become to the other outfitters in the area. He thought she would become a shop staple that clients, mainly male clients, coming in from all over the country would view as a welcoming sight. She was friendly and very good-looking, and someone Josh thought would bring visitors back, if for nothing else, to flirt with her. Rose didn't see it that way. As a serious guide, she wasn't going to be put on a shelf for window shopping. She wanted to be on the river and actually loathed the men who would come into the shop and tell stories to try to impress her.

Other guides did the same. Rose often pretended to listen to them and stroke their egos, but inside, she would feel the burning behind her eyes and the gritting of her teeth. She always told herself to just shut up and listen, and soon she would be out of the shop and on the river chasing her own dreams, and these indignant encounters would soon be behind her.

Rose was passionate about her craft and was learning the river and honing her skills as a guide, and just wanted to be taken seriously. She knew why Josh had hired her, and she resented that, but she played the game because she also knew that this hill wasn't worth dying on. The other outfitters respected her and were putting her on the river because she was a quality guide. Calling someone out and burning bridges was not going to benefit her, so she stifled the burning resentment and kept quiet.

Josh had another motive for helping Rose out that first year. Josh was single and was attracted to Rose and wanted to be with her. Rose, however, wasn't the least bit interested in Josh and didn't want anything to get in the way of her career. Rose did everything she could to thwart Josh's advances. In the end, the situation created a sense of bitterness in Josh, and Rose soon saw herself slipping further and further down High Banks' guide list.

Seeing less experienced guides booking trips before

her frustrated Rose. Even on the April morning when she picked up Ron and Buzz, there was Billy Packer, another guide, picking up his clients. She was well aware he had been called before her for that trip because her trip was booked at the last minute. Billy was much less experienced and had only been guiding for High Banks for a month, and now he was getting called before her.

"Little fucker," she thought to herself as she turned to Buzz and, while smiling, said, "Hi, I'm Rose. You must be Buzz…"

Blue-wing olives were hatching on the Missouri, and Rose knew where those little critters would most likely bring fish up. Just downstream from Craig was a big flat the locals referred to as "The Hemingway Flats," due to the son of the legendary author, Ernest Hemingway, owning a house on the banks overlooking the river there. The water was only a few feet deep on the flat that ran for about a quarter mile along the west side of the river before dropping off into a deep bend and a pool with a cliff overhanging the river known as Jackson Rock.

Hemingway Flat was the perfect depth for springtime bugs as the sun would warm the rocks lining the bottom, causing nymphs to pop and trout to come up from the deeper pools to take advantage of the warming riverbed and those early hatches. Hundreds of fish would migrate to the flat and form pods, rising in a manner that, from a distance, looked like shallow riffles breaking the surface. Clients coming from other rivers across the country were always amazed at these pods of fish when Rose would point them out. They actually mistook them as shallow riffles until they were made aware of the fish and studied their noses, disrupting the surface as they gulped down bug after bug after bug. So many fish in such a tight space—it was hard to pick out a target.

"Just throw it out there, right?" There was often an error of assumption that clients would make. "How could you miss?"

A wing shooter might make the same mistake on a flock of cupped-up mallards setting into a spread of decoys. You would think all you had to do was point and shoot into the flock and something would drop, but that was rarely the case. Without picking out a target, all the shooter was destined to accomplish was donating pellets to the pond.

The pods of fish on the Missouri were so big and ate so readily, how could they not eat an imitation if you just put it in front of them? The reality, however, was that these trout weren't stupid, and although they look easy to trick, they are not.

Rose dropped her boat into the Missouri off the Craig Fishing Access Site about a mile upstream of the Hemingway's. She got Ron and Buzz into the boat and went through the initial instructions of casting and mending to get a perfect drag-free drift. They fished their way down to the flats, the whole way, Rose coaching Ron and Buzz into hooking fish on their nymphing rigs, but they were having a difficult time landing them. During the early stages of the trip, Rose learned about her clients and their abilities while nymph fishing before she would test them on dry flies.

As they fished, Rose could tell Ron and Buzz were going to need a lot of instruction. They were great guys, and she genuinely liked them, but they were not very experienced anglers. When they got to the first pod of fish coming to the surface to sip emerging bugs along Hemingway Flats, Rose dropped her anchor. They watched the pod of rising trout, and she shared with them the importance of the perfect presentation to trick those fish into taking their fly.

"The drift has to be perfect," she told them. "If it's got any drag at all or it's not right on their noses, they won't eat it."

Rose continued explaining the difference between freestones and tailwaters and what makes the Missouri such a technical river to fish.

"The biggest differences are one, the amount of food these fish have to eat, and two, just how flat and relatively slow-moving the water is. They get a long time to look at your bug, and if it doesn't look right, they don't eat."

Rose recalled the story of two guys she had guided a couple of days before.

She had parked her Clackacraft drift-boat on this same pod with the two clients earlier that week. Parking the boat just upstream of the fish at an angle to cast 45 degrees downstream to them was common practice on tailwaters. The client would have to throw a reach-cast, dropping their fly upstream from the target, and feed it into the pod with a perfect drag-free drift. The trick was to align the fly, the leader, and the fly-line in a manner to get that perfect drift, but still not let the fly-line drift over them. If the pre-sentation wasn't perfect, the trout wouldn't eat it.

"That's close," Rose shared the coaching she gave to the clients as she recapped what had happened the other day, "but it's got to be perfect."

"That's bullshit," the client in the front of the boat said. "That should have gotten eaten. They don't want that fly."

"It's got to be perfect," Rose said calmly, biting her tongue, knowing that if it were a male guide telling them that, they would probably have taken the constructive criticism as truth.

This went on for about twenty minutes when the client in the front of the boat became frustrated and told his fishing partner in the back of the boat to give it a try. Rose continued to share with Ron and Buzz the story; how the guy in the back of the boat switched with the guy in front and gave it a try. Again, none of the fish would take the fly.

Rose did change flies just to appease the client and again got the same result. As the fly drifted into the pod of fish with just the tiniest bit of drag, the fish went down, let the fly pass, and then came back up to gulp down the naturals (or real bugs) in the exact same spot they were previously eating.

"Fine, Rose," said the client as he looked back at her with skepticism, "show us how it's done."

Rose stood up in the middle of the boat and grabbed the rod from the client. She made three false casts well upstream of the pod of fish and then angled her cast downstream, shooting fifteen feet of line to add to the 10 to 12 feet she was carrying into her back cast. As the line shot through the rod tip and the fly rolled out, straightening the line, she reached upstream with the tip of her rod. The result was the fly settling gently on the water with her line landing upstream from the fly, creating the perfect drift. She stacked more line on the water and fed the size 18 Parachute Adams right onto the nose of the closest fish on the edge of the pod.

The two clients watched in disbelief as the 18-inch rainbow sipped the fly. Rose lifted the rod firmly and came tight on the trout.

Not even looking at either one of the clients, Rose

calmly said, "It's not the fly…"

Ron and Buzz both chuckled at the story while they watched this pod of fish eagerly eating emerging mayflies—partly because they now realized why they couldn't catch fish on the Missouri by themselves and also because they understood the plight of a female guide breaking into the business. Both leaned left of center, politically, and they had a fair amount of sympathy for women who were often discriminated against in many professions, let alone a profession like guiding that's comprised of 99% males. They admired Rose and liked the fact that she was able to put these guys in their place.

The sun was rising higher as mayflies were building in numbers on the surface of the river. Rose knew they only had an hour or so before the water would warm too much, and the bugs would stop hatching. She grabbed another rod out of the rod-holder in the boat and asked which one wanted to take a shot at these rising fish.

"Screw it, I'll give it a shot," answers Ron. "What's the worst that could happen, these little bastards completely embarrass me?"

"Aw, it's not that bad. If you put these guys down, you'll have more chances," Rose assures him, trying to minimize the inevitable humiliation Ron would likely soon feel.

Ron strips about 30 feet of line off the reel and, while trying to pick the majority of it up into his back-cast, turns downstream and throws it out onto the water in the vicinity of the pod with a clumsy "splat." The entire pod erupts as they spook, turn tail, and take refuge on the bottom of the river.

"You can't slap the water," explains Rose.

"Nice work," Buzz proclaims as he gives Ron a

sarcastic pat on the back. "It only took you one cast to put the entire pod down!"

"You'll get your turn, asshole," Ron fires back.

"Sweet!" Rose recognizes, "I'm guiding the actual 'Grumpy Old Men.'"

Rose grabs hold of the anchor rope and pulls, lifting the 30lb diamond-shaped piece of lead off the stream bed, allowing them to drift. She draws on the oars while looking to the far side of the flat.

"There's another pod over there. Let's check them out," Rose suggests while sliding towards them. "This time, try to carry less line on your back-cast and shoot more."

Before Rose can slide the boat ten yards towards the pod, she hears a voice yelling at her from 80 yards upstream.

"Rose! What the fuck are you doing?"

Rose jumps in her seat and snaps her head back. She feels the blood rushing to her face. Her heart is racing, partly out of fear and partly out of humiliation. She looked back upstream to see the boat of Jake Trapper. Everyone knew his boat as it was an old-school, wooden McKenzie River style drift boat that was a little higher-sided and a little heavier than what most of the guides rowed. He used this classic boat because it fits his persona of being the OG of the river. He was standing up in the middle of the boat with his arms open and hands splayed out to emphasize his disgust. His clients were sitting faces down and shaking their heads, either as a gesture of disapproval of her actions or embarrassment for Jake yelling profanities across the river. Regardless, Rose quickly turned the boat from the pod, slamming on the brakes by pulling on her oars, backing away from the rising fish.

"Pick a side!" Jake yells out.

"We're going to find some other fish," Rose quietly tells Ron and Buzz.

Buzz looked back at Jake and then at Rose. He didn't say anything out of compassion for not wanting to make Rose feel more embarrassed. Ron wasn't as sensitive.

"What the hell's that guy's problem?" Ron asks.

"Nothing. He's right. I should have looked behind me before making a move." She replies while pulling hard on the oars.

"He doesn't have to be an asshole," Ron adds.

"It's all right. He's right. We'll find more fish."

The two fly shops in Craig are High Banks, which is where Rose got her start, and the Missouri River Angler. Neither shop has an owner who is an outfitter to run trips through, so they rely on local contracts with outfitters to keep their books legit. Jake Trapper is one of the outfitters for MRA and has a reputation in town for being one of the heavy hitters. He is very experienced and has guided on rivers all over the world. Every guide's goal is to get on MRA's list and in favor of guys like Jake and the other outfitters that contract with MRA.

Rose hadn't broken into that crowd yet. When she decided to get into guiding, her first contact had suggested talking to Josh from High Banks. Josh was a little easier getting in with because, to be honest, he had a way of turning over staff and burning bridges with partners. He was always looking for new relationships to replace the ones left in a pile of metaphoric ash along the bank of the river.

Before Rose arrived on the scene, she had limited knowledge of the political dynamics of Craig. She just wanted to guide, but she found out quickly how important it was to make the right connections, not just any connections, and if one was to align themselves with the wrong folks, the ceiling wasn't only limited by her gender, but also by her allegiances. Rose was on strike two and wanted to change that quickly. Pissing Jake off was not going to help.

The rest of the day went as well as it could have for Rose, Ron, and Buzz. In fact, it went so well that they wanted to book her again for the next day. Being on a bit of a high and totally forgetting the interaction she had with Jake, she stopped by Izaak's for a drink and to touch base with some of the other guides. Let's be honest, Rose wanted to brag a little bit and let others know how good the day was.

Izaak's is the only restaurant in Craig. Most of the guides wind up there at the end of the day. The owners, Steve and Kim Maddow, were becoming close friends with Rose, although it didn't start that way. While Rose lived in the camper behind the shop, her first year in Craig, she and Kim met for the first time. Kim was walking her dogs on a leash, and Chase was running free, doing his sniffing and marking fence posts. As Chase approached Kim and her two pups, one being a wiener dog and the other, an older, fattened-up chocolate lab, Kim waved to Rose as the little yapper started giving Chase the "what for."

"Don't worry," Rose called out. "Chase will be alright. He's chill."

Not even thinking anything about it, Rose hadn't realized Kim had misheard the exchange and let it brew. Instead of asking Rose what she had said, Kim thought the worst. Her dog was barking at Chase, and she didn't hear that all Rose was saying was that Chase was harmless. It impacted her so much that she went to the bar that night and told the guides who were hanging out that Rose had confronted her about her dogs attacking Chase.

"Who is that little fly-girl bitch?" Kim asked before she started her venting.

From that day on, Rose was referred to as the "Fly-Girl." She thought it was cute and a little enduring, but the reality was, they were really referring to her as the "Fly-Girl Bitch" only they left off the "bitch" moniker. At some point, it was shortened to "Fly." Rose accepted that as her nickname and wore it proudly until a year later, when she and some of the other guides were hanging out at Izaak's, and Kim shared the story and the little inside joke.

"What?" Rose asked, "I was just trying to be nice."

"I know," Kim admitted, "But now you're 'Fly'. There are worse things to be called."

Rose pushed through the doors, entering Izaak's on this night, and still got the "Hey, Fly" from the guides sitting at the bar. "What's up?"

As she recounted the day with the others, not even remembering the exchange with Jake, Josh walks in from High Banks.

"Hey Rose, how'd the day go?" Josh asks.

"It was great. Fish were happy. Ron and Buzz were cool," Rose was trying to downplay a little. "They said they were glad they got a guide. They actually caught fish instead of rowing in circles all day."

"Yeah, I know," Josh says while looking down at his feet, "I booked them for tomorrow with Billy."

"What the fuck, Josh?" Rose was obviously pissed. "Those are my clients. I fished with them. It's because of me that they're getting a guide for tomorrow!"

"Hold on, Rose. You don't have clients. You're a guide. Those are my clients," he explains. "And to be honest, they're actually Pete Strom's clients because he's the outfitter I ran them through. You don't want to turn over the apple cart, Rose."

"Fuck that," Rose blurts out. "Absolute bullshit."

Rose stormed out of Izaak's and found a place on the patio to sit down. She is pissed. Her face is flushed, and she feels her eyes burning and her teeth grinding again. She is going through all the scenarios in her head of what she should do next. Does she go back in and tell Josh off? Does she apologize? She is furious.

A few minutes later, Keith Merchant, another local guide who got his start a couple of years before Rose, walks out of Izaak's with two Budweisers and two shots of Sinfire. He sets the drinks down on the picnic table and pulls out a pack of Camel Lights. He offers one to Rose, and she takes it in her fingers. Keith ignites his lighter and holds it out for Rose to light her cigarette.

"Fucking asshole," Rose says in a soft, low voice while exhaling.

"Yep," says Keith. "But what're ya going to do?"

Keith was the quintessential trout bum with a goatee that dropped to the middle of his chest, nipple piercings, earrings, and tattoos that covered just about every inch of his forearms and biceps. One of the tattoos was that of a rainbow trout that was stretched out along his forearm with distinctive markings that were used to measure fish as he laid them out against his skin. At twelve inches, the words "small fry" denoted a less-than-impressive catch. At fifteen inches, the words "getting there" told of at least an adult trout. At eighteen, "cookie-cutter," and at twenty, "Toad." Keith also had a mark at twenty-four inches, but at that point, the mark was so far up his arm that his sleeve always hid the letters. Rose thought it read,

"Monster," but she felt a little too proud to ask.

Keith had taken Rose under his wing from the first day she arrived in Craig. He was serving drinks at the Craig Bar in the mornings before the guide season got rolling. Rose stopped by every morning for those first few weeks to check emails using the bar's Wi-Fi, and they would chat. Keith had no interest in Rose on an intimate level since he was living with his fiancée, Kelly. Rose could tell that Keith was safe and had wanted nothing from her. He was just a nice guy lending a helping hand, the same way guys helped him when he first started. For Keith, it was a way for him to "pay it forward."

"It's not fair, Keith. Those guys are paying for another trip because of me, and now Josh is farming it out to fuckin, Billy? You gotta be kidding me." Rose exhales again.

"Here's the deal, Fly," Keith explains, and when he uses the nickname, it actually sounds respectful and makes Rose feel good. "Regardless of how much of a dick that guy is, it doesn't do you any good to piss him off. You gotta take care of yourself, which means don't worry about Josh or High Banks. Don't piss them off, but start forming relationships with the big boys—the real players. You're a good guide. Start working for real outfitters."

Keith holds up a shot of Sinfire. Rose takes the other shot, and as they clink, Keith says, "Cheers."

"Prost," Rose replies.

The two take their shots and then slam the glasses down on the picnic table. Keith grimaces and shakes his head as the Sinfire burns down his throat.

Rose takes a drag off her cigarette and says, "Pussy."

A SLEAZY TRAPPER

Rose stubs out her cigarette and stands up. Keith follows suit, hugs her and says, "Let's get another drink."
Rose is still reeling as she walks back into Izaak's and sees Josh standing by the bar, talking to Billy.

"A-hole," she whispers under her breath, and she heads to the other end of the bar.

She doesn't want to confront Josh any more than she already has and realizes Keith's advice is sage. The balance in the guiding community is tricky. On the one hand, you have to stick up for yourself. On the other hand, you never want to piss anyone off because you know that someday, and probably someday soon, you are going to end up working for or with them. It's always better to be seen as a team player than someone tough enough to stand up for themselves until you've been on the scene for long enough to earn street or river cred.

In Rose's second year in Craig, she had yet to build the clout needed to put other guides and especially shop owners in their place. Plus, she's a woman, and that never gets lost on her or anyone else. Just the other day, a few of the guides were hanging out on the porch at High Banks, drinking a beer. Billy commented on Rose's sunglasses.

"Hey, Fly, where's the flight jacket? Did you park your jet around back?"

Rose always wore aviator glasses. They were lighter, and she just felt they fit her face better than the typical guide series glasses everyone else was sporting.

"Fuck off," she snapped back.

"Oh! Fly's got a little attitude," needled Billy. "Why don't you back that ass on over here for a little adjustment? Give me 15 minutes, Fly, and I'm sure I can put a smile back on that cute little face."

"Give me 15 seconds, Billy, and I'm sure you'll be splooging all over yourself." Rose fired back.

"Dick." She whispered to herself as she dropped her head, shaking back and forth just enough to get her point across.

Had Billy said that to a male guide and that guide fired back with a stern, "fuck you," they would have all had a little chuckle, and life would have moved on. But if a woman tells the offender to "fuck off," it's an entirely different story. Instead of her standing up for herself, she's got an attitude problem and needs to be "put in her place." She's a bitch or weak, or can't handle having someone give her shit. There's a different set of rules for women in the guide world, and because there's not a lot of precedence for female guides, those rules are less defined, and the greys tend to be left up to interpretation by the ruling class. In this situation, the ruling class is the arrogant bro-bras like Billy.

Back inside Izaak's, Keith orders another round of shots and again, "cheers" and a "prost" are declared, shot glasses clink, and then slammed on the bar as the cinnamon whiskey burns down their throats to eventually nestle in their bellies. Rose snaps out of her head and joins the conversation that Keith and another guide are having about presentation versus fly selection.

Paul, who towers over everyone at 6'6", is all about the fly selection and declares, "Nobody gets the perfect drift, but if you have that fly that fish eat like crack, they're gonna eat."

"No way, man." Keith cuts in. "It's all about drift and presentation. You could put the best-looking fly on the planet in front of a fish's nose and if it's not presented well, they ain't eatin it."

"That's such bullshit," Paul defends. "You think that fly is just drifting along in a perfect flow like everything else as it goes through riffles and bounces over rocks and shit? There's no such thing as a 'perfect drift.' What do you think, Fly?"

"You're both right, you dumb-asses," Rose says while sitting up a little higher as she realizes that someone is actually asking her for an opinion. "Are we talking dries, streamers or nymphs? Flat water? Riffles? All these things matter, right? Honestly, I'm a presentation kind of gal, but I also know conditions and situations matter."

"Shut the hell up, Fly," Paul says as he wraps his arm around her and gives her a proper noogie.

"God damn, Paul," Rose contests. "I spent all day on this hair, and look what you did!"

Paul looks back at Scotty, who's been standing behind the bar waiting for an order.

"Set 'em up!" he yells. "Shots for the house!"

"Cheers!"

"Prost!" and a slam as a dozen or more shot glasses hit the bar. The party is in full-on NASCAR mode now as more guides filter into Izaak's after their day on the river.

"Hey, Rose!"

The baritone voice cuts through the crowd like the bark of an overweight Rottweiler. She wheels around and feels her heart sink. The voice is coming from Jake Trapper.

Jake is an imposing figure on the river. He's even more impressive in person, towering over most other guides, although he's not nearly as tall as Paul. As large as he is, he also has a reputation for being a loose cannon. He's not at all obese and has the shoulders of someone who's spent most of his life rowing, but also the gut of someone who's drank his share of cheap beer over the years. His face is weathered, and he almost always has a five o'clock shadow. Like most guides, he also sports raccoon tan lines around his eyes because he's on the water eight days a week, wearing the guide-series shades. Seeing him standing there makes Rose shrink into her barstool. She feels herself wanting to run, but there's nowhere to go.

Remembering the interaction they had earlier on the river that day, Rose tries to get out in front of the conversation to tamp things down.

"Hey, Jake. I'm so sorry about…." She starts.

"Shut up for a second," Jake interrupts. "Scotty, let me buy Rose a beer."

"You don't have to…" Rose tries to get out.

"Just…shut up," Jake insists. "Listen. What I did earlier was uncalled for."

Rose could tell how difficult it was for Jake to apologize, and in this moment and in this role, she sees the tiniest bit of vulnerability in him. With most other guides, Rose might exploit this, but this is Jake Trapper, and she knows that vulnerability could morph into a heartbeat. She also finds it endearing, so she decides to let it play out.

"No, Jake. I cut you off, and I'm sorry. I should have been looking behind me, and I just wasn't paying attention," she explains.

"Regardless," Jake continues. "I don't own the river. You have just as much right to those fish as anyone else, and I'm sorry."

Rose is dumbfounded by this. She doesn't know what to think or say. She knows not to make a big deal out of it and realizes what she says next could either build a bridge, setting herself up for trips in the future, or could drive a wedge between her and this 'heavy hitter.' She sees Keith studying her out of her peripheral.

"Well, thanks, Jake. I certainly appreciate that," she says. "But just so you know, I'll do my part in the future to be more observant—maybe even mount some rear-view mirrors or something."

"Fair enough," Jake answers as he holds up his bottle of Bud Light to clank bottles with Rose. "Fair enough."

Rose doesn't know how to feel. Part of her wants to jump out of her Chacos for joy. A feeling of vindication pulses through her, but part of her also wants to cry. She doesn't fully understand where that comes from, but it's real, and holding back the tears has been a common feeling lately, especially as she's been fighting so hard to be respected in the guide community. Rose feels relief, but it's also degrading.

"Fuck it, Scotty!" Rose turns to the bar. "Let's do shots!"

Scotty sets up the next round of shots for the group of guides huddled around the bar as Rose reaches into her pocket to pull out a hundred-dollar bill, which was her tip for the day. She sets it on the bar, and Scotty says in a low voice, "You're short fifteen bucks, Fly."

"I got it," Keith butts in as he gives Rose a look as to say, 'don't worry about it.' He puts two twenties on the bar and says, "Keep it."

This entire interaction goes unnoticed by the rest of the bar as Keith and Scotty make sure of that. They want Rose to succeed. They want her to gain the street cred she desperately needs to stand up to the rest of the guides, and they will do anything they can to help.

Rose mouths the word, "Thanks."

The party rolls on as it did just about every night in

Craig. The guides are pros on the river and at the bar. When clients want to hang out and party, they think everyone is on vacation and expect the guides to participate too, and the guides don't want to disappoint.

At around 2 am, Scotty pipes up, announcing to the patrons, "Two o'clock folks! It's time to shut'er down. You don't have to go home, but you can't stay here!"

Scotty thinks it's a pretty funny way to end the night, not realizing that saying the same closure every night has made his salutation a little cliché and uninteresting for the locals. The new guests might think it's funny, though, so he keeps it in his repertoire.

As hard as Rose tried, she was no match for the other guides. She kept up with them drink for drink, but at a slight 126 pounds, she doesn't have the body mass to absorb the alcohol like the dudes in the bar do. As she stands up from her stool, the floor rocks out from underneath her, and she plops down on her butt. She laughs as Keith and another guide help her up.

"You're not driving home," Keith says.

"I'll be fine," Rose contests. "My Chaco caught one of those nails sticking up out of this shit floor."

"Yeah, yeah, yeah. I know. But you're still not driving home."

Jake steps up and says, "Hey, Rose, the Sutton Place is open. I had clients bail early so you can stay there."

"I'm fine," Rose continues to protest.

"No. You're not driving," Jake says. "It's a done deal."

The Sutton Place is one of four cabins owned by a local businessman from Helena that is managed by the Missouri River Angler. It's able to sleep 4 clients and is usually booked up solid throughout the season. For this cabin to be open is a rarity, and since it's been paid for already and nobody is in there, Rose takes Jake up on the offer.

"Ok, ok. I'll crash at the Sutton."

Jake and Keith help Rose out the door of Izaak's, across the street, and to the steps of the cabin.

"You got this?" Asks Keith. "I gotta get going. Kelly just texted, and she's not happy. She's been stuck up at the house with two lab puppies tearing each other apart."

"Yeah, I'll take care of it," Jake replies.

Rose drapes her arms around Keith, "Thanks, Keith. I'm sorry. I'm drunk."

"Yes, yes, you are," Keith says. "It happens to the best of us."

As Keith walks away, Jake pulls the key for the cabin out of his pocket and inserts it into the keyhole. The door unlocks, and Jake turns the knob, and it swings open.

"After you," Jake says as he holds a hand out, gesturing for Rose to enter.

As Rose enters the cabin, Jake follows her in and turns on the lights. The cabin has been recently updated with new wood trim and wood-looking vinyl floors. Although the finishings lend to the rustic look folks expect, the newness provides a bit of contradiction. There's a couch in the middle of the room, a kitchenette in the back, and stairs leading up to a bed in the loft. Rose plops herself down on the couch.

"How's your season looking?" Jake asks.

Rose opens one eye and squints to try to stop the room from spinning. She sees a number of Jakes in the fog that has consumed her brain, and tries to focus on the middle one.

"What?" She asks.

"How's your season looking? You getting enough days?"

"I guess," Rose responds in a slurred stupor. "Could always do more."

"I could help you out with that," Jake tells her in what appears to be a genuine tone of compassion.

"Thanks, Jake. You're sweet." And with an alcohol induced bout of courage and honesty, she adds, "You're not nearly the a-hole people make you out to be."

Rose feels herself lifting up to the sky and opens her eyes. She looks down to see the river below as she gains altitude. The water is a beautiful greenish-blue with sun shimmering off riffles dumping into deep pools below. She looks to her right and sees an eagle only a few feet away, soaring by her side. The eagle turns to her and winks before banking off into the clouds and out of sight. Rose furrows her brow and thinks, "That's weird."

She feels weightless as she ascends higher and higher until the river becomes a series of thin green lines meandering through burnt grass, cutting through golden fields, and disappearing into dark green clumps of trees.

At some point, what was a peaceful scene slowly starts to rotate as she feels her body slipping into a flat spin. She reaches out to try to stop the motion, but her body spins faster and faster, quickly spinning out of control.

Rose opens her eyes and sits up. She bursts out from under the sheets and comforter on the bed in the loft of the Sutton Place. She's confused. She doesn't know where she is or how she got there. She does know one thing: she needs to find a toilet fast.

Jumping from the bed, Rose runs to a lit doorway that she can only assume is an acceptable target for what she knows is going to be projected from her face very soon. Fortunately, Jake left the light on in the bathroom just in case something like this happened. Rose kneels in front of the toilet and violently hurls everything up from her stomach, and when she thinks she's got it all out, her body convulses and pushes even harder trying to extract whatever could be left. And then her body convulses again and again as if it's not even her anymore. Tears stream down her face. Sweat beads on her forehead. She screams in defiance of the demon that has taken over—that demon is Sinfire.

Eventually, she regains control over her body and stands up. Rose looks into the mirror over the vanity. She's a mess. Tears have stained her face, and her hair is matted against her forehead. Her mouth tastes like acid. Her abs are burning from uncontrolled convulsions.

She runs some water and washes her face. She also notices a bottle of mouthwash and takes a pull off of it to rinse the devil from her tongue, which only makes her want to hurl again, but she fights it back.

"What the fuck…" she murmurs.

Her eyes drift down to notice what she's wearing. Rose in a T-shirt that's big enough to shelter a family of Hobbits and nothing else. She feels cold and knows something is not right.

As she makes her way out of the light of the bathroom and back into the main room in the loft, she begins to make out some of the dark objects. The bed is destroyed. Her Chacos and her clothes are piled up in the corner. There's another pile of clothes she doesn't quite recognize.

"You all right?" She hears Jake's voice coming from the mess of covers on the bed.

"Jake!?" Rose blurts out as Jake lifts his head from the pillows and looks back at her. "What the fuck, Jake? What the actual fuck?! What are you doing here? What am I doing here? Jesus!"

"What?" Jake protests. "We were messing around. You were into it."

"Jake! You're fucking married!" Rose yells.

"Well," Jake confesses, "that's not going all that well and…"

"What?" Rose interrupts. "Jesus Christ, Jake. I was passed out!"

"You weren't passed out," Jake argues. "Passed out chicks can't do what you were doing."

"Fuck, Jake. Seriously?"

Rose doesn't even bother with her underwear as she pulls her thin, quick-dry guide pants over her hips. She rips off the T-shirt that she now realizes smells like Jake, consisting of sweat, beer, and Copenhagen, and his scent is making her want to throw up again. The tears swell. Pulling the hoodie over her head, she gathers up her Chacos and, without taking the time to slip them on, stumbles down the stairs and out the front door of the cabin.

"Hold on," Jake yells down the stairs.

"Don't worry about it, Jake." Rose turns back to direct a whispering, yet yelling kind of response, "I won't say anything. I'm not going to be the bitch that ruined your marriage."

Still drunk. Still in a daze, Rose runs across the street to the overflow parking lot of High Banks to find her red Jeep. It's the only car left in the lot except for the shop rig used to run shuttles. She fumbles through her pockets to find her keys and opens the door, and jumps in.

"What did I do?" She thinks to herself as she starts the Jeep. "What if people find out? How could this happen?"

Rose shifts the Jeep's transmission into drive and steps on the gas. The Jeep still has some gid-y-up as she spins the tires on the way out onto Bridge Street, which is essentially the main street in Craig. She turns left and crosses the Craig Bridge on her way to the Recreation Road, which runs along the Missouri River from Wolf Creek all the way to Cascade. All she wants is to just get back to Wolf Creek. She could take the highway, but she's worried that a State Trooper could be making the rounds and decides the Rec Road would be safer.

As she approaches the intersection of Bridge Street and Recreation Road, she glances down at her clock on the Jeep's radio. It's 6:21 am. The sun is just starting to chase the darkness from the sky.

"Fuck," Rose thinks. "Chase! God dangit."

Rose realizes that Chase has been locked inside the cottage all yesterday and all last night. She steps on the gas and peels out onto the Rec Road and cries uncontrollably as she speeds upstream along the Missouri River back to Wolf Creek.

IN A SPLIT SECOND

The two months leading up to the draft were two of the longest months of Trick's life. Although he was overwhelmed and thought there just wasn't enough time in the day to get everything done, he also felt the paradox of time moving at a snail's pace during those days. The one thing he looked forward to was the fishing getaway with Mike and Bret, and some of his former teammates.

Mike had planned the entire trip with the help of Sara. They reached out to a number of lodging options in the Craig area, from the super bougie full-service lodges to the do-it-yourself rustic cabins. They settled on the Fly Fisher Inn, which was just downstream from Craig across the Recreation Road from the Mountain Palace FAS. They chose the lodge for its location and modest amenities, and for its price, since most of Trick's buddies were also just graduating from college and had yet to find jobs. The Fly Fisher was really more like a travel motel with decent accommodations for eight guests to sleep, and a log-style, shared dining area with a fireplace and a kitchen to convene in the mornings and evenings.

Out of the eight men going, three of them had drift boats or rafts they were towing to the Missouri with them. That would allow for three guys per boat with an extra spot open. Some of them had rowing skills, while others did not, and only a few could actually fly fish. Mike planned to split them up so that nobody would get stuck rowing the entire time and everyone would have to do their share of the work. This wasn't going to be a guided trip; just eight buddies hanging out on one of the most prolific trout streams in the U.S., trying to figure it out.

Food was also a logistical challenge Sara and Mike

planned for. They put together menus for three dinners, breakfast foods, and lunches. Everything was so well planned out; all each of Trick's friends had to do was show up with a check to cover their portion of the cost. The plan was to cook the dinners and breakfasts in the kitchen at the lodge, and lunches would be done on the river. Beer and alcohol were left up to each individual.

Everyone was to arrive at the Fly Fisher Inn on Friday evening on the 11th, fish Saturday and Sunday, and leave Monday morning. Except for Bret, everyone would be driving over from Missoula. Bret would fly into Helena late Friday night, stay in a hotel, and be picked up early Saturday morning by either Mike or Trick, or one of the other guys.

The plan was set. Mike and Sara sent out multiple emails to all the guys, keeping in constant contact with them to make sure it would all go off seamlessly. The trip was incredibly important to Mike. He wanted so badly to give this gift to Trick as a symbol of how proud he was of how hard Trick had worked the last few years.

Most of the guys showed up that Friday evening packing layers of fleece, rain gear, waders, and fishing rods. A few bottles of whiskey circled around the group, and multiple cases of beer filled coolers that were being double-teamed as they unloaded supplies and brought them into the lodge. Mike had originally planned to drive over with Trick, but because someone had to pick up Bret Saturday morning, Trick decided he would take his Nissan Frontier so that Mike didn't have to mess with unhooking his boat and leaving it somewhere while they ran into town. They also figured they could use Trick's truck as a shuttle rig to transport drivers back to their rigs at the end of their floats.

Mike rolled into the parking area of the lodge around 4 pm. Getting out of his F-150, he greeted the group, introducing himself to those he had not officially met yet. Most of the guys were familiar with Mike, as many had been invited to Mike and Sara's for those Sunday lunches during the college football season. A couple were not, however, so Mike took a few minutes to exchange pleasantries before getting things set up.

"Beer?" one of the players asked Mike.

"No thanks," Mike replied. "I gave that up a while back. Don't let me stop you from getting your drunk on, though. Anyone hear from Trick?"

"He was right behind us when we left Missoula." One of the players responded. "I think he said he had to run back to his house for something. I'm sure he's close."

Trick had to run back for something. He was also incredibly grateful for all the work Mike had put in to help him meet his goals, and he wanted to show his gratitude. He didn't run back to his house. Instead, he stopped at the Grizzly Hackle, a fly shop in Missoula, to pick up a gift for Mike.

At around 5:30 pm, Trick turned his Frontier off the Rec Road and into the parking area. The temperatures were starting to drop, so the group had moved into the dining area of the lodge. Mike had been in the kitchen putting things away and getting ready to start cooking. Trick stepped through the doors of the lodge, with his hands behind his back, ducking his head, avoiding the door jamb.

"Trick!" reverberated throughout the lodge as Trick's teammates jumped up from their recliners and couches to greet him.

Mike busted out from the kitchen to give Trick a

proper hug. He picked Trick up and shook him so hard he almost dropped the package he was hiding behind his back.

"What you got there, Tricky, Trick?" Mike asked with a big grin on his face.

"I got this for you," Trick replied as he pulled the rod tube from behind his back and extended it towards Mike.

Not being that much of a gearhead, Mike never had a new rod. He made do with what had been passed down from his grandpa, occasionally picking up an old fiberglass or a cheap graphite rod from second-hand stores or pawn shops. He was of the school of, "it ain't the bow, it's the Indian." In fact, he often said those same words as he plucked the fly out of another trout's lip, looking back at Trick with a shit-eaten grin as Trick looked on with a little bit of jealousy but mostly in awe of how successful Mike was at catching fish regardless of how ratty his gear looked.

Mike took the rod tube from Trick's hand. "What's this?"

The rod was a brand-new 4-piece, 9-foot, 5-weight Winston Boron made in the good 'ole USA. In fact, it was actually assembled and wrapped in Twin Bridges, Montana, almost in their backyard. It had the classic dark green blanks with deep green thread wraps on the guides and the handwritten insignia on the furrows. The rod was absolutely gorgeous.

Chuckling, head cocked to the side and grinning ear to ear, Mike lets out a, "You 'ole dog, Tricky, Trick. What's this for?"

"Your gear sucks, Mike, and if I'm going to keep borrowing shit from you, I think you ought to step up your game a bit."

Trick continues, "Dude, there is absolutely no way I could have gotten to this place without you. This rod? This is the least I can do. I just want you to know how much I appreciate you and what you've done for me."

"You did all the work, man," Mike replies. "I didn't do anything."

"You made me believe in myself," Trick confesses. "Thanks."

Mike wraps an arm around Trick's neck and pulls him into a one-armed headlock and says, "Let's get this party started. Thanks, Trick."

Mike took on the cooking details with a couple of the players helping out. He cooked his signature spaghetti using elk burger. It was a sweet and hot red sauce, where he unabashedly started with your plain old store-bought, generic pasta sauce as the base, but then added a little brown sugar, Italian seasoning, crushed red pepper, cloves, onion, garlic, and fennel.

Trick walks into the kitchen, "Holy crap, what's that smell?"

The fennel and cloves gave off a licorice aroma that filled the entire lodge. That, with the garlic, onion, and tomato base, brought out the more traditional savory fragrance of the typical Italian offering. As the smells drifted out into the dining area of the lodge, the players unconsciously started feeling hungry, moving towards the chip bowls and veggie trays.

"Secret recipe, Trick," Mike declares. "It's just about done. Grab the guys and let's do this."

What was becoming a louder and louder roar with the guys drinking beer and telling stories about their time as Grizzly football players, quieted down to clanking of silverware onto porcelain plates and the occasional,

"Holy shit, this is some good pasta," as they all dove into dinner. The food was amazing. The guys were happy, and the weekend was well on its way down the path towards everything Mike was hoping for.

By 9 pm, the dishes were done, and the kitchen was cleaned up by a few of the other players who hadn't helped with the cooking. Now everyone was relaxing either at the table or the bar, or draped over the reclining chairs next to the fire that was crackling in full force. They were still drinking beer, but now a bottle of whiskey had made its way out into the group and was being passed around. Mike was declining as the bottle circled past him. Trick took a pull off it as he had done everything he could up until now to impress the NFL scouts and general managers, and now it was pretty much out of his hands. He might as well celebrate.

Bret called at around 11 pm. He had landed at Helena Regional. He was taking a short shuttle ride to the hotel, as Mike and Trick didn't feel it was necessary to rent a car only to have him arrive at the lodge as the party was dwindling. Trick decided he would run into Helena on his own in the morning while the others got their gear ready for the day.

By midnight, the whiskey was cashed as well as a case and a half of some local beer that was brought over from Missoula, along with some cheap alternatives. Moose Drool and Cold Smoke were the predominant beers for the Missoula locals. If you couldn't handle the hard stuff, Coors and Coors Light with a few Rainiers were thrown into the mix.

"If you want to drink cheap beer, it might as well be Rainier!" One of the players shouted out as he raised his can for another toast.

The first casualty hit the floor right in front of the fireplace at around 12:30 am. He was the quarterback, so not very big and definitely not able to hang with the rest of the guys, who comprised of mostly linemen and a full-back. It wasn't really a fair fight as the starting QB was outweighed by anywhere from 40 to 100 pounds.

A couple of the offensive linemen lifted their quarterback up off the floor. Mike piped in, "Huh, looks a lot like what was happening all day against Wofford."

A sarcastic, "Fuck you," came out of one of the players. That game still stung a bit to the seniors.

"I'm sorry, man." Mike consoled. "Too soon?"

"It's all good," came the response. "It's all good."

The two players picked their QB up and carried him out the door and to an empty room in the motel. They didn't undress him. They didn't even take his shoes off or pull the blankets over him, but they did make sure he was fully on the bed.

By 1 am, the party was winding down. The guys were heading to their rooms and saying their goodnights. Mike and Trick were the last to call it a night.

"You picking Bret up in the morning?" Mike asks Trick as he yawns.

"I am. I should get going early. I'm thinking around six or six-fifteen." Trick answers. "I can just meet you guys at the shop in Craig. We'll take care of Bret's gear when we get off the river."

"Sounds good," Mike responds. "Time to get some sleep."

"Hey, man," Trick adds. "I really do appreciate everything you've done for me these past few years. I don't think I would have had the chances I'm getting without you…you and Sara."

"Well," Mike tells Trick. "I appreciate that. Sara and I love you. We are both really proud of you. Now let's get to sleep."

The alarm on Trick's phone went off at 5:45 am. Confused and disoriented, he reached for the phone to snooze the alarm. Becoming aware of the throbbing in his head, Trick realized how much beer he had drunk the night before, and the pieces of the puzzle were slowly coming into focus. The room was dark and smelled of the musk that infiltrated the various fabrics in the motel's rooms, such as bedding, chair covers, and drapes hanging over the windows from a winter of stagnant, damp storage.

Trick picked up his phone and turned on the flashlight function, pointing it into the darkness. He scanned the room. His roommate was still a lifeless lump on the adjacent bed. Trick located his clothes in a pile at the end of his bed and fought off the temptation, defying the voice in his head to just go back to sleep. He made a move towards his clothes and as quietly as he could, trying not to wake up the other player, he pulled on his pants, draped his flannel over his shoulders, and headed out the door.

It was still very dark outside, and to say brisk, it would be a bit of a romantic understatement. It was cold. A streetlamp hanging outside the lodge gave just enough light for Trick to navigate the broken sidewalk from the motel. He quickly scurried down the path to the front door of the lodge and went in while rubbing his arms, trying to get his blood to circulate.

The kitchen light was on, and he smelled the comforting aroma of rich, dark coffee. He heard it percolating and couldn't think of anything he wanted more than a cup of this lifeline with some cream and sugar. Trick loves the smell of coffee but isn't sold on the taste so he does everything he can to make it resemble hot cocoa.

Mike steps out from the kitchen. He doesn't have the handicap of a hangover, so he was already up, starting coffee and prepping for breakfast.

"How you feelin'?" Mike asks Trick.

"I think a dog snuck into my room and shit in my mouth," Trick answers. "That was cheap-ass whiskey. Between that and the Cold Smokes, I guess I'm doing as well as can be expected."

"There's a solution to that," Mike states with a hint of condemnation.

"Yeah, yeah, I know," Trick says. "Sometimes ya just gotta let loose."

"You won't have time to eat what I'm cooking, but grab a muffin and some coffee," Mike instructs.

"Oh, you better believe it."

Trick grabs a travel mug sitting on the bar and fills it up. He wolfs down a muffin and heads towards the front door.

He yells back into the kitchen, "Hey, dude, I'm heading into town. I'll meet you guys in less than two hours at the shop. Do I need to pick up anything?"

"Nah, we're good," Mike yells back. "Sara made sure we had everything we needed. See you at the shop."

Trick jumps in his truck and fires it up and waits for a few seconds to let the engine warm, and then throws the shifter into drive. The Frontier has a snappy little six-cylinder engine. Trick spins the tires as he goes from the gravel of the parking area to the asphalt of the Rec Road. He turns left, back upstream along the Missouri River, finds the right lane, and accelerates.

The sun was just starting to show itself over the canyon walls of the Mighty Mo. Trick elected to drive the Rec Road to Wolf Creek before getting onto I-15 to head south. Getting on the road early, he had time. He has coffee, and he just wants to take in the sights of this amazing place and this amazing time.

Speeding past the Canyon Access point where he could have jumped onto the freeway, Trick follows the Rec Road back upstream, heading south. It was difficult to wrap his head around the idea that he was, indeed, heading south and upstream. That's just not the way his brain worked. Trick has been in Montana for a few years now and realizes water flows downhill, which doesn't always mean it flows south, but assumptions and habits are hard to break, even in an individual only 22 years old.

Trick passes the confluence of the Dearborn River, then Spite Hill, and Stickney Creek. He takes a mental note of where these access points are since he knows it will be important information for when they are floating down the river. He sees the turnoff to Craig and keeps heading upstream on the Rec Road to Wolf Creek.

As Trick speeds past the Craig turnoff, he looks down at the clock on the radio of his truck. It's taken a little longer than he thought to navigate the winding Rec Road, and he knows he's cutting it close on time. Bret will be waiting for him at the hotel. Trick steps a little harder on the gas and speeds on.

A mile upstream from Craig, the road banks left following the contour of the river. A cliff wall rises off the river, creating a bluff looking out over the landscape with the old Fly Way Ranch in the background. A crude parking area had been created by locals years ago on top of the bluff. Fish, Wildlife, and Parks had recently designated the parking area as a fishing access site, naming it "Lone Pine." The guides refer to it as Cell Phone Bluff because it's the only place that's high enough near Craig to get an adequate cellphone signal to do business. Many of the outfitters and guides stop off at the parking area regularly to check their messages and to respond to trip requests.

A few hundred yards before Trick reaches the bluff, his phone dings. He looks down and sees he has a text message from Bret. Picking up his phone to look at the message, his eyes are down for only a second or two. When he looks back up, he sees a vehicle on the road in front of him. It's too late.

Trick locks up the brakes. His truck goes into a skid and slides sideways. He's going too fast to avoid contact with the vehicle that seems to have stalled in front of him. Steering to the right would send him off the bluff and into the river. Huge boulders on the left side of the road prevent him from using the opposite ditch. Time slows. His heart stops for a moment. Trick grips the steering wheel, and as if he were taking on a defender trying to rip his head off, he braces for impact and actually lowers a shoulder to deflect the blow.

Trick doesn't smash into the car in front of him. It's more of a glancing blow that sends him into a spin and the other vehicle, just a nudge, propelling it down the road. The Frontier slides across the bottom end of the parking area, wiping out the jack fence protecting vehicles and people from the steep embankment dropping off into the river.

The metal of the truck buckles around him as it bounces off boulders on the way down. Each boulder he slams into throws his body from one side of the truck to the other, straining against the seatbelt he has secured across his chest and waist. His head slams against the door window, shattering it.

The Frontier keeps rolling and slamming into boulders, and Trick wonders how long this can last. He is on a ride that feels like eternity, like when he was a little kid the first time on the Zipper at the fair, and he can't stop it. There's no button or lever or carny he can call out to that can slow the ride down. Tumbling down and down, the truck flips up, and he feels himself going airborne.

The feeling of weightlessness only lasts for a second as the truck slams down onto the bed of the river, bouncing up only to slam down again. The sound of the truck crashing was horrific. Angry growls of metal on rock and then the thumping and crunching, echoing against the cliff walls, sending magpies scattering. Water sprayed up around the truck and fell back to the river in droplets, creating ripples circling the carnage.

Trick's truck landed on its passenger's side with the nose of the vehicle facing upstream. It rocked as if it wanted to roll upside down, but fortunately, it lost the momentum to carry it all the way over and came to rest in that position. The depth of the river where the truck came to rest was only a couple of feet deep. The windshield was shattered but not busted out, which protected the cab from the rushing water, creating a pocket of air.

Trick was unconscious and hanging lifeless from the seatbelt that had not failed. His body was contorted, with his head supported just high enough to keep his mouth and nose out of the water that had filled the cab about a third of the way up.

Jeff Thomas, a local mechanic and volunteer firefighter, was heading down the Rec Road towards Craig from Wolf Creek. He lived just outside Wolf Creek, but his shop was in Craig. He was on his way to work when the crash happened. From his vantage point about a quarter mile upstream of the bluff, he saw the truck as it went airborne and violently smashed onto the riverbed. He saw the water spraying up like a geyser and then falling back to the river, leaving a cloud of dust and mist that lingered for several seconds in the dim light of the morning.

"Holy fuck!" He said out loud, although there was no one else to hear.

Having been a volunteer firefighter for 30+ years, Jeff had been to a lot of accident scenes in the area. Because of how far Craig is from any hospitals or ambulance services, the volunteers are usually the first ones on the scene. Jeff is usually one of those volunteers, but actually witnessing the accident was not something he was all that familiar with.

The first thing Jeff did was pull over and radio for help. It was obvious this accident was severe, with at least one serious injury, but potentially more. He knew he would need help immediately, so putting first things first, he made the call to initiate emergency medical services.

Jeff pulled back onto the Rec Road. He could feel the adrenaline rush. That wasn't new. Anytime he would get called out, there was that element of nervousness and sense of urgency that he learned early on to use as a resource for action. Seeing the accident happen, or at least watching the tail end of it, ramped up this adrenaline rush to a heightened level, and Jeff knew he needed to get a hold of it. He backed off the accelerator of the old Chevy pickup and told himself to take a breath and calm down.

As Jeff traveled towards the wreck, following a bend in the road, a familiar sight came towards him. Jeff knew just about every vehicle in the canyon, due to him being the only mechanic for miles. Guides are notorious for misusing, abusing, and just neglecting their rigs, so Jeff often sees them in his shop. This vehicle coming towards him was Rose's red Jeep.

"Fly?" he contemplated.

Jeff's focus was on the wreck. He knew he needed to get to the bluff and down to the vehicle before it filled up with water. But as Rose passed him, speeding in the opposite direction, their eyes locked for a brief moment. She looked stressed. Her hands were gripping hard on the steering wheel. That split second when their eyes met notwithstanding, she was staring intently forward—never letting her eyes leave the road in front of her. Her hair was a mess, and for that brief second, he thought he could see her sobbing.

Jeff's focus quickly left Rose and moved on to the Frontier that was lying on its side in the Missouri River.

WHEN TOMORROW COMES

Jeff's quick thinking that morning to immediately initiate EMS most likely saved Trick's life. Along with a severe head injury, his left arm was severed to the bone just above the elbow with multiple compound fractures to his humerus. Both the ulna and radius bones were also crushed at the elbow. Apparently, as the driver's side window shattered, Trick's arm flung out of the window and was rolled up on before the truck went airborne. The brachial artery in the anterior of the upper arm was also severed, and had Jeff not responded as quickly as he did, Trick would have bled out while hanging from the seatbelt, half submerged in the river.

A second vehicle, a dark blue, late model Dodge Durango, was also on the scene with obvious damage to the front-right bumper and passenger side as it came to rest in the opposite ditch facing downstream. It appeared to have suffered the brunt of the damage by glancing off boulders lining the ditch along the road. The driver of the Durango, a middle-aged male, sporting the typical guide attire of the button-up fishing shirt, Simms hat, and Buff, was struggling to open his door and exit the vehicle.

Jeff's initial assessment of the accident was to prioritize care for Trick. From his vantage point above the river, he could tell Trick was in critical condition. He was not moving, and Jeff could see his arm with the bones protruding and blood spurting out of the wound. He needed to get the bleeding under control above all else.

Jeff yelled to the driver of the Durango, instructing him to have a seat and relax, and that help would be there soon, then grabbed his medical kit he always carried behind the seat of the old Chevy, and scrambled down the embankment of the river towards Trick. As he entered the water, he gasped as the cold water nearly sent him into shock. He wanted to jump back out of the river, but he knew he needed to get the bleeding from Trick's arm under control.

Jeff was in the water for about 10 minutes before the first of the volunteers showed up. Knowing how cold the water was, the volunteers took shifts with Trick, tapping out every few minutes until the rescue crew with appropriate gear, including wetsuits, arrived.

A flight for life air ambulance left Great Falls and landed in the clearing on top of the bluff 24 minutes after being called. Two ambulances from Helena arrived at the scene within 45 minutes. All the volunteer firefighters from Craig and Wolf Creek were on the scene to offer support. Jeff was able to stabilize Trick's bleeding in that initial trip into the water. The other firefighters were able to keep the bleeding under control as they took shifts.

At this point, Trick had lost a lot of blood, but that wasn't the only concern. He had been in the water for approximately 30 minutes, and hypothermia was looming. Paradoxically, it was the cold of the water that may have helped to save his life. With capillaries constricting as a natural response to the cold water, the bleeding from Trick's arm was slowed down. However, the crew needed to get him out and warmed up without causing more damage to any potential head or neck injuries. Still unconscious and with the EMTs fearing the worst, he was carefully removed from his truck and strapped to a backboard before carrying him upstream along the riverbank to a safer extraction point.

When Bret didn't hear back from Trick after texting him, there was some cause for concern, but he also understood that the guys had been hanging out at the lodge all night, and there was a good chance they all got a late start. Plus, cell service along the river is spotty at best.

It was around Eight O'clock that Bret's anticipation of fishing the Missouri and potentially missing out, along with a fear that something might have happened, created enough anxiety to call the lodge. There was no answer, so Bret called the shop.

"Missouri River Angler, this is Mike," was the answer from the shop.

"Yeah, my name is Bret and I'm looking for a group of guys meeting up there for a fishing trip?" he responded, knowing he probably was a bit vague. "I know, there's probably a lot of those guys, but these guys you can't miss. They're all football players and pretty stacked."

"Yeah, I think they're all standing outside. Can I grab one of them for you?"

"Yes, please. Mike Morley is the guy's name." Bret answered.

The 'shop' Mike walked outside and, with the receiver of the cordless phone tucked against his chest, yelled, "Mike Morley?"

"That's me," Mike yells back.

Mike runs up onto the shop's porch and grabs the phone. "Hello?"

"Dude," Bret starts. "What's up?"

Mike was waiting in the parking lot of the shop with the rest of the guys watching the commotion of volunteer firefighters and state troopers, and the helicopter landing, and finally two ambulances speeding across the Craig Bridge. That was about twenty minutes before the call came from Bret, but at that very second, with Bret's voice asking that simple question, panic consumed Mike's body.

"Oh my god, Bret. I'll call you back on my cell phone. Oh my god!"

Mike gave the shop employee standing behind the counter just enough time to make eye contact before throwing the phone to him from the doorway.

"I'm sorry, man. I gotta go."

Mike ran to his truck and, with his boat still in tow, threw the transmission into gear and started out of the parking lot onto Bridge Street. The players watched as Mike turned right towards the river. Another rig coming into town slammed on its brakes to avoid a collision.

Mike raced through town, past the boat ramp, and over the bridge. He barely slowed down as he turned right onto the Rec Road, going back upstream towards Cellphone Bluff.

As Mike approached the bluff, EMTs were transporting Trick from the ambulance he was originally put in at the extraction point to the helicopter on top of the bluff. Mike couldn't tell yet who was on the gurney, but deep down inside, he knew. His truck barely came to a stop, and Mike was jumping out, running toward the air ambulance.

A state trooper held out an arm to stop Mike. "I'm sorry, I can't let you go over there."

"That's my best friend. I have to!" Mike pleaded.

"Hold on," the trooper directed and ran over to the chopper.

He shouted some things at one of the technicians and then looked back at Mike and waved him over.

Mike didn't hesitate. He ran to the helicopter and was given a hand by the tech and helped up. Mike looked down, and sure enough, his fears were confirmed. With Mike buckled into a spare seat, the helicopter lifted and banked north, following the river downstream.

The first ambulance had already left for St. Peter's Hospital in Helena with the driver from the Durango. Trick was en route to Benefis Hospital in Great Falls via Flight for Life. However, on the way to Great Falls, Trick's breathing stopped, and due to his deteriorating condition, he was rerouted to the level II trauma center at St. Patrick Hospital in Missoula.

It took 45 minutes for the air ambulance to reach St. Patrick Hospital. In that time, Trick was intubated and given an IV of plasma to help stabilize shock and manage his blood loss. He never regained consciousness on the transport. Mike held his hand the entire way, quietly saying prayers, encouraging Trick to hang in there.

The first call Mike made was to Sara. She would be the one to get the wheels turning, calling Trick's parents and making sure everyone was contacted who needed to be contacted. Mike also knew she was the best person, in the moment, to oversee the care that Trick was being given. She canceled all her appointments and was at the hospital within the hour.

The next call was to Bret.

"What the fuck's going on, Mike?" It was the first thing out of Bret's mouth as he answered the phone.

"I'm sorry, Bret," Mike answered. "I'm sorry, but I had to go. Trick wrecked on the way in to pick you up."

"What?" Bret asked with a sense of urgency. "How bad?"

"I don't know, Bret. It's bad, but nobody really knows. He was air-lifted by flight-for-life to Missoula."

"God dangit," Bret responded. "Can you tell anything?"

"All I know," Mike admitted, "he was unconscious

and never woke up. I rode in the chopper with him. He stopped breathing at one point. His left arm was pretty mangled. I don't know, dude."

"Shit," Bret sighed. "I didn't know what was going on, so I rented a car. I'll head over to Missoula right now. I'll be there in a couple of hours."

"All right, dude," Mike added. "Just be prepared. It's not good and listen, I know how much you care about Trick, but I also know you and Trick are business partners…just be prepared."

"Mike," Bret interjected. "Let's put first things first. Let's just make sure Trick makes it through this. Football can wait. The NFL isn't going anywhere."

Trick opened his eyes for the first time on April 26th, two weeks after the accident and the first day of the NFL draft. He had minimal response to external stimuli, but was showing promise that he was not paralyzed because he responded to pin pricks on his feet.

The extent of his head injuries was unclear. Luckily, he didn't have any fractures to his spine that might cause permanent damage. He suffered from a fractured femur, a broken nose, multiple lacerations across his face and forehead, and his left arm was nearly cut off eight inches from the shoulder.

It was on day three after the accident that Trick's parents had to make the most difficult decision of their lives. With Trick still unconscious, his left arm developed a bacterial infection, and he went into septic shock. Doctors tried treating the infection, but given Trick's condition, he was not responding to the medications. Doctors suggested removing his arm in an effort to save his life. Trick's parents consented.

Little by little, day by day, Trick regained cognitive

ability. During the first few days after regaining consciousness, he woke up and scanned the room, noticing people in the room he recognized and forcing out a smile. He only stayed awake for a few moments before drifting back to sleep. Each day brought a few more minutes he could stay awake, and his interactions became more nuanced and sophisticated. It would take Trick another week and a half to be able to put sentences together.

Mike and Sara, along with Trick's parents, Roy and Genene, became regulars in the recovery unit at St. Patrick Hospital. In those first few weeks of recovery, the four got to know each other very well. In fact, Roy and Genene often referred to Mike and Sara as family. When talk of Trick's condition and who would eventually address the elephant in the room once Trick was able to receive such information was too much for Genene, she and Sara took walks along the Clark Fork River that flowed through Missoula and talked about things like wedding plans and children and anything but the accident and what that would mean for Trick's future.

Roy and Mike spoke often as well, but mostly about Trick's future. It was decided early on that Trick would not transfer back to California because they both agreed that Trick's heart was in Montana, and being here, playing for the Griz, he had developed the support system he would need to recover. Roy suppressed his initial reaction to the thought of not taking Trick home but knew, in the end, it was the right thing to do.

When the topic of football came up and the discussion turned to who was the best to break the news to Trick, no one was confident that there was a right or wrong way to do it. Even the mention of having that conversation brought tears to Roy's eyes. He knew how important football was to Trick. He knew how hard Trick had worked to make it as far as he did. To even be considered by NFL teams, given where he started, was incredible. But to have it all right in front of him and now ripped away by something out of his control was gut-wrenching.

"It's not fair." Roy would often say as he cradled his head in his hands, fighting off the tears. "It's just not fair."

It didn't help that there wasn't a lot of information about what actually happened that day at Cellphone Bluff. Authorities were able to recover Trick's phone, but because it was submerged in water, it took a while to access anything useful from it. They were able to conclude that a text message from Bret had been delivered just moments before the accident.

The Durango that was involved in the accident was heading north and had swerved off the road and into the ditch, striking the rock wall, trying to avoid impact with Trick's Frontier. The middle-aged guide driving the Durango admitted he had just checked his phone for a text message that had chimed through as he came into cell coverage and looked up barely in time to see the Frontier swerving in front of him. He hadn't remembered seeing anything else and had also been unconscious for a few seconds, so his testimony to what may have happened was useless.

Mike often fell back on his faith to offer some solace to Roy, and when that didn't work, he would redirect Roy into focusing his energy on Trick and his recovery. Mike was angry, too. Mike had seen Trick through many of the challenges that would eventually position him for a shot. Yes, it was frustrating for all of them and incredibly sad, but the focus, as Mike would always come to, was doing what was best for Trick now.

As much as Bret wanted to be there for Trick, this was the most important time for him and his other clients, as the draft had come and gone, and the window for unsigned free agents was quickly closing. He called Mike every day for updates, even after it was a forgone conclusion that Trick would never play football again. Mike and Bret talked often about when to give Trick the news and who should deliver it. Bret insisted on being there, and as Trick started gaining some strength and was able to process information a little better, Bret flew back to Missoula.

Mike put the word out to a couple of the players he had contact information. They contacted other players and coaches. They all showed up at the hospital and flooded the recovery unit. Knowing how devastating the news would be to Trick, it was decided that only Trick's parents, Mike, Sara, and Bret would be in the room to deliver it.

Trick was awake when the five entered the room. He gave a painful smile and then his eyes fell to his chest.

"Son?" Roy asks. "Are you in pain?"

Trick shook his head. "It's not that, Dad."

Trick was struggling to get words out. He continues. "My leg…hurts. My face…feels like hell. Whole body, sore." After a pause, "Can't feel my arm."

Roy sits on the edge of the bed and reaches out to hold Trick's right hand, "Son, I'm sorry. They tried to save it…I'm sorry. There was an infection, and the medicine wasn't clearing it up. We had to do something, and if it wasn't the arm, you probably would have died."

Trick closes his eyes. A single tear slowly rolls down the side of his face.

"I'm so sorry, Trick," Genene adds. "I'm so sorry."

Bret enters the conversation, "Trick, we're here for you. I promise. I know you don't want to hear this, but it's going to work out. I'm just glad to see you're alive."

"Hey, Trick?" Sara asks gingerly as she clears her voice. "I don't blame you if you don't want to see anyone right now, but there are a few people who would like to say hi."

Trick shrugs his shoulder as if to say, "What does it matter?"

The door to the room opens slowly as a couple of players poke their heads in. "Is it alright? Can we come in?"

One by one, Trick's teammates file into the room, give Trick a couple of words of encouragement, a hug, and turn back to exit. Every teammate, from the seniors who he had played their last game with him to the red shirts he barely knew, came in to offer support to Trick. The coaches were last.

It was Trick's tight end coach, Bryce Josephson, who brought up the rear and, while holding Trick's hand, leaned down and whispered in his ear, "You didn't get this far, Trick, because you had some fuckin, God given talent. You were undersized. You came from nowhere. You worked your fucking ass off to make the team. You worked your fucking ass off to turn the heads of all those scouts and GMs. God did give you something, Trick. Fall back on that. We all love you."

As Bryce left the room, Mike entered again before the rest of Trick's family.

"You alright, buddy?" Mike asks.

"What am I going to do, Mike?" Trick replies.

"Well," Mike answers. "For starters, you're gonna live. And when tomorrow comes, we'll figure that day out and then the next."

RIVER THERAPY

It's been over 13 months since Rose took her last drink. It hasn't been lost on her how much better she feels physically, especially in the mornings. Emotionally, however, she's still got a lot of work to do. She hits the snooze button one more time before she knows she has to force herself to get moving. Chase jumps up on the bed, and the gradual waking of the day slowly progresses to sitting up, rubbing her eyes, and then realizing that he needs to go out.

Rose jumps to her feet and opens the front door out into the small fenced-in yard. Ross, Rose's landlord, is making his way to one of the sheds in the backyard of the historic hotel. He's wearing old, ripped-up Carhart bibs and looks like he's about to tackle a dirty project. The sheds are filled with old tools and farming equipment, no doubt left by either the previous owners or even the owners before them. Every once in a while, Ross gets a wild hair and decides to rummage through the sheds in search of a pot of gold or just something he thinks might be useful. Rose guesses that he feels that if he just keeps picking away, eventually he'll have some usable space to store things that are actually worth something.

"Morning, Rose," Ross greets her.

"Morning, Ross," Rose answers back.

Chase lifts his leg, relieving himself on the fence. He then pushes the gate open with his nose and, while wagging his tail violently side to side, saunters off towards Ross to give his own greeting, knowing it will elicit a scratching of his ears.

"How are you feeling, Rose?" Ross asks with a fatherly kind of empathetic voice.

"Oh, I'm fine," Rose replies.

"How's your back?" He asks.

"A little stiff," Rose admits. "Won't keep me off the river, though. Yoga's been helping."

"Gotta trip today?" He asks.

"Yeah. It should be pretty lax. Taking out some recovery folks," she answers. "They're usually pretty chill. Take 'em out, catch a couple of fish… let 'em take their minds off of things for a little while. And I told the sheriff I would so…"

"How 'bout you, Rose?" Ross raises an eyebrow. "Are you able to take your mind off things?"

That night with Jake Trapper, a little over a year ago, led Rose down a path of self-loathing and self-destruction, which, had it not been for Ross and Karren, may have been too much of a hole for her to climb out of. She had been raped. She lost her dignity, and as she fled the cabin where the assault had taken place, she got into her Jeep and piled up a tally of poor decisions she is now slowly chipping away at.

"I'm fine," she insists with a shortened tone. "Gotta go."

Rose calls Chase back, and they retreat to the cottage together. She needs to get moving. She looks up over the canyon walls surrounding Wolf Creek and notices clouds building and churning. It's usually a little more humid and a little more shaded in the canyon, which makes it feel cooler than it actually is. The clouds building tell of rain. That's kind of a bummer to Rose, as today is meant to be pretty low-key and fun for folks that don't usually have the means to float the river.

Rose leaned on Ross and Karren heavily for support in the weeks and months after she was raped. She opened up to them about Jake, and Ross took it much like a father would and immediately went to the gun rack. It took all Karen had to talk some sense into him. Rose was taken aback by Ross's reaction and found herself even more endeared to him. That didn't mean she didn't get equally frustrated with Ross for asking personal questions, much like she did with her biological father while he was alive.

Montana Healing Waters Project provides an opportunity in the form of fly-fishing for victims recovering from head injuries and other neurological conditions as they try to get back on their feet. Spending a day on the water helps build some confidence in patients as well as take their minds off the rehabilitation process, helping alleviate some of the frustration of a slow-moving recovery. It also does wonders for breaking free from the grip of PTSD for a little while.

Today's trip consisted of six anglers from across the state of Montana with varying levels of disability. They were also at different points along their road to recovery. Along with the six anglers, there were three guides; all meeting at the Missouri River Angler at 8 am.

Rose arrived in the parking lot of the shop a few minutes before eight. The anglers were there along with one of the other guides and the project coordinator, Tom Owen. She liked Tom. He was a little bit on the heavy side with a fluffy white beard and white hair. Although she had not yet confirmed this, she was certain Tom played Santa during the holidays. Tom had a heart of gold. He worked as a therapist with his own private practice. His role with MHWP, coordinating these trips, was purely a volunteer arrangement, and Rose respected that about him.

"Hey Tom," Rose announces herself as she bashfully makes her way to the group.

"There's my girl," Tom proclaims as he wraps an arm around Rose and pulls her in tight. "How are you doing this morning?"

Tom had a way with making her feel like a little girl—not in a subordinate way, but like he protected her as if she were his own. It made her feel warm and valued. Those feelings were feelings she had a hard time with ever since her dad became ill when she was a little girl. Where she kept everyone else at a distance, she felt comfortable with Tom showing affection and giving her accolades. Other people might get a sharp tongue lashing at any sign of a compliment.

"I'm good," Rose replies with her head tilted down and a crooked smile emerging on her lips.

"Hope you got a good night's sleep. You might have your work cut out for you today," he says right in front of the group, not even caring he might be offending the two anglers he was pairing Rose up with. "This is Rose, she's one of your guides."

"What, these guys?" Rose asks. "I'm sure they'll be fine."

Rose scans the group. The two guys to the left of her in the circle they naturally formed as she approached appeared to be in their late sixties, maybe early seventies. One of the gentlemen has a bit of the tremors going on, like that of someone experiencing the early onset of Parkinson's. He is leaning into a walker. They both have similar facial features, a similar build, and if Rose were going to bet, she would put her money on them somehow being related.

Tom introduces them as "The brothers, Pat and Dave McDermott."

Folks with Parkinson's weren't the population the

project normally served, but Tom was generous in his definition of trauma and included Pat and Dave, as he knew they would both benefit from a day on the river. It's a horrible disease, and Tom was quite certain the donors to the program weren't going to hold it against him.

The man to their left was much younger and dressed in a tattered Simms shirt, tattered Simms hat, and Simms waders stained with mud and mayo from guide sandwiches and whatever else that may have dropped out of his long, scruffy beard.

"You must be one of the other guides," Rose assumes.

"I'm Riggs," comes from her cohort.

"Riggs?" she confirms as she raises an eyebrow. "Well, Riggs, it's nice to meet you."

She holds out a hand, and Riggs reaches across the circle to shake it.

"I'm John," another participant says as he holds out a hand.

"Randy," comes from the next in line, and another handshake.

"Bob," and a nod from the next gentleman.

The last of the participants didn't play along like the others. He had visibly pulled back from the group and was standing a little sideways as if he had something to hide. His head is down, and he's yet to engage. He's younger than the rest of the participants and much taller and quite good-looking.

Rose thinks, "If he would just lift his head up..."

As Rose trains her eyes on him, she asks, "So, who are you?"

He lifts his head and turns towards her. She notices the left sleeve of his button-down Columbia PFG shirt is hanging empty with the cuff tucked into his belt. Their eyes meet. His stare rips through her. She feels the pain and anguish of what must be an incredibly difficult road this last participant is traveling.

"My name's Trick."

"Hey, Rose," Tom cuts in. "Have you seen Billy?"

"Billy?' she asks with a condescending tone, she quickly reels in as she turns to Tom.

She knows two of these guys are going to be fishing with him. It would be unfair to reveal her disdain, which would no doubt cause a predetermined bias for what they could expect out of him.

"I haven't seen him," she continues with a much softer delivery. "I'm sure he'll be here soon."

Her eyes go back to Trick. They continue to stare into each other, which is becoming increasingly obvious to the rest of the group and even a little uncomfortable to at least a couple of the guys as their heads drift down and they start picking through the gravel of the parking lot with the toes of their boots. She reveals a shy smile and cocks her head slightly, squinting, giving him an inquisitive look. He hints at a reciprocal smile and then lets his eyes fall back to the ground, and he joins in with the rest of the group to shuffle gravel.

"All right!" Tom claps his hands together, shocking the group to attention. "Let's get rolling. Rose, you've got Dave and Pat. Riggs, you're with John and Bob, and when Billy gets here, he'll take you, Randy, and Trick. The guides know the drill. They will take care of you guys. We'll be back at the shop around four?"

Rose and Riggs both nod.

"Sweet," Tom finishes. "Let's do this."

Rose gestures to Dave and Pat to come with her, and the group disperses. She grabs Pat by the arm to help him cross the parking lot as the wheels on his walker catch the stones in the gravel. As they head to Rose's rig, Billy comes rolling into the parking lot in his truck. In an obvious hurry because of his tardiness, he's driving fast enough to kick up a cloud of dust, making the patrons of the shop turn to see who this ignoramus is, barreling through the lot like a buffalo trying to outrun a cloud of biting flies. He locks up the brakes, slams the transmission into reverse, and backs up to the tongue of his boat trailer he has left in the yard of the shop.

Billy flings his door open and jumps out. A crumpled Bud Light can tumbles out of the door with him and rolls across the gravel. Billy shoves a lit cigarette into his mouth and pulls his pants back up over his waist, and then bends down to pick up the can and chucks it into the back of his truck. He waves towards Tom.

"Dumbass," Rose says to herself under her breath.

She turns her attention to Dave and Pat. "So, how are you guys doing on this fine spring morning?"

"Great," Dave answers. "Looking forward to this. It's been a while since Pat and I have been able to get out."

Pat struggles, "We used to fish together all the time."

His words are tired. Rose can tell he's having trouble putting sentences together. It's a sad thing to watch people who have lived their lives getting out, doing things like hunting and fishing on their own, now having to rely on others for those few moments when they might relive the glory days. Pat isn't the first client she's had who has struggled with getting older and, more profoundly, dealing with this nasty disease at a relatively young age.

"Oh yeah?" Rose asks. "Ever fish the Mo?"

"You know, it's crazy," Dave says. "We both live in Bozeman and have fished all over the State—the Yellowstone, Madison, Gallatin when we could get out and wade-fish, and even the Big Horn, but we've never fished the Missouri."

Pat adds, "We used to take one out-of-state trip a year. We fished in Alaska and Idaho…"

Showing a little impatience, Dave continues for Pat, "Yeah, we've fished all over the country, really. It was kind of our thing up until a couple of years ago."

"Nice," Rose says. "So, you might be teaching me some things today."

"Hey, Rose!" Riggs yells across the parking lot. "Where you heading?"

"Oh, probably Lower Canyon. You?"

"Wasn't sure. Mind if I tag along?" Riggs asks.

"Not at all. The more the merrier," she fires back.

The two guides and four participants gather their lunches, fill their coolers with ice, load up into their trucks, and head downstream to Mid-Canon, which is located just a few miles north of Craig. As they begin the ritual of putting their gear together and situating their boats, Billy's truck careens into the site. The truck jounces over potholes and speed bumps. The trailer bounces off the road and slams back down like he's towing a string of cans off his hitch. Billy's crew rocks back and forth, fighting the inertia from slamming their heads against the windows of the truck. They slam to a halt next to Rose's rig.

"What's up, Rose?" Billy announces his arrival as he jumps out of his truck.

"You decided to join us," Rose answers.

She watches as Billy's two participants climb out

of the truck. As Trick straightens up, she notices him looking down and shaking his head, scratching the back of his neck with his right hand.

"That poor boy," she thinks to herself. "He's going to have a long day."

Riggs and Rose quickly get their gear together and launch their drift boats into the river. The water is cold, and the clouds have built. Everyone is wearing raingear and waders. Rose stands in the water next to her boat and helps Pat lift a leg over the gunwale and into the bow. All the extra layers of clothing make it even harder to move. While grabbing the casting brace in the bow of the boat, Pat pulls his body into the boat while Rose guides his trailing leg and then plops down into the front seat.

Rose pushes the boat away from the bank with the anchor down, holding the boat from drifting away. With the boat floating free of the gravel, Dave climbs in and sits down in the back. Rose folds Pat's walker and places it along the front seat. There's just enough room in her boat for all the gear, the walker, and the three of them to barely fit. She sits down in the rower's chair in the middle of the boat. They are off.

The easiest way to get people into fish on the Missouri is to drift wet flies, imitating nymphs. Clients cast their line with weighted flies that drift along the bottom of the river where the majority of the fish live. A strike indicator that floats along on the surface of the water will tell the angler when their fly either hangs up on the bottom or a fish eats it. As soon as the indicator gets pulled underwater, the client sets the hook and hopefully comes tight on something other than a rock. The quicker the client is, the more opportunities they get for hooking fish.

As the boat drifts downstream, Rose watches Pat's indicator for any movement or signal of a trout eating his fly. Each time the indicator moves, Rose yells, "Hit it, Pat!"

Due to the Parkinson's and, more likely, his medications, his reaction time is slower than it used to be, and by the time he lifts his rod to set the hook, the trout he would normally catch spits out the fly, and Pat comes up empty. Meanwhile, Dave is hooking fish and landing them with little effort.

"Hit it!" Rose yells, but again, Pat is too slow.

At around noon, the three boats pull over onto a gravel bar off an inside bend of the river. They set up a table and chairs and served lunch to the participants. The guides grab a sandwich and huddle up together.

"How's it going for you?" asks Riggs.

"Nymphing's pretty good," Rose responds. "Or at least it would be, but Pat's a little slow on the trigger. It's kind of sad. I think his Parkinson's has really taken its toll."

"Dude," Billy cuts in. "I bet we put thirty in the net this morning."

"Hey, Billy," Riggs steps up. "Shut the hell up, alright. Not everyone can be as awesome as you."

Billy looks at Riggs as though he's going to say something and then thinks better of it as Riggs gives him a contemplative stare.

"You got something to say, Billy?" Riggs asks.

"What the fuck, dude?" Billy responds.

"Let me tell you something, Billy," Riggs continues. "Be a pro. Show some humility. This isn't a dick swinging contest, and if it were, I'm sure this little lady would make you piss yourself. Tighten it up, dude. Your truck is trashed; everyone who has to ride with you smells like smoke. You drive like a fucking maniac…you think these guys enjoy getting thrown around the cab of your piece of shit Tacoma on the way to the river; scared shitless that you're going to wrap it around the next telephone pole? Grow the fuck up."

Riggs walks back to the group to make sure they all have what they need.

"What the fuck was that?" Billy asks Rose.

She shrugs, "You tell me. I don't even know the guy."

Rose turns and walks back to the group with a shit-eating grin on her face.

She turns her attention to Trick and notices a prosthetic for his left arm. It's a synthetic arm with two hooked pinchers for a hand. He didn't have it at the beginning of the day, but must have put it on once they got in the boat.

"Where do you put your wedding ring?" Rose asks Trick while nodding towards the prosthetic.

He looks up at her and responds, "Fortunately, I don't have to worry about that."

"How's the fishing?" She asks.

"Well, the drill sergeant over there has gotten us into a lot of fish."

Billy is off by himself, licking his wounds and smoking a cigarette.

"He can be a little intense," Rose offers. "We're not all like that. How's the prosthetic working out?"

"Oh," Trick begins to answer, "rather have the real thing, but it's working out."

"Hey, Rose!" Riggs calls her. "Look at that pod of fish working."

The group looks out into the shallow flat along the inside bend where they are eating lunch. It's about one o'clock, and the March browns, which are large springtime mayflies, have started popping. With the heavy cloud cover, their wings don't dry very quickly, which gives them time to collect in mass on the surface in a blanket-hatch of bugs. About a dozen fish have worked their way up to the flat and are now porpoising in unison to gulp bugs down. Less than a second between each time their noses poke up through the film on the surface, they eat bug after bug after bug. It's beautiful how efficient and effortless they look; staying in one place in the river waiting for the bugs to come to them as they only move an inch or two, to rise again and eat the next one.

"I bet Pat would like to stick one of those pricks," he puts a hand on Pat's shoulder and gives him a little shake. "What do you think, Pat?"

The color drains from Rose's face. "Um…yeah. Hey Pat, you want to give 'em a try?"

If only Riggs could hear her inner dialogue right now as she curses him up and down the river to herself. "I've been working with Pat all morning, and now I'm supposed to get him to be able to present a dry fly to these fish? What the hell, Riggs?"

She's doing all she can to not actually mouth the words she wants to say… "There's no fricken way! And then I'm going to waste all the time to re-rig his rod and then have to change it back…"

"Yeah," Pat declares. "I would like to try."

"Shit." She suppresses holding it to herself.

"Awesome," she actually says. "Let me just rig this rod up and we'll teach these trout a lesson."

As Pat finishes his lunch, Rose grabs his rod and switches out the leader that has been kinked up due to crimping on sinkers and a strike indicator with a fresh leader. She stretches the memory out of the leader by running the length of it between her fingers, she protects with the tail of her shirt. She adds tippet material and ties on a single, size 14 parachute March brown. Trick watches intently, admiring how efficient she is with the entire process from tying a surgeon's knot for adding tippet to the leader to the Davie's knot to tie on the fly.

"Ready, Pat?" She asks as she dresses the fly with flotant and blows hard on it to fluff the wing hackle.

"Go get 'em, Pat," Riggs encourages.

Rose glares at Riggs.

As Pat gets up from his chair, he grabs his walker and heads towards the river and the pod of fish. With rod in hand, she locks her arm around Pat's and helps him push the walker through the river-stone lining the beach. They walk out into the water together. She positions Pat upstream from the pod and at an angle to make a good reach-cast and to feed the fly downstream to the pod. Pat takes some line off the reel, throws about 10 feet of line into his back cast, and lays out an almost perfect cast just upstream from the pod.

The lunch group entirely stops what they are doing and watches on.

"That was awesome, Pat." Rose praises. "You were just a couple of feet short."

Pat slowly strips in line and tries it again, setting the fly down on the water like a feather, barely disturbing the water, in the perfect line to cover the closest rising trout. The trout porpoises up to eat the parachute.

"Oh!" Rose grunts. "Get 'em, Pat."

With a nymph rig, the flies are a good five or six feet from the indicator or even more, which causes a delay between a trout eating and the indicator moving. The angler has to be on it and could never be too quick. When a trout eats a dry fly, you want to slow it down and not have too hard of a hookset. With Pat's condition, his timing is perfect. He lifts his rod tip and comes tight. It is just a little rainbow trout, and Pat is able to bring it in without much finesse or struggle, but it is a win.

"Nice work, Pat!" Rose proclaims with a big pat on the back.

The entire lunch group erupts as Pat turns to give an "I've got this" kind of look and a thumbs up.

Rose helps Pat back to his chair, and as he sits down, she asks, "You doin alright, Pat? You look a little cold."

"No, I'm ok." Pat retorts.

"What do you think, Dave?" Rose asks.

"Well, I'm kind of over this bobber fishing," he responds.

"Sweet," Rose confesses. "Me too. You want to chuck and duck?"

"What's that?" Dave asks.

"Big 'ole streamers," Rose answers back with a smile and a nod. "When we see more fish up, we'll give Pat a shot at them."

"I'm in," Dave replies with an eager grin.

"You want to just keep that dry fly rigged up, Pat?" Rose asks. "We can look for more heads?"

"Yeah," Pat answers. "Let's just do that."

As they all loaded up into their respective boats, Trick walked by Rose. He's starting to warm up.

"That was pretty cool, Rose." He tells her.

"Well, it was Riggs' idea." She admits.

As Rose and her sports float down the river, she notices Pat slumped over in the front seat, with the butt section of his rod on the floor, leaning up against the casting brace in the bow. She looks back, motioning to Dave.

"Oh, he's alright," Dave says. "He's just napping. He does that."

Rose slides the drift boat into a side channel with willows hanging over the water and seams running past boulders, creating pockets for trout to hide.

"Throw it under those willows," she directs Dave. "Strip it hard. Get that thing moving."

As Dave follows her orders, a brown and yellow streak rushes towards his streamer, and he makes contact.

"Got 'em!" Dave yells. "That was fricken awesome."

Rose nets the 16-inch brown and lets it slide back into the cold Missouri water.

"Let's get another one," she says.

"Absolutely," Dave eagerly agrees.

Rose pulls the drift boat back out into the current, and they continue downstream. Rose is rowing, looking back at Dave and pointing out structures to chuck his streamer into. Dave is doing his best to hit every seam along every rock. Pat is sleeping in the front seat and doesn't even flinch as Dave and Rose both shout and laugh, and giggle as another brown trout comes out from behind a rock at a hundred miles an hour. Hooking up on them doesn't even matter to Dave as he's just having the time of his life watching the action.

At the end of the channel, as the current meets the mainstem of the river, a seam merges where March browns are collecting, creating a food trough for a pod of about 10 rising trout. Rose sees the risers and pulls on the oars to hold the boat in place against the current. As the boat stalls, she studies the pod and strategizes her next move.

"See that pod, Dave?" She points out.

"Oh yeah. Awesome." Dave says. "What do you think? We should get Pat on them, huh?"

Rose slowly lets the boat drift down towards the pod of fish. It's a little tricky because there is a current-line coming in from the main channel and another conjoining with the side channel they are in. She needs to slide the boat over to the port side just a few feet to give Pat a shot. She slides the boat over and slowly lowers the anchor so as not to slam it down into the rocks and spook the fish. They are in the perfect position.

"Hey, Pat," Rose nudges him. "Do you see those fish coming up?"

Pat lifts his head and doesn't say a word as he slowly reaches down and grabs his Sage. He pulls the fly from the guide it was hooked on and lets it drop into the water. He methodically strips the line off his reel, about two feet at a time. One pull off the reel after another, Pat strips off line until he feels like he has enough out to reach the pod.

"You see that one closest to us, Pat?" Rose asks. "That's the one you want. See how much water he's moving when he eats? That's a big fish."

Pat doesn't say a word. Shaking the tip of his rod to let some line out, he allows the fly to drag downstream. He slowly lifts the rod, pulling the line towards the boat against the tension of the current, and then, with a burst of energy, thrusts the rod tip towards the pod.

Amazingly, that compact cast with the least amount of effort shoots 35 feet of line out of the rod tip, straightening out to lay the fly softly on the water just six feet upstream of his target. He feeds another few feet of line out and, with the angle, has just enough to put the fly right on the sipping trout's nose. One cast and Pat center-punches his target, and the trout gulps down his fly.

Rose doesn't say a word. She just watches in awe as Pat, in his own time, lifts his rod, setting his hook on the twenty-one-inch rainbow. The trout goes airborne as it tries to throw Pat's fly. Rose reaches up and pats him on the back as he fights this Missouri River trophy.

"Absolutely astounding," she proclaims in a soft, admiring voice. "Astounding."

Pat brings the rainbow towards the boat. Rose jumps out into thigh-deep water to assist with the net.

"You want a pic of this one?" She asks.

"Ok," Pat replies.

Rose holds the fish, Pat points at it with a big grin, and Dave snaps a picture with his Olympus digital camera. Rose lowers the trout back into the water, facing into the current, and it slowly slips from her hand and swims away.

As Rose climbs back into the boat and takes her seat, she looks back at the seam. With all the commotion, the pod moved up about ten feet and started rising to the surface to feed again.

"Pat," she calls out. "They're still coming up. You want to take another shot?"

"Ok," he says.

Pat goes through the process of pulling the line off the reel again and again, drops a dime just upstream from the fish on the outside edge of the seam, and again, a fish sucks down his fly. Pat comes tight and fights this fish for a few seconds before it pulls the hook. As Pat gathers up his line, the pod comes back to the surface for more feeding.

"You want to take another shot?" Rose asks.

"No. I've molested these fish enough for today," Pat decides. Then he puts his rod down by his side and drifts back to sleep.

GETTING UP THE NERVE

Pat slept the rest of the float while Dave fished out of the back of the boat. Rose and Dave talked and laughed and shared stories of past lives. The three boats with anglers and guides reached Pelican Point within 15 minutes of each other. Boats were trailered, rods secured, and participants loaded up. They headed back to Craig. Rose and Dave continued their conversations as Pat slept in the back seat—no doubt dreaming of the last fish he might ever land as his Parkinson's would eventually take over to a point where he couldn't be the angler he wanted to be. It was better to just go out on top.

Dave thanked Rose for spending the time with Pat and allowing him to have one final victory with a fly rod in his hand. Rose thought back about the feelings she had while re-rigging Pat's rod with a dry fly and started feeling a little guilty.

"I gotta be honest, Dave," Rose admits. "I wasn't really feeling the dry fly thing with your brother. If it wasn't for Riggs, I probably wouldn't have even tried it. I guess there's a lesson there."

"Yeah, I know," Dave replies. "But you did, and you were great."

"Well, Pat was great," she says. "It was pretty awesome, watching him cast like that; so methodical and wasting no energy. And his reaction time—perfect with the dries where he was late on the nymph-rig. Lots of lessons in there."

"That streamer stuff was fun, too," Dave admits.

"Chuck and duck, Dave. Chuck and duck."

As Rose turns her rig into the MRA parking lot, she sees Tom walking out from the shop porch. He waves as he makes his way towards her Jeep. She pulls around to the side of the shop, lines up her boat with an empty parking spot on the lawn, and backs her boat in. Rose jumps out of her Jeep and walks around to the back to unhook her boat.

"What's up with your bumper?" Tom asks as he walks around to the back of the Jeep. "I hadn't noticed that."

"Oh, just a little fender-bender," Rose answers back. "Just haven't had the cash to fix it yet."

"The red duct tape is a nice touch," he notices.

"Yeah," she says. "Nothing like a little redneck body-work. I didn't even realize how many colors duct tape comes in. Pretty impressive."

Tom turns his direction to Dave and Pat as they have made it out of the Jeep and are now standing, watching Rose do her thing.

"How was it?" Tom asks.

"We had a great time," Dave answers. "This lady knows her stuff."

"Did you get some fish, Pat?" Tom asks.

"I did," Pat answers. "It was perfect."

Just then, the other two guides with their anglers turn into the parking lot—Billy's truck first and then Riggs. Billy is driving noticeably slower than he was that morning. They both back their boats into an empty spot, and their clients pile out of their vehicles. Tom walks over to the group to ask them how the day went.

Rose finishes tidying up her boat, picking up any used leaders and tippet material, and runs them, along with the garbage from lunch, to the trash can next to the shop. As she makes her way back to her rig, she notices Trick leaning against the MPHW van, looking up into the sky. He was by himself, but didn't look like he was bothered by that. He was occupied by something in the air a few feet above his head.

"What you looking at?" Rose asks Trick as she approaches him.

"What are these?" He points to the sky.

Above his head, there are dozens of bugs dipping up and down in a sort of dance with each other. They are flying with their heads up and fine, thin bodies pointed straight down. Their tails are disproportionately long and wispy.

"Well," Rose starts to answer, "Did you see all those bugs on the water today?"

"Yeah," Trick says. "The March browns?"

"Nice," She responds. "You know your bugs."

"My entomology is a bit lacking," Trick admits. "I know some of the main bugs, but I could probably use a bug course."

"So, yes," Rose continues. "The bugs on the water were the 'dun' stage of the March browns. They stay on the water until their wings dry, and then they go airborne. At some point, they molt into spinners and become sexually mature and mate. That's what those are."

"So, that dance they're doing? That's them mating?" Trick affirms. "Huh…"

"Kind of cool, right?" Rose states.

"It is," Trick admits. "It's like they're courting by dancing."

"Courting?" Rose snickers. "What, were you born in the 50s? They're hooking up!"

Trick laughs a bit, embarrassed. "Yes, I guess you're right. They're hooking up."

"You lost the pincher?" Rose points to Trick's arm.

"Yeah," he says. "I haven't really gotten used to it yet.

I only wear it when it helps. Pretty tough to work the reel without a second hand of some kind."

Trying not to pry, Rose asks, "You must have been fly fishing for a while, huh? I saw you out there getting it done. Casting looked good."

"Yeah," he admits. "I started a few years back while in college. My trainer used to take me out when he thought I needed a break from football."

"Oh yeah? You played?"

"I did…"

Rose was definitely curious but also wanted to be respectful of Trick's feelings. It was obvious that whatever happened to him was post-college days and post-football, which meant it couldn't have been too long ago.

Treading lightly and wanting to change the subject, she asks, "Where did you go to school?"

"I transferred to Missoula after spending a couple of years at a community college in California." Trick says.

"So, you stuck around?" She probes.

"Yeah, my mom and dad are in California, but after my accident," Trick nods towards his missing arm, "I decided to stick around Missoula for rehab. My trainer, my best friend, really, is in Missoula. He and his wife are just as much family as anyone. Plus, some of the guys from the team are still around, and it was just a better situation."

"How did you find the healing waters project?" Rose asks.

"Well, like I said, my trainer and I fished quite a bit before the accident. I was getting into it—hadn't fished since, but his wife knew about this program," he explains. "She's a counselor and knew about it through her work. She thought it would help me."

Trick felt Rose's stare on him. He had been looking off into the distance while talking to her with quick, shy glances back at her occasionally, just to make sure she wasn't getting too bored with his story, something guys do to protect themselves from vulnerability. Her gaze made him flush. It felt like a ray of sunshine warming his face.

Trick turned to Rose with deliberate intent. It wasn't like Trick to take chances with asking women out. Because he was so focused on football, he never really put the time into meeting girls. His teammates and friends and even Sara would ask him why he wasn't going after some of those girls who would woo all over him.

"For god's sake," Sara would say. "Why don't you get after one of those cheerleaders or something? You're a football player. Isn't that what you guys do?"

Attraction to women wasn't the problem. Trick was just too busy. And because of that, he lacked any sort of *game,* and now, he had no idea how to pursue one except for just being honest.

"I was pretty apprehensive," Trick says, now staring back at her. "But now I'm kinda glad I did."

Now Rose's heart thumped loud enough that she thought, for sure, Trick heard. She, however, had too much experience with guys hitting on her and had developed some calluses and an auto-response to advances from men to deflect, even though this interaction seemed innocent and genuine.

She plays it off. "Yeah, the Missouri. It is pretty amazing."

Trick's eyes looked down to his feet, and then he turned his head to the group of MHWP participants that had gathered near Riggs' boat. He was hoping for the door to open a crack. He was hoping Rose would give him a sign that she was interested. When she didn't, his mind went to his arm and what he thought she must be thinking, and now he was feeling a flighting impulse he rarely ever felt before the accident.

"Why would she ever want to be with a gimped-up guy like me?" Trick thinks to himself.

As he starts to turn towards the group, Rose struggles with her own inner dialogue: "Why do you have to be such a bitch?" She thinks.

"Hey, Trick." She blurts out. For the first time in a long time, she felt nervous and scared and vulnerable. "You want to go fishing sometime?"

The color now back on Trick's face, and he turns back to her, "Yeah! That would be awesome!"

Knowing he is a bit overly eager with his response, he searches for words to temper his excitement, "but don't expect me to row too much."

"Ha!" Rose shoots back. "That's funny. Don't worry, I'll take care of it."

Their conversation hadn't gone unnoticed. Tom had rallied the group and was herding them towards the van. As they moved, Rose and Trick caught up with them. Rose, still a little bit in "guide mode", walked around to the tail end of the group to help Pat navigate the gravel of the parking lot with his walker. That left Trick open to some not-so-subtle pats on the back and a couple of "at-a-boys" from John and Randy.

"Would you guys grow up?" Trick quietly admonishes.

"Come on," Randy responds. "We're too old to have our own lives, can't we live yours?"

"Listen," Bob chimes in. "If I knew then what I know now, I'd be…"

"You'd be what?" Randy cuts him off. "You never had any game."

"How old are you guys?" Trick asks. "So, when you become an old man, does that mean you can act like a 15-year-old?"

The two older men laugh and give Trick a bit of a shove from the back, pushing him towards the van. Trick stumbles forward but quickly gains his balance. The day was a good one for Trick. For the first time since the accident, he's been able to interact with people in this way. The cloud that consumed him now opened, just a little bit, letting rays of sun warm him. He actually smiles and feels some things he hasn't felt for what seemed to be forever. He felt shy. He felt embarrassed for a moment. He felt his heart race. He felt alive. Trick feels hope again.

On the ride back to Helena, the older men spent their time reliving the day with Tom. They told him about the fish Pat caught at lunch, how he stood in the river leaning up against his walker. They talked about the hippy guide, Riggs, and the drill sergeant, Billy, and also talked about all the 'ones' that got away, and compared the 'fish of the day,' to which Pat was the obvious winner. Trick took a seat in the back and remained silent until Randy piped up about who really had the catch of the day.

"I don't know, Pat," he declared. "I think Trick's got you beat."

"Oh, yeah," Bob agreed. "As impressive as that rainbow on the dry was, Pat, Randy's right. I'd have to give it to Trick…tricky, Trick. Boy howdy."

"What?" Trick turned from staring out the window to the group that was now turned back, looking at him. "What'er you old bastards talking about?"

The entire van erupted.

"Ahhh, Trick. Good for you!" Congratulated Randy. "That Rose. Wow. Quite the *catch*."

A second wave of chuckles and cheers signaled approval of the pun.

"What?" Trick downplayed. "It's not like that. She just asked me if I wanted to go fishing again. She probably just felt sorry for me."

"Sorry for you!" Randy chortled. "Sorry for you? I saw the way she looked at you. She wasn't feeling sorry for shit. Look at you, man. That girl had one thing in mind, and it sure as hell didn't have anything to do with pity."

"Whatever," Trick, again, playing it off. "We're just going fishing."

A third wave of chortles filled the van. Trick shook his head and went back to staring out the window—the noise of the boisterous group of old men faded into the humming of the wheels. Trick's mind went to a place of self-doubt and deprecation that's been commonplace these past few months—thoughts that have been occupying space in his head, robbing him of the hope he felt for a few moments not even 30 minutes ago.

"There's no way a girl like that is going to want to be with someone like me," he thought to himself. "I'll never hear from her again. She was just being nice."

Tom parked the van at their rendezvous point, which happened to be a grocery store parking lot. The participants again piled out of the van, with Trick being last, and said goodbyes while scanning the lot for their rides home. Sara and Mike had driven Trick to Helena from Missoula that morning. They were going to spend the day in Helena to check out the Capitol and museum, and a couple of antique stores. Sara's Subaru was nowhere in sight.

Tom walks over to Trick, "How are you doing, Trick?"

"I'm good," Trick answers. "Today was fun."

"You got a little quiet back there. Care to share your thoughts?"

"Not really," Trick responds, realizing he is coming off a little churlish. "I mean, I'm sorry. I had a great time, Tom. I really appreciate it."

"That's not what I was asking," Tom clarifies. "You've gone through a lot, Trick. Your world has been turned upside-down. Your entire plan—everything you worked for has been taken from you. Who you are, in some respects, has been taken from you."

"It is what it is," Trick replies as he stares off into the distance.

"But it's not fair, Trick, and it's ok to feel that way. If it were me, I'd be fucking pissed."

Tom continues, "You're being forced to accept changes you didn't want. Your dreams…your story. It's all changed now, and that must suck. Your body has changed, and I would guess, the way you see yourself has also changed."

"How much is this costing me, Doc?" Trick replies flippantly.

"It's ok to feel angry, Trick," Tom sympathizes. "I just don't want you to *be* angry."

"What do you mean?" Trick asks.

"Yes, all these things changed, and you didn't have any control over it," Tom explains. "You didn't choose to be in the accident. For all I know, you probably weren't even at fault for what happened. Accepting that change and developing a plan that really gives you hope is going to take work—a lot of work. But there are things about you that haven't changed, and maybe recognizing those things would be a good start."

"Like what?" Trick asks.

"Your physical attributes may have changed. But what's in here?" Tom puts a finger in Trick's chest. "What's in here is still there, and you can draw on those attributes, or you can let your anger suppress them. That's your choice. And then *that* becomes who you are. You're a kind person, Trick. You have a big heart. And I'm sure you have a thousand other things to be grateful for."

"I'm a gimp," Trick tells Tom. "Who wants to be with a gimp?"

Tom tilts his head back and looks inquisitively at Trick. "Rose?" he asks.

Trick turned to look at Tom for the first time since they began talking. "It's not just Rose…"

"Today it *is* Rose, Trick. And tomorrow it might be someone else." Tom continues, "What do you want her to see? An angry dude missing an arm? Or a kind man with a big heart who has two good legs, a good arm, and doesn't give up?"

"Easy for you to say," Trick responds.

"You're right, Trick. I have no idea what you're going through or the pain you feel. That pain is real. I get that. All I'm saying is control what you can control. Find those things that haven't changed, that you want people to see about you, and then let the chips fall how they may."

"Tight lines," Trick murmurs.

"Yeah," Tom agrees. "Tight lines."

Trick sees Mike and Sara roll into the parking lot of the grocery store and lifts his head, motioning to them.

"Guess my ride's here," Trick says to Tom.

Mike and Sara park, and Sara steps out of the car and hugs Trick, and then Tom.

"How you doin, Tom?" She asks.

Mike walks up and shakes Tom's hand.

"We haven't met," Mike says. "I'm Mike Morley."

"Oh, yeah, I've heard some great things about you," Tom tells him.

"Ah, shucks…" Mike gives his best Goofy impression.

"Quit it," Sara orders as she slaps his shoulder.

"Ouch!" Mike protests as Sara pushes him away, tickling him at the same time.

"Holy…" Trick interjects. "Do you guys ever stop flirting?"

"Speaking of flirting…" Tom says.

"We're just going fishing," Trick cuts Tom off.

"What?" Sara asks emphatically. "Did you meet someone?"

"What? Did you guys set all this up or something?" Trick asks defensively.

"If that were the case, you would have been fishing with her all day instead of Billy," Tom admits.

"Yeah, I gotta be honest," Trick reveals. "I would have much rather fished with Rose."

"Rose?" Sara asks. "Who is this Rose?"

"It's just fishing!" Trick declares. "Fishing!"

"Doesn't sound like it," Mike interjects as he grins ear to ear in the Mike Morley way.

"All right," Trick says, trying his best to diffuse the interrogation. "I'm getting hungry. Can we just get some food?"

Trick was feeling like a little kid being teased by the "adults." On one hand, he was a little embarrassed, but on the other, it was kind of exciting and reassuring all at the same time. The fact that these adults saw something there to tease him about meant they saw a real possibility that something could happen.

"Did they really feel that way?" he wonders to himself.

"Okay," Mike puts an end to the harassment. "Pizza or Suds Hut chicken?"

They all nod and at the same time declare, "Suds Hut."

They say their goodbyes to Tom and turn to the car. Before Trick can climb into the back door of the Subaru wagon, Tom yells to him, "Hey, Trick! It's ok to feel a little hope. Tight lines, bud."

"Thanks, Tom," Trick replies as he works his way into the tiny back seat.

It was around 10:30 pm that night when Trick, Sara, and Mike arrived back at the house in Missoula. Trick had taken up residency at the house in the mother-in-law suite above the detached garage out back. Mike built the apartment for Trick after the accident, knowing Trick would need a place to stay and some help recovering. Trick said goodnight and headed off to the garage.

Once settled in, Trick takes out his phone and scrolls through his contacts. Before Rose and Trick said goodbye in the parking lot of the Missouri River Angler, Rose asked Trick for his phone and saved her number to his contact list. Trick finds Rose's name and number. He takes a breath. He tries as hard as he can to chase the butterflies and the nerves and the doubt from his stomach.

"What's the point?" He thinks. "Could she really be with someone like me?"

Rose was sitting alone in the cottage with Chase. She was often alone these days because the alternative was to hang out with everyone else at the Frenchman Bar next door or Izaak's in Craig, and she knew that wasn't an option. She picks up her phone and double-checks for any notification of a new message. She decides she has had a long day and gets ready for bed.

Trick recalls the things Tom told him. He also remembers what his tight ends coach told him those early days in the hospital after the accident, when he learned of how the accident would change his life.

"This is going to be hard," he admits to himself.

Rose finished washing her face and brushing her teeth. Her face is buried in a towel when she hears the chime of her phone. She pokes her head out of the bathroom and looks at the phone, not sure if she had actually heard the notification chiming through. A green light flashes, telling her a new text had indeed arrived.

A FAVOR FOR A FAVOR

Trick and Rose text messaged each other for hours that first night. Much of what they talked about was fishing different rivers in Montana. Trick admitted he had only fished on the west side of the Divide and mostly with Mike. Rose had fished all over but primarily on the Missouri and surrounding tributaries. The conversation was light and without mention of Trick's unfortunate turn of events with the exception of learning how to land a fish with the use of his prosthetic.

Rose shared stories of messing around with her dad's old, auto-retrieve reel and wondered if something like that would help. Trick was politely dismissive of the idea as he wanted to try to get back to life without crutches. He didn't want special treatment. He just wanted to be seen as a normal functioning human being. Part of that was his desire for her to see him that way.

It was around 2 am when Rose texted: "OMG, it's 2 am! Need sleep!"

Trick replied: "K, ttyl?"

Rose: "Wait! When we going to fish??"

Trick: "Umm. Tomorrow 😊?"

Rose: "Can't tomorrow. Working. Monday?"

Trick: "Love to. I'm not cleared to drive yet ☹"

Rose: "That's ok. I'll come there? We can fish Rock Creek. Heard salmon flies are coming off."

Trick: "Perfect!"

As Rose put her phone down on her nightstand and plugged it into the charging cord, she looked at Chase, who was lying on the bed. He looked up at her and cocked his head to the side, and lifted a brow.

"You're not supposed to be on the bed," she scolded.

She grabbed Chase by the ears and ruffed him up a bit and then rolled him on his back. Chase hated being rolled on his back because Rose tickled him under the armpits when he was a puppy, too often. He would kick Rose with his rear legs, trying to get out of her grasp.

He twisted out of her grip and jumped to his feet on the bed and launched himself onto her, almost knocking her over. She grabbed him with both hands by the scruff of the neck and continued wrestling with him. Chase nipped at the cuff of her shirt sleeve and nibbled and pulled until he accidentally grabbed skin.

"Ouch, you little shit," she whimpered.

Chase let go and backed up, still on the bed. He was grinning, and his tail wagged uncontrollably, knocking the lamp off the nightstand.

"Ah, you're gonna get it," she lunged towards him.

They played and wrestled for a while. Rose was wound up and knew she couldn't go to sleep even if she wanted to.

"We have a date," she told Chase as she continued to rough him up. "We have a date!"

Monday morning, Rose woke up early, ate a bowl of Greek yogurt with blueberries and granola, then loaded Chase up into the Jeep and hit the road. She followed Highway 434 North to 200 and took a left towards Missoula. Highway 200 climbs up the Rocky Mountain front and crests the Continental Divide at Rodger's Pass. From there, the roadway drops down into the Blackfoot drainage. If Lewis and Clark had only known that they could have been on the Blackfoot in a fraction of the time it took them to travel over the Bitterroot Mountains, which would have taken them to the Clark Fork and then out to the Columbia, they would have saved themselves months on their search for a Northwest Passage across the continent.

Rose knows she's getting close to Missoula as Highway 200 reaches Bonner and travelers are forced to slow down to residential speeds. That is also where the Blackfoot flows into the Clark Fork, doubling the Clark Fork in size. A nervous feeling she hasn't felt in years creeps in, and she is not sure if she likes it. She pulls the Jeep into the Exxon station before taking the on-ramp to I-90 West.

As Rose makes her way to the bathroom to wash her hands and her face, she looks into the mirror and takes inventory. "Should have I put makeup on?" She thinks to herself. "We're going fishing, right? Who wears make-up when they go fishing?"

To be fair, Rose doesn't often wear any makeup. She has been blessed with amazingly clear skin with just enough freckles to stand out and naturally long, thick lashes.

"Maybe a little lip gloss, or some eye color?" She thinks. "Screw it. If he doesn't like me, he doesn't like me."

Rose storms out of the bathroom with obvious defiance. She goes to the drink cooler and picks out a lavender kombucha and walks to the back of the line, waiting for an open clerk. The candy bar P.O.P. jumps out at her as she reaches the head of the line. She's usually incredibly conscientious about what she puts into her body and, for the most part, eats and drinks healthily. Rose doesn't smoke (only while she drinks, and she gave that up a while ago) and tries to keep down her sugar intake. However, she does have a weakness for Reese's Peanut Butter Cups.

"Screw it," she says to herself as she picks out a King

Size pack and places it on the counter.

"Is that all?" The clerk asks as if she had a few more seconds to decide, she might just take the entire box.

"I'm good," she answers with a bit of a smug grin.

Rose pays and quickly makes her way to the door and out to her Jeep. She rifles through her purse and center console and finds the remnants of an eyeliner pencil, eyeshadow, lip gloss, and mascara, and applies a modest amount of each.

"What are you looking at?" She asks Chase as he looks on inquisitively.

Throwing the Jeep into gear, Rose steps on the gas and takes off towards Missoula. She takes an entire Reese's cup into her mouth and washes it down with the kombucha.

"Oh, my…," she thinks. "That's a horrible combination."

Rose takes the Van Buren Street exit off I-90, turns right, and heads up Rattlesnake Creek. She has written down the directions and the address of Mike and Sara's house while looking for street signs and house numbers, realizing she's getting closer and closer, and eventually pulls in front of their house, parking along the curb of the street.

Looking into the rearview mirror, Rose cleans off a tiny bit of chocolate from the corner of her mouth. She parts her hair and fluffs it a bit, then pulls out a scrunchy she knows she had from rummaging through her purse, and pulls her hair back into a ponytail.

"It's as good as it's going to get," she says to herself as she pushes her door open and steps out. Chase jumps over the console and takes her seat behind the wheel.

Rose shuffles her way up the concrete walk towards the front door of this modest house. Hyper aware of an audience judging her, she walks with an awkward gate as if she's walking out onto stage at her grade-school choir recital, trying her best not to trip. Two old-growth Douglas firs frame the walkway to the porch. Roots from the trees have lifted a couple of concrete slabs, tilting portions of the walk, which compromises her efforts at a graceful entrance. The needles and shade from the firs have prevented grass from growing in the bulk of the front yard. The dampness and shade have taken their toll on the natural wood siding of the house.

As she takes three steps onto the front porch, she notices the new redwood planks that have replaced the old wood of the decking. There has obviously been some construction going on to address some of the issues an original house of this era is bound to have. The porch is solid. The new wood hasn't been stained yet. As she knocks on the screen door, it rattles, and it is apparent that fixing the door hasn't been a priority.

As Sara opens the solid oak entry door, Rose pulls open the screen door.

"Hi'ee…" Sara greets Rose, extending the hard vowel sound, emphasizing her excitement to meet her. "You must be Rose."

They both go in for a hug and embrace.

"Sara?" Rose asks. "It's so good to meet you."

"Come on inside," Sara directs. "Would you like some coffee or anything?"

"Um..sure," Rose replies. "Coffee sounds great."

"Do you take anything with it?" Sara asks.

"No, thank you. Just black," Rose answers with a smile. "I love your home. It's such a beautiful part of Missoula."

"Thank you. We were so lucky to find it," Sara admits.

"The market in Missoula is ridiculous. This place needs a lot of work, but it has potential, and thankfully, Mike is a wizard with a hammer and a saw."

"It's so nice to see people taking on these older homes and doing something with them." Rose admires.

"Well, it's a process…How was the ride over?" Sara asks.

"Great! I love that drive." Rose answers.

Rose follows Sara through the house and into the kitchen. It's obviously had a lot of work done to it. However, the style remains that of what one would expect from a 110-year-old house. The cream-colored cabinets with oil rubbed bronze pull handles and hardware screams of classic, farmhouse. The stone countertops are elegant, offset with stainless steel appliances that pop with a modern, clean look.

"Wow," Rose says to Sara. "Your kitchen looks amazing."

"Thanks!" Sara responds, smiling. "I love it. Mike did an amazing job. He really is good."

"But wow," Rose compliments. "The style is so…so antique, but not. You know?"

"Yeah, that's what we were going for. I'm glad you like it."

"I do." Rose tells her and asks, "Where is Mike?"

"Working," Sara answers. "He's so good at this. He started his own business, and now he's so busy he can barely find the time to work on this house. He finished the apartment out back for Trick, and now he's running, non-stop, doing everyone else's houses."

"Yeah," Rose says empathetically. "It's a good problem to have, right?"

"Yeah, but life's too short to have to work so much. I'm

sure at some point, we'll figure out a good balance for him."

The back door to the kitchen opens suddenly, and Trick walks in to see Sara and Rose sitting at the breakfast bar in the corner of the kitchen, Sara had repurposed out of a Hoosier Hutch they found at an antique store in Gallatin Gateway. Noticing the coffee cups were almost empty, he figured they had been talking for more than a minute or two.

"Ladies," Trick greets them, pointing at the cups. "I see you've had some time to chat?"

"Just getting the dirt," Rose says as she gives him a wink.

"Trick," Sara interjects. "Do you think I'm going to let one of my guys go off with a strange woman without getting to know her a little first?"

Rose stands up and walks over to Trick and holds her arms out. Trick wraps his arm around her awkwardly, and she embraces him.

"It's good to see you, Trick," she says.

Trick's eyes light up. He struggles to find the words. "Ah…you look amazing…We're still going fishing, right?"

"Trick," Sara says condemningly as she feels Rose's embarrassment.

"What?" He backpedals. "All I'm saying is that it's going to be hard to focus on fishing with her looking like that. How's a guy supposed to concentrate?"

Sara and Rose both raise an eyebrow, lower their chins, and give Trick an all-out "mm, hmm."

Rose, however, enjoyed how Trick had climbed his way out of the hole he was digging. As they walked out the front door towards the Jeep, she lifted herself up on her tiptoes and gave Trick a peck on the cheek.

"You have gear?" Rose asks.

"I do. If we pull around back, I can grab my stuff," he says. "You really do look great."

As Trick walked around to the passenger side of the Jeep, Chase quickly jumped from the driver's seat to the front passenger seat. Trick opened the door, and Chase didn't move. He sat in the seat, facing forward, not even acknowledging.

"Get in back," Rose directs Chase with a stern voice.

Chase didn't move; he just kept staring forward from *his* seat.

"Chase," Rose tells him again. "Get in back."

This time, she reaches across the seat and grabs him by the collar and pulls him over the console and into the back seat.

"Is he always that stubborn?" Trick asks.

"Takes after his mama," Rose answers.

They drove around back to the garage where Trick's gear was stored and loaded his waders, boots, rod, and prosthetic into the hatch of the Jeep. With all of Trick's gear loaded up, they headed back down Rattlesnake Creek towards the entrance to I-90.

"You like Tool?" Rose asks as she fiddles with the radio.

"Can't say I know a lot from Tool, but I'm open to listening," Trick responds. "I gotta to be honest, I'm really big on good vocals. Have you listened to much Edwin McCain?"

"Not a ton, but if you like vocals, you have to check out Maynard."

"Let's do it," Trick agrees, and Rose cues her favorite Tool song, *Sober*.

They continued talking music while driving East on I-90 to Rock Creek Road, where the infamous Testy

Festy billboard towers over the Rock Creek Lodge, sig-nifying the turn-off.

The Rock Creek Testicle Festival has been an annual event since 1982. It's not just an excuse for people to travel to Montana and get drunk. They also get to indulge in something that truly is Montana—Rocky Mountain oysters. The sign almost always gets a chuckle from folks new to the area, but elicits deep disdain from many of the locals. The festival often gets out of hand, and stories of drunk bikers showing off their own testicles while riding Harleys up and down the highway are common. It's not something the locals are particularly proud of.

"Ever had 'em?" Rose asks as she points to the sign.

"What's that? Bull nuts?" Trick asks and then answers with a short, "Nah."

"Why not? They're good," she insists.

"I'm good," Trick concedes. "I trust you."

As Rose pulls off the highway and turns up Rock Creek, she starts to get her game face on. She wants to impress Trick and has heard salmon flies are hatching, but she's much more comfortable with the Missouri River and other tailwaters. The problem with salmon flies is that they migrate upstream, so one day you might find them close to the mouth, and the next, they could be 15 miles upstream. One thing is for sure, however, it's pretty obvious when you have missed them because of the carnage they leave behind.

As salmon flies emerge from the river, they cling to anything they can crawl up on, which at that time of the year is usually a boulder, or willow branch, or a sweeper that hangs into the water. The big stone fly nymphs will climb to a place where they are safe and can hatch out of their exoskeleton that protects them as nymphs and into an adult. It takes a while for their wings to dry, and once they do, they go airborne and head upstream. Unfortunately for them but extremely fortunate for trout, salmon flies are not the most graceful in flight and are often a bit ambitious, trying to take off before they are ready. The result is a three-inch cripple, often referred to as the T-bone, splashing into the water and eventually, into the gut of a trout.

You know if you're too late for the hatch if you're finding those exoskeletons, or shucks, hanging off the limbs, and no adults flying. Thousands of them could be hatching, and at a few inches long, you can't miss them. When you see the shucks and no adults, you might as well pack up and head further upstream.

Driving up Rock Creek a few miles, the threesome came to the Tamarack Creek access site. Rose parked the Jeep, and they all jumped out, including Chase. As he began the all-too-familiar task of marking fence posts and rocks and everything else that might be holding a rival scent, Rose and Trick walked to the river and were met by spent shucks. They needed to go higher.

After loading up in the Jeep, they followed the road as it turned to gravel, and what seemed to be a treacherous road at first now felt like a death trap. They stopped at Norton, Harry's Flat, and Bitterroot Flat and kept seeing the same thing—loads of shucks but no bugs.

Eventually, they came to Squaw Rock Campsite, parked the Jeep, and headed to the creek. The sight was magical. Salmon flies had just started coming off and looked like drunken hummingbirds fluttering in the sky with the grace of a toddler taking his first steps. Watching, Rose and Trick caught themselves rooting for the bugs as they pointed them out, witnessing their struggle to stay up off the water and then ohing in disappointment as they flopped down to the river.

"Watch that one," Rose pointed as she noticed one hit the water. "Watch!"

As the bug fluttered on the surface and was swept through a riffle, they watched splash after splash as the little dinks smashed the surface with no luck at putting the bug in their mouths. Eventually, the bug pooled out under a willow branch along the bank, and a more substantial nose from a large cutthroat slowly appeared in the shadows, opened its mouth around the bug, and sank back into the dark water, leaving only a couple of rings in its wake.

"Oh, my!" Rose shouted with excitement. "Did you see that?"

"That's a big fish," Trick added. "The bigger the fish, the smaller the rise."

"Damn straight," Rose said. "Damn straight…let's get 'em."

They both started the process of putting their rods together and threading the line through the guides. Rose was acutely aware that Trick wanted no special treatment. That was apparent the first time they met on the Missouri when she had mentioned his prosthetic, so she didn't offer. She also realized a flaw of hers was to be a little impatient, and she was cognizant that her impatience might put stress on Trick, so she purpose-fully took her time putting her gear together. When she had finished with her rod, she tied on a big orange sofa pillow that would emulate a big salmon fly, secured it to one of the guides on the rod, wrapped the line around the reel seat, and tightened it up.

"I'm going to use the bathroom before I get my waders on," she told Trick. "I'll be right back."

When Rose returned, Trick had gotten his rod together, line threaded, and had his prosthetic on. He was in the process of tying on a fly. He was obviously struggling.

"Want some help?" Rose asks.

Trick looked at her with a bit of contempt. He hated feeling disabled. He hated having to ask for help, especially with things he was able to do before the accident. He was frustrated with this simple task that he couldn't complete, and was embarrassed and felt like crying, but instead of crying or showing any vulnerability, he did what most guys did.

"Fuck it," Trick responds. "I can't even tie a damn fly on. What kind of fly fisherman can't even tie his own fly on his line?"

"Well," Rose answers. "It's a good thing you're hot, cuz I'd be willing to trade you. I'll tie your fly on but you gotta give me something."

Rose's effort to flirt with Trick was lost in his frustration and anger.

"I don't want you to have to tie my damn flies on for me!" Trick burst out.

He looked at her. She looked back with a stunned brow, and now Trick could add shame and guilt onto what was becoming a cocktail of emotions that was about as enjoyable as accidentally sipping a beer bottle full of chew spit. (That was something he experienced in college and will never forget.)

"I'm sorry," Trick explains. "I'm sorry. I just can't…"

"What?" Rose asks. "Tie a fly on yet? How long did it take you to learn how to tie a cinch knot the first time?

With two hands?"

Rose gave him a minute before continuing.

"How many times have you been fishing since the accident, Trick? Once?" She answers for him. "I'm sorry, Trick. I really am. Your life isn't the same anymore. There are probably going to be a lot of things you're going to have to re-learn."

Trick stares at the ground while shaking his head and pursing his lips.

"Dude, it's ok," Rose tells him. "I know you don't want to feel like a burden or helpless or whatever else you've got going on there. So, I tell you what. Let's figure it out. Let's learn how to tie on your own fly."

For the next half an hour, Rose and Trick worked at learning how to use his prosthetic pinchers to hold the shank of a fly and tie a cinch knot. It took a while, but together, they figured it out, and when they were done, they went after the fish that slowly rose and ate the salmon fly when they had first arrived at the campsite.

They didn't catch that fish, but they did find a number of others that were willing to eat as they floated big orange bugs along the banks of Rock Creek. Rose helped Trick out when she could, but often just let him flail until he figured it out on his own or he was able to suck up his pride and ask for help.

As they walked back to the Jeep, Trick apologized again. "I'm sorry I got so frustrated. I do appreciate your help. Thanks."

"Well, Trick," Rose turned to him and grabbed his forearm. "I enjoy helping out where I can. You just have to be willing to ask. But…you still owe me."

Trick gave her the inquisitive look, and knowing now she had him in a safe place, she lifted up on her tippy toes again, but this time kissed him on the lips.

"Now we're even." She declared.

"Um," Trick struggled to find words. "Could you help me with my water bottle?"

Rose turned him around and pulled his water bottle out of his pack, and handed it to him. She gave him another kiss.

"You're learning." She said and kissed him again, then turned to walk along the bank back to the Jeep.

HABILITATION THERAPY

With spring run-off winding down and anglers from across the country wanting to get out after a long winter, Rose found herself picking up an overflow of guide days, which kept her incredibly busy but also kept her from visiting Trick as much as they would have liked. Most of her work was on the Missouri River, and with Trick living in Missoula, the two-hour drive was a bit much for an evening rendezvous. They spoke nearly every night, however, and Rose's admiration for Trick's perseverance drew her closer and closer.

Trick's rehab was going well, and he was eventually cleared to drive again. In the middle of June, he took his driver's test and was issued a Montana license. Although his Frontier was obviously totaled in the accident, Trick was able to use the insurance money to put a down payment on a 1998 Toyota 4Runner. Payments on the loan were made by working as an assistant football coach at Hellgate High School in Missoula.

Although Trick wouldn't take handouts and hated the idea of cashing in favors, he did accept the position with Hellgate that was offered through a friend of Trick's tight ends coach at the University. It was painful for Trick to see the players doing their thing at first, but soon became a source of therapy and a catalyst for self-reverence as he helped coach players that would be exploring a path he was formerly on—if not at the professional level, at least in setting them up for college football. Trick's work ethic was infectious to the players and was where he was able to make his biggest contribution.

Rose was also on her path to recovery, and every chance she had to help Trick learn a new way to tie a knot or handle a fish or any other seemingly mundane task for those who have the use of two hands, it gave her a sense of self-worth and social capital that had been lacking for a while. They had both been through a lot and fed each other, giving each other the prospect of redemption.

Pity was not what brought Rose and Trick close, however. Rose loved the way Trick looked at her with a hint of shyness she found charming. Trick couldn't help but stare at her when he was with her. She often caught him in the act as he quickly and bashfully would look away, only to look back at her, acknowledging his guilt with a grin as their eyes would meet. Compassion and empathy colored both their gazes as well as their chemistry and a deep infatuation. That passion was realized after they made it back to Trick's apartment following the first fishing outing they took together to Rock Creek.

Rose had opened the door for intimacy by flirting with Trick and rewarding him with a kiss for simply asking for help. That first kiss was like spring run-off on a freestone river for Trick, flushing any lingering doubt he felt over what Rose might be thinking or wanting from him. He was incredibly attracted to Rose, but was engaging in an inner dialogue where his confidence was trampled by insecurity and self-pity. That first kiss washed enough of the doubt away, which gave him the courage to invite Rose up to his room as she parked the Jeep in the alley behind Mike and Sara's house.

"Getting late," Trick noted.

"Sure is," Rose acknowledged.

"Driving back to Wolf Creek this time of night might be dangerous. You could stay here." Trick gingerly walked. "I've gotta couch?"

"I'm sure you'd be real comfy on your couch," she responded.

"You think I'm sleeping on my couch?" Trick asked.

"I guess we'll find out," Rose teased.

The two made their way up the dimly lit stairs to the apartment. Chase followed them up the stairs and pushed his way into the front of the line, knowing somehow, there would be food on the other side. Trick reached for the key above the frame of the door and slipped it into the deadbolt.

"Saves me having to dig through my pockets," he revealed as he turned back to Rose.

"Makes sense," she agreed.

Trick turned the knob, and Chase flung the door open with his nose and rushed in. He didn't need an invitation. Trick and Rose followed behind.

As they walked into Trick's apartment, they continued to find things to talk about, including the ones that got away and how impressed Rose was with Trick's casting and his command of the art of fly-fishing, even though he had only been doing it for a couple of years. Trick was also enamored with Rose's ability to compliment him without sounding patronizing or showing sympathy for his condition.

Trick went to the fridge and pulled out some summer sausage made from an elk a buddy had gifted him. They were both famished from their day out on Rock Creek. They had brought some fruit and crackers to hold them over, but were now in need of something a little more substantial. However, neither wanted to waste time cooking so summer sausage, cheese, and crackers were going to have to do it.

They sat next to each other on the couch while they

ate. Trick had turned on some music he stored on his iPod that was plugged into a portable speaker resting on the end table.

Ewin McCain's "I'll Be" started to play, to which they both blurted out, "I love this song!"

As they reached the chorus, Trick and Rose both sang along at the top of their lungs, "And I'll be your crying shoulder…"

"You have a really nice voice," Rose complimented Trick.

"Thanks," Trick responded and then self-handicapped with, "I used to sing and play a bit, but it's been a while."

"Why don't you sing anymore?" She asked.

"Well," Trick thought of a response, being careful not to be too self-deprecating. "Football took up a lot of time and then…"

"Yeah, I know," she let him off the hook. "You got busy. Maybe someday you'll get back to it."

"I've got a lot of other things to work on right now," he conceded. "Trying to get back to some kind of normalcy before I tackle playing the guitar again."

"Hey, I've got an idea," Rose declared.

"What's that?" Trick asked.

"We should work on some more 'habilitation therapy,'" she suggested while using air quotes.

"What do you mean?" Trick asked again.

"Well," she began. "You learned how to tie a fly on today with your one hand, right?"

"Yeah," Trick proudly responded. "That was no small feat."

"Ok, so here's the deal," Rose explained. "I'm going to give you a task that normally would be a piece of cake with two hands, but you'll have to do it with one. And when you succeed, you get a reward."

"A reward?" Trick asked while raising an eyebrow.

"For instance," she continued. "How about that bottle of water? Open it."

Trick grabbed the unopened bottle of water and placed it in the armpit of his left shoulder. He pinched down on it like a vice and turned the cap with his right hand. The cap spun off, and water spilled out onto the floor before Trip could grab the bottle with his right hand, preventing the spill.

"Well, practice makes perfect," Rose suggested. "But you did it, so you get a reward."

Rose leaned into Trick and kissed him on the lips. This time, she left her lips on Trick's mouth for a few seconds. She opened her mouth and sucked on Trick's bottom lip, licking him with her tongue.

"I like this kind of therapy," Trick admitted excitedly.

"Ok," Rose replied. "How are you with buttons?"

"Um," Trick tested the water. "Mine or yours?"

Rose looked across at Trick. She doesn't smile or frown or give any expression at all. She just cocked her head slightly to the side and responded with, "Your call."

Trick reached out with his right hand and pinched the uppermost button on Rose's shirt that was still secured. He rolled the button between his thumb and index finger, and with a motion that resembled the snapping of his fingers, only much slower, he unbuttoned that first button.

"Nice work," Rose whispered, and she leaned over and kissed him again.

Trick moved down to the next button without asking. And then the next, not waiting for his reward.

When he had completely opened up her shirt, Rose kissed him again and whispered in his ear, "Now my bra. And by the way, the clasp is in the front."

Trick's heart was racing. His breath was short and quick, but a sense of calm enveloped him. He didn't have to guess anymore. He didn't have to wonder and found himself poised and in control. He reached over and slid his index finger between Rose's breasts and the clasp on her bra. Lifting his finger, applying just enough pressure to fold the clasp over, with a flick of his thumb, the clasp released, and her bra fell open.

This time, Rose didn't reward him with a kiss. Instead, she looked down at her naked chest and then back at Trick with a surprised smirk.

"Well, Tricky, Trick." She shrugged her shoulders. "You earned it."

Rose stood up, swung a leg over Trick's lap, and sat down. She slid her hips into him and pushed her chest out. Trick touched her naked breasts with his hand and then kissed her skin. Goosebumps radiated across her body, around her flanks, and down the small of her back.

She cupped Trick's head in her hands and lifted his chin up so that their eyes were aligned. Bending down, she kissed his lips deeply. Sliding her body further into his lap, she pushed firmly against him and felt him getting excited, and continued kissing his lips, forcing her tongue inside his mouth.

After a few minutes of making out, Rose stood up and grabbed Trick's hand, helping him stand. She walked him into his room and said, "It's my turn, Trick."

Chase, who was lying next to the couch this whole time, exhausted from all the exploration he had done throughout the day, lifted his head up to give a shallow whimper of disgust with their behavior before dropping his head, closing his eyes, and falling back to sleep to dream about squirrels.

The next morning was more comfortable for Rose than she had ever felt with a man. There was no guilt or shame, or embarrassment. She didn't want to run or hide. She woke up with her head on Trick's shoulder and didn't want to leave. Everything felt so natural—so safe. So amazing.

She lay on Trick's shoulder, awake for a few minutes, before feeling his breathing accelerate and body flex. His legs stretched out, and he yawned. Rose curled up to hide in Trick's armpit, only to peek up at him as his eyes opened.

"You all right?" Trick asked.

"Perfect," Rose answered.

With Rose's calendar filling up that spring and Trick not having his license until mid-June, it was heart-wrenching for the two to not be together. That first night was better than either could have ever anticipated, and the distance was killing both of them. They had gotten together a couple of times over the past month as Sara and Mike drove Trick to Trixie's in Ovando for dinners, but that just wasn't cutting it.

Ovando is the halfway point between Missoula and Wolf Creek. Trixie's is the favorite local bar and restaurant for guides finishing up their days on the Blackfoot River. Sara and Mike liked Rose and were more than happy to bring Trick to see her for a couple of hours before she would have to go back to Wolf Creek to work the next day. But those encounters were obviously not the same. It was like having parents as chaperones, and Rose felt like they were about to get caught every time they said goodbye to each other with hugs and kisses that would last for more than a few minutes while Sara and Mike waited in the Subaru.

By the first of July, Trick had his driver's license, and Rose kept the weekend of the Fourth open. She had blocked it off her calendar, well aware of all the rec-floaters that would be hitting the river. The kayakers were all fine as they tend to have a pretty good grasp on steering their way down the river. However, the tubers and pleasure floaters and unicorn rafts don't usually come with paddles or anyone who knows how to use them, so Rose was happy to have the days off. She was also excited to spend those days with Trick.

As the weekend grew closer, Trick and Rose talked about the exploring they would do to some of her favorite places together. She told Trick about the Dearborn River and couldn't wait to take him there. While she described it to him, she was sure not to reveal too much, as one of the best things about the Dearborn is the first time a person gets to see it. It was breathtaking, and she didn't want to spoil it for him, much like stealing a punchline to a joke or blurting out the ending of an epic movie before you're halfway through.

They also talked for hours about how they wanted to explore each other, and the anticipation of being alone together occupied much of their time—so much so, they didn't spend very much time on their past, particularly not the hurt they had both been through in the last year and a half. The rape, the accident, and all the painful rehabs felt like distant memories—memories that lacked detail as if their infatuation for each other was the river wearing down all the sharp edges of the stones that lined its bed. However, that memory would be something they would both have to resolve before truly being rehabilitated.

THE FOURTH OF JULY ON THE DEARBORN

Wanting to bring Trick somewhere special for their first major trip together, Rose chose the Dearborn because it was by far her favorite place on the planet—a place she often came to in the first couple of years living in the area and a place Trick had never seen. It's where she honed her fly-fishing skills and also where she came to slow down her brain after all the noise and clutter with the breakup of Lyndsey. That time in her life now felt so distant, and she thought she might not even recognize him if she bumped into him. It's also where she came to rid herself of the memory of that night with Trapper and all the fallout that ensued. The Dearborn River was her church, and now she wanted to invite the person she revered most and had quickly come to love.

The two had only known each other for a couple of months, but there was something different about this relationship for both of them. There was an obvious attraction. They both enjoyed many of the same things as music, the outdoors, and fly-fishing. But they both experienced events that created significant trauma, and both shared an admiration and empathy for each other that became the mortar in the foundation they were building, and strengthened and solidified their bond. Without even speaking the words, they just knew that together, the past could not ever denigrate the relationship they were constructing, so talking about the past just didn't feel necessary.

The Dearborn in June and July is a crap shoot for floating. If there's enough of a snowpack in the Scapegoat Mountains, the window for running the river begins in

May but usually closes by the Fourth. This particular Spring, however, the Rocky Mountain Front was blessed with late storms that extended the window well into July.

Three access points to the Dearborn allow floaters to spread out, with the lower section being the easiest to access from the bridge on Hwy 287. It was a long float for day-trippers, being 18 miles to the confluence of the Missouri, with most of that cutting through amazing canyons with modest rapids and rock gardens, which is a good challenge for novice rafters and kayakers. The middle section, starting at the Hwy 200 bridge, was much shorter and often had the least traffic as it wasn't as scenic and a little harder to drag a boat out of. However, the fishing in that section could often be better with less pressure, and being a short trip, it was easier to fish harder. The upper stretch, which began a few miles upstream from the infamous High Bridge, was something only the more experienced floaters would want to tackle. Rapids and wave trains made for technical rowing, and a 10-foot waterfall about halfway down forced either an hour-long portage or running the falls, hoping to keep upright and not lose gear.

A person could choose to float any of these stretches in a day or take all three stretches and make a three-day trip out of it. Since the Fourth was on a Saturday, Rose had taken Saturday, Sunday, and Monday off. Traffic on the Missouri and Blackfoot rivers was going to be insane. The Lower-Dearborn was also going to be crazy, so Rose planned to put in above the High Bridge with Trick and take the long trip. Rose had purchased an old 13-foot Maravia raft just for such rivers last year and was excited to have the chance to test it out.

Trick met Rose at her cottage in Wolf Creek on

Friday evening, the third of July. Rose had gotten off the Missouri at around 5:30, parked her drift boat in the yard at MRA, and hitched up the trailer with the raft. The two began transferring gear from Trick's Four Runner to the Jeep.

"You ever gonna get that taillight fixed?" Trick asked.

He had never really noticed it because his mind was always elsewhere when the two were together, but something about it caught his attention, and he thought he might ask.

"Yeah," Rose replied as she threw a couple of stuff sacks into the hatch of the Jeep, "I either have to get it fixed or maybe step up my game and find a real truck. With the A/C out, clients are complaining about the heat. The back seat's too small, so not super comfy for bigger dudes. I just need to get something better."

The two finished loading up the Jeep and decided to grab dinner at the Frenchman. Tim, the owner, watched as Rose walked in. Grabbing the remote control for the TV above the bar, he switched it from Fox News to the History Channel and looked back at her.

"Fly," he says as he nods.

"Tim," she replies and gestures to the TV. "Thanks."

As Rose and Trick find a table in the corner of the bar, Trick notices, "Wow, you've got them trained."

"Yeah," she says. "I was in here one morning and these three rich white people were on Fox talking about 'Obama Care' and how we have the best healthcare system in the world, so why do we need to change anything, and I said, 'yeah, for those who can afford it.' And then this old guy at the end of the bar called me a socialist. It got ugly."

"I bet," Trick replied.

Trick never really had much interest in politics, but

he knew Rose did, and he not only appreciated that about her, but he also learned from her and found himself listening and taking in how she would frame her thoughts about things that most people didn't care about. He loved that about her, and she loved that he didn't try to contradict her like most of her guy friends and most of the people who hung out at the Frenchman.

"So, yeah. The next time I came in here," she explains, "Tim turned the channel from that propaganda spewing crap to the History Channel, and it's been that way ever since."

"You do have an effect on people," Trick admits.

The two finished dinner and walked back to the cottage, holding hands. Chase met them at the gate of the chain link fence, and they all entered the small house. They embraced, kissed deeply, and began helping each other out of their clothes. Their passion for each other was intense and mutual, and they spent the next few hours exploring each other as they had been both fantasizing about for the past few weeks when they'd been unable to get together.

The next morning, they were on the road well before the sun came up. Rose had set up a shuttle through MRA the day before so they wouldn't have to take time shuttling rigs before dropping in above the High Bridge. That way, they could have the river to themselves for at least the morning, and if it all worked the way she had planned, they would keep downstream from everyone floating that stretch and could find a good place to camp before anyone caught up.

As the Jeep rambled down the gravel road approaching the High Bridge, Rose stopped talking and just let the sights and the beauty of the canyon that was opening up in front of them breathe. The sun was now up, illuminating the cliff walls of the Rocky Mountain Front that reached up for a thousand feet in front of them. On top of the step of the plains, they could see the Front extending for miles to the north, but as they dropped into the canyon, the walls closed in, and the cliffs looked close enough to reach out and touch.

Rose stopped the Jeep and trailer in the middle of the one-lane bridge. They took a minute to look upstream and then back down. The air was crisp, and the roar of the river was enough for both to feel it was better not to compete with and try to speak over. Rose took her foot off the brake and let the Jeep roll across the bridge and then parked on the other side and turned off the engine.

"Let's get a better look," she suggested.

As they gazed upstream, standing next to each other, leaning against the supports of the bridge, they were able to talk comfortably without shouting.

"This is amazing," Trick said.

"Yeah," Rose agreed. "This is where I come to find peace. It's my church…or my chapel, I guess."

Rose told Trick the abbreviated story of the day she had with the young client and his dad, and then the trip she took by herself a few days later. She told him about the Old Woodsman and the monster rainbow and sending the size 12 parachute Adams back to the earth. She told him about the reason she came up there on that day and the emotional space she had been in for so long, but wanted to make it crystal clear to him that it was all in the past. Rose wanted to tell Trick she loved him, but the time wasn't right—not after just sharing the pain she had felt with the break-up.

"Do I get to meet this Old Woodsman?" Trick asked,

showing an interest in that part of the story, trying to put distance between the hurt.

Trick had a way of doing that. Without saying anything germane, he could comfort Rose and let her know she was safe—that she didn't have to explain or dwell on the past, and even though it wasn't him that broke her, all was forgiven. He wasn't going to judge her for past relationships and past failures.

"Of course you'll get to meet him. He's just up there about a mile," Rose pointed upstream. "We'll be dropping in about five miles upstream and floating through here, go down another 10 miles or so, and find a place to camp. Tomorrow we'll get through the flat part and back into the canyon, and by Monday, we'll be in good shape to finish off the bottom and then out to the Missouri. It's probably about 35 miles altogether. We should get going."

Rose whistled to Chase. He jumped into the back seat of the Jeep, and as he tried to jump over the console, into the front passenger seat, Trick swung his way in, blocking the lab from the shotgun position.

"Ah, I gotchu you old bastard," Trick cheered, reaching back to ruffle his ears.Chase let out a snort, shook his head, and settled back into the rear seat, head between the front bucket seats, staring out through the windshield.

The threesome drove another 12 miles or so and then turned into a washed-out beach along the river just downstream from the next bridge access above the High Bridge. Rose took to unstrapping the raft and pumping air into the tubes before sliding it off the trailer onto the river stone covering the beach.

Dumping gear out of the hatch, Trick strategically placed it out on the beach in order of priority for how the day would unfold. Camping gear would get stowed first, as it would be the last to access. Fishing gear and life jackets would be placed on top with easy access to lunch. Everything would get rigged so that in the event that something crazy happened, the gear would stay with the raft.

Once rigged, Rose drove the Jeep around to the road so that the shuttle driver could just jump in and head out without backing or maneuvering through tight corners. Trick dragged the raft further into the river to a point where it would float and held it until Rose could get back and jump into the rower's seat. Once in, Rose yelled for Chase to load up into the back of the raft on top of the rear tubes, and Trick took the pole position in the front seat. They were off.

It was a gorgeous summer day. There wasn't another person putting on at that bridge. They guessed it was too much effort for most folks who had multiple plans for the Fourth, which was great for them. With the warmth, both Rose and Trick left the waders behind for shorts and Chacos, wide-brim hats, and lightweight wicking long sleeve hoodies. Fleece layers and rain jackets were stowed away just in case.

They drifted along for a couple of hours before the walls of the canyon pinched the Dearborn into a single channel. Like a garden hose being restricted, the river became smaller and faster and started feeling more and more like a water park with waves splashing over the tubes, spraying just enough water to cool them off without completely soaking them.

As they rounded a bend in the river, the current slowed down a bit as the flows flattened and spread out. Up ahead, a cliff wall protruded out from the canyon almost as if it was leaning out to look over a pool that was forming below it.

"There it is," Rose shouts.

"There, what is?" Trick shouts back.

"The Old Woodsman!" She responds. "Don't you see it?"

"Oh yeah," he yells back, pointing up at the cliff wall.

Rose pulled the raft over onto the beach before dropping into the pool. She released the anchor from the stern bracket, dumping it into the gravel. She jumped out and grabbed the anchor, throwing it up onto the bank.

"Grab your rod," she commands. "Let's go!"

"What are we doing?" Trick asks.

"Ah, just saying hello to a friend."

Golden stones were fluttering in the air, catching the sun as the rays shone down into the canyon. Shadows from these big bugs flickered on the water. Cliff swallows chased the bugs like F-16s chasing MIGs—diving and swooping down on the bugs as they did their best to stay airborne.

"Here," Rose holds out a bullet head, stone. "Tie this on."

Rose works her way down along the bank, gesturing to Trick to follow. The river has washed out a big swath through the elders and cottonwoods, which gives them plenty of room to circle around the pool without being seen or casting shadows.

As they get into position downstream from the pool, she asks, "You ready? Take a cast up into the run that dumps down into the pool and let it drift. I want to see if this guy wants to play."

There's a lot more water dumping into the pool at this point than what would normally flow towards the end of summer. The pool is still obvious as the green water of the deep pool contrasts with the clear water that spills out over the shallow bed, along and over the banks. Trick throws a cast above the pool into the run and watches as the fly bounces over a ledge and into the churning froth at the head, and then releases to float above the green pool. With that first cast, a large rainbow slowly rises and gulps down the fly.

"Get 'em," Rose grunts.

Trick lifts the tip of the rod and comes tight on a nice, 16-inch rainbow. Getting really good now at grabbing ahold of the line with his prosthetic and stripping the line in, Trick lands the trout as Rose scoops it up in her hand, not even bothering with a net. As she releases the hook from the trout's lip and lets it slide back into the transparent water, the trout disappears, and Rose turns to Trick.

"Nice work," she says. "Just had to let him know I'm still here."

Rose knows this wasn't the same trout from a couple of years ago, but appreciates the symbolism of the place she has come to love and the feeling of peace she gets when she fishes this pool. Every successful cast and take from any trout triggers a memory, but not one of sorrow or strife. Rose remembers the lesson of finding peace when one is ready for it and the strength she takes from that. It's an exercise of learning to focus on the present and, through that focus, learning to let go of the past.

"Let's go," she says, and they head back to the raft. She tells Chase to load up, and they are off again.

As they float through the run and dump down into the pool, Rose looks up to the Old Woodsman and blows a kiss.

"See you next time," she yells, and they continue downstream.

They spend the next couple of hours drifting the Dearborn in the warm summer sun. Rose pulls on the oars, slowing down just enough for Trick to fish the pools, and then pushes through the dead water. Trick is catching a few fish as they make their way through canyon walls and pinch points until he hears the roar of what obviously is heavy water rolling over giant boulders into a deep pool.

"Do you hear that?" He yells back at Rose.

"Yep! Let's go check it out!"

Rose pulls on the oars and slides the raft into the bank, and again, drops anchor, jumps out, and pulls the raft up onto the gravel. Chase has already leapt into the river and is shaking himself off. Trick follows, and they head to the waterfall that boils downstream.

As they stand on the bank looking over the waterfall, Trick asks, "What do you think?"

"Well," she begins. "There's a run on the far side over there. If we take that chute and then spin the raft to the right, we can follow the current past that boulder in the middle, and we should dump down into the pool still upright."

"Should?" Trick gulps.

"Or we can dump all the gear and portage. It will take a little bit of time, but it's probably our safest bet," she concedes.

"You're the pro, Rose." Trick replies. "The last thing I want is to turn a pretty fantastic day into a tragedy."

"Tell you what," she says. "Let's carry all the gear down below the falls. I'll run it with just the raft. Without all that weight, I think I'll be able to push it around a lot easier, and I should be fine. I'll wear a jacket, and if I flip, it'll just pool out, and we can flip it back up and reload. Piece of cake."

"Your call," Trick agrees.

Quickly, Rose and Trick transport the gear around the falls and pile it up along the bank. Rose releases the anchor from the carabiner off the back of the raft and walks it to the bottom. As she turns to head back to the boat, Trick grabs her arm and turns her back towards him, and gives her a quick kiss on the lips. She turns and runs back up the trail to the raft with butterflies still fluttering in her stomach.

With Trick waiting at the bottom of the falls, she pushes the raft out into the current and yells, "Here I come!"

Rose feathers the raft over to the other side of the river and lines it up where she estimates the line to be where she can drop in and follow the run down into the pool. It's about a ten-foot drop with a step and a boulder halfway down. She won't be able to see any of the run until she's looking straight down from above. She feels her body pucker up as she leans over the front tubes to get a look.

Pulling back on the oars, she can keep the raft from tumbling into the run as she musters up the nerve to go for it. She can see Trick waiting on the bank. He's yelling something, but she can't hear him. He's also waving his arm, motioning her to move further out.

"What?" Rose yells.

"Go further right!" Trick yells back as he waves his arm.

"Shit," Rose thinks to herself as she pulls on the left oar to slide the raft further to the right.

A little panic sets in, realizing that if she misses her spot, the raft will drop off to the left of the boulder and most likely, flip into the rocks at the bottom of the falls. Without headgear, Rose knows she could get pretty banged up, not to mention she's got nothing protecting her arms or legs, or torso.

She stands up again to take a look, and as she relaxes her rowing strokes, the current grabs the raft, and there's no holding back. Rose has committed to the line and now will have to deal with the consequences.

Positioned just far enough into the run to avoid the straight down drop to the bottom, she lands the raft on the ledge halfway down the waterfall, then pulls on the right oar, spinning the stern to the left, pointing the bow down the run as it dumps off to the right. The inertia of the raft falling slams the raft into the boulder on the ledge, which nearly sends Rose catapulting through the air. Fortunately, she has hooked her foot in between the side tube and the bladder of the self-baling bottom of the raft, which barely keeps her in the chair.

Using her left oar to push off the boulder, she releases the raft down into the run. Rose then pulls back on the oar and straightens the raft out, and lets out a big "whoop! Whoop!"

"Whoa!" Trick yells as he wades out into the river as if he's going to catch her. "Holy crap! Are you alright?"

"Yee haw!" Rose yells back. "I want to do it again!"

"I don't think so, Fly."

It was the first time Trick called her that, and Rose didn't know how to take it. Just about everyone from that world who knew her as Fly was part of a fraternity she may have respected, but she didn't want Trick to cross into. That world was filled with egos and bro bras, and Trick was nothing like that. As 'Fly', she wasn't a woman. She was more like one of the boys, and that's the last thing she wanted Trick to see her as.

"Really?" Rose asks. "Fly?"

"Yeah," Trick answers. "Others call you that. I think it's cool."

"Yeah," she explains. "But I'm not sure I like how those people see me. Maybe just Rose?"

Feeling a little embarrassed and as if he'd offended her, he suggests, "How about Bud? Like Rose Bud…"

"Um, got another?" She asks.

"Hmm…sex kitten?"

She grimaces and shakes her head with short gyrations.

"Love of my life?" Trick inquires as he further tests the water.

Rose feels her face becoming flushed again. It's not the first time he's made her feel that way. Did he really feel that way? Is this where they are going? Is this where they are?

Rose jumps out of the raft and treads through knee-deep water to where Trick is standing in the river and gives him a kiss on the lips.

"We'll work on it," Rose says and then pushes Trick back hard enough for him to lose his balance.

As he takes a step back, Trick trips on a small boulder, falling backwards into the knee-deep water, completely submerging his body in the river with a wave of displaced water slapping him in the face. Rolling over, he picks himself back up and rushes her.

"Now you've done it," Trick declares.

Trick wraps his arm around Rose's waist and pulls her in. Rose drapes her arm over his shoulder and gives a half-assed effort to pull away. He lifts her like a doll. She kicks her legs just enough to protest, but quickly submits as he wades out into deeper water and drops her, and now, they are both soaked to the bone.

"Oh, that's fricken cold," she complains as she splashes water back at him.

"Tell me about it." Trick replies.

And then Trick puts his hand gently on Rose's neck and looks deep into her. She feels weak yet confident and safe all at the same time. He kisses her, and just like every other time he kissed her, her world spins.

"You are the best thing that's ever happened to me, Rose." Trick continues, "I thought my life was over before that day with the healing waters project. Sara had to push pretty hard to get me out the door that morning. I really didn't think anything could help me. I didn't think there was any point in going. I wouldn't have ever expected that I would meet you. You saved my life, Rose, and I will always love you for that."

Rose kisses Trick again, but this time they kiss as though the world around them is burning down, and the kiss is the only thing saving them. He holds her tight and squeezes her, letting her know he'll never let her go. She feels warm and safe, even in the 50-degree water they are standing waist-deep in.

"How about we do this?" Rose suggests. "Let's start a fire and camp here tonight. We can make up some time tomorrow. I'd rather play more right now."

Trick and Rose changed out of their wet clothes and started a fire. They spent the evening and all that night on the bank of the Dearborn below the rapids. Not a single boat came by. The sound of the river drowned out the rest of the world as if a curtain was drawn, protecting them from the rest of humanity. They made love and then fell asleep in each other's arms. The first day together on the Dearborn, and now the night was absolutely perfect.

LOBSTER BAKE

Day two on the Dearborn begins with the squawking of a merganser mother and her 14 babies. As they swim upstream towards the waterfall and past the couple's campsite, Trick lifts his head and peers out of the tent. Mama mergie gets startled and scoots across the water, paddling vigorously with her webbed feet. Three of her babies climb on her back to catch a free ride as the others jealously fall in line behind. Trick taps Rose on her naked shoulder.

"Hey, check that out," he whispers.

Rose rolls over and rubs the sleep from her eyes and catches the tail-end of the merganser's great escape. "Fish-eating sons-a-bitches," she says with a bit of disdain for the mergansers and reverence for her trout.

"You ever watch those little bastards hunt for fish?" She asks Trick.

"I don't think so," he answers.

"They are fish killing machines," she notes. "Too bad they're inedible. Maybe people would hunt them. I guess they taste like rotting fish. I've never tried 'em but I trust the reviews."

"It's a good thing we have bacon," Trick says. "I'm starving. I'll cook. You've been doing all the work so far."

Being in bear country, Rose and Trick took the appropriate measures to hang a bear rope and suspend all their food and anything else that smelled like food well away from camp the night before. Trick slips a pair of fleece pants on, a sweatshirt, and then Chacos, and stands up out of the tent. Taking a big stretch, reaching towards the sky first, he then tacos forward to touch his toes. Feeling the freshly circulating blood reaching his extremities, he walks along the bank of the Dearborn to the tree where the food was hung.

"Hey," he shouts back to Rose. "Check this out."

Rose follows his lead, standing and stretching, and then comes to his side.

Pointing down to the mud, still wet from receding high water, he says, "Look at that. We had a visitor last night."

"Hmm," she acknowledges. "That's a big track. You see those claw marks?"

"Grizzly?" Trick asks.

"I mean," she ponders. "I'm not a professional tracker, but looking at the size and the claw marks, I would say, yeah, it's probably a griz. We should get the bear spray."

"Well, what do you think?" Trick asks.

"I say we quietly get the hell out of here," she responds. "Breakfast can wait. We'll get downstream a couple of miles and then stop for food."

Chase appears from the brush along the bank and gives a "woof." His hackles are up, and he's prancing around in an obvious state of agitation. He doesn't even acknowledge the mergansers that have continued their hunting expeditions on the other side of the river.

"I think Chase agrees," Trick adds.

Rose helps Trick with the bear bag and rope. They re-rig their gear into the raft with a sense of urgency, yet still being careful to suspend the Yeti cooler off the floor of the raft and secure anything else that could fall out if the raft were to capsize, as they know they'll be encountering more rapids before they get to the next good place to camp. Trick jumps into the front of the raft, Rose sits in the rower's chair, and Chase sits on top of the cooler in the back. They push off, and a sense of relief comes over them.

"I saw a griz up here a couple of years ago," Rose tells

Trick. "I didn't get a good look at it, but it scared the shit out of me. I was fishing up by the High Bridge. It was getting dark. I had to climb straight up the scree to get to the road to avoid him. The last thing I want to do is run into a griz out here."

"No shit," Trick agrees. "I think we're fine now, though."

"Yeah. We'll be far enough downstream soon enough," she says. "Just a reminder, you gotta be bear aware out here."

Rose continues to navigate her Maravia through rock gardens and rapids while Trick fishes out front. She leaves her life of guiding behind as she allows Trick to pick out his own spots, working on placement and presentation. She is at peace with being in the moment and not feeling like Trick needs to catch every fish. In fact, she doesn't even care if he lands another one. She's just happy pulling on the oars and dodging rocks and sharing stories and listening to Trick as he shares his truths. Every once in a while, she parks and pulls the raft up on the bank and grabs the rod from Trick, takes a few casts, lands a fish, shrugs her shoulders, and gives the look of, "Well, what do you expect? I'm a professional."

They make their way past the Hwy 200 Bridge and on through the flats along the Dearborn Ranch. By about 2 p.m., they reach the Hwy 287 Bridge, and Rose starts looking for a place to camp. By this time, all the rafters that have launched at the bridge are long gone. The parking lot is still three-quarters full of rigs waiting to get shuttled down to the Missouri, where they will eventually take out. They've timed it perfectly to give the illusion of having the entire river to themselves. They have yet to even see another raft or kayak, or any watercraft of any kind.

"Let's get downstream another three or four miles," Rose suggests. "That will get us out in front of the boats putting on tomorrow morning."

"Sounds good," Trick agrees. "You're the captain."

At around 5 o'clock, they turn a corner in the river and come to a beach on the inside bend. The beach is devoid of river rock with fine, black sand; perfect for a campsite site and with the water receding drastically over the past few days, they can camp well below the high-water mark. Montana's river access laws are quite favorable to recreational users. As long as a person accesses the river legally, either through a public access site or bridge crossing, once you're in the river and stay below the historic high-water mark, you can pretty much go wherever you want. Some landowners either don't understand the laws or don't care and try to keep people from passing through what they believe is their property; however, Rose knows the law and is confident she is in the right.

Rose jumps from the raft and pulls the stern up onto the beach.

"Give me some rope," she instructs, and Trick pulls up on the line that is wedged in the cleat along the frame of the raft, letting out about eight feet.

Rose throws the anchor up into the sand and brushes off her hands.

"I think this will work," she says as Chase leaps from raft to beach, clearing the water without getting wet.

"You've got an interesting pup there, Rose," Trick lets out. "He's not like other labs I know. He doesn't seem to like to get wet."

"Yeah, I know," she says. "And I'm grateful. I used to take him down to the dog park in Helena. It would rain, and the lower part of the park would fill up with water—pretty much just a big mud puddle. I would watch as people would let their dogs off leash, and they would all bust down to the water like kids running to the swing sets. The dogs, mostly labs, would roll around in that crap. I would watch as their owners would just shake their heads like, 'What do you do?' Chase never liked getting dirty. I mean, he's not afraid of the water. He just needs a reason."

Rose picks up a piece of driftwood and chucks it into the river. Chase launches himself into the water and chases it downstream.

"There's no real rhyme or reason to it," she says.

Trick has now jumped from the raft and is handing gear from the rear of it to Rose. They continue telling stories while setting up camp. Building a fire ring out of small boulders they find along the bank, they start a fire in the pit and cook dinner. After dinner, they hang their bear rope and bag and settle down for the evening.

The sun retreats behind the canyon walls, and the temperature drops a good fifteen degrees. Rose sits next to the fire with her sleeping bag, and Trick sits down next to her. She covers his legs with the bag and snuggles into his shoulder.

"Let me ask ya, Rose," Trick begins. "Do you believe in destiny, or do you think things just happen randomly?"

"Like, chance or coincidence, or is there a greater plan?" She asks.

"Yeah," he continues. "And if so, I mean if there is some great plan, how does that contribute to love? Like, how do people fall in love? Do you think it's random or do you think there is one person we are supposed to be with, and if you wait for that person, eventually they come to you?"

"Hmm," she thinks out loud. "I don't know. I guess there's a chance we're all magically living out some plan. It's a pretty elaborate plan, though, right?"

"Yeah, but somehow doesn't that give everything a sense of purpose?" Trick asks. "I mean, look at how we met and look at where we are now. Were we supposed to meet or was it just a random act of chance? And if it is just chance or coincidence, does that mean it's more or less meant to be? And what does that mean for what love really is or isn't?"

"You're blowing my mind, Trick," Rose says sarcastically. "I never thought you were such a deep thinker."

"Ha," he says. "I'm not just a pretty face…but seriously, don't you want to think that *it's* meant to be? Like the person pulling the levers wants you to be with the person you are with? Like, that's what makes it real and what the Universe wants?"

"Yeah, I guess, but I'm here now and that's really all I care about," she admits. "Just being here with you is enough, regardless of what I think the Universe wants. Just being here in the moment and that makes me truly happy."

"So, along those lines," Trick continues. "Why did you start volunteering with the healing waters project?"

"Well, Trick. It's a long story, and I suppose there's no better time than right now to start sharing how fucked up I am." She admits.

"Nobody's perfect."

"Yeah, well, some of us are a lot less perfect," Rose continues. "The sheriff kind of *suggested* I volunteer. I made some mistakes."

"Yeah?" Trick pries.

"Getting into guiding for a chick is hard, Trick," she

reveals. "I was spending a lot of time, too much time really, competing with the boys. Not just on the river but in the bar. One night, I was at Izaak's and drank way too much. One of the outfitters…"

"I'm sorry," Trick apologizes, recognizing the shame she was feeling. "You don't have to…"

"No. It's alright," she says.

Rose hadn't shared the story with anyone since she had been interviewed by the sheriff the day after she was raped, except for Ross and Karren. She didn't think it would be this hard, but now she was finding herself searching for the words that would give just enough detail to cause Trick to be sympathetic, but not so much as to make her out to be the monster she had seen herself as since that morning.

"Anyway," she continues. "The next thing I know, I'm waking up next to the guy. It was disgusting. I was passed out, and he took advantage of me. I took off. I got in my Jeep and just took off and pulled out in front of a truck, and it went off the road. I kept going. I was scared, and there were other vehicles there, so I just left. It was about six hours later when the sheriff knocked on my door. He must have felt bad because of the circumstances. Plus, there was no indication I was drunk, so he didn't charge me with anything. He just swept it under the rug, which I guess is what they can do if they feel bad for you or they know that charging you isn't going to fix anything. He did make one request as far as some kind of restitution, though. I had to volunteer for the healing waters program. Honestly, I felt like it was the least I could do."

"Well, Rose. Again, I'm sorry," Trick says, showing compassion. "Looks like you've grown from it."

"I just want to move past it now," she says. "As

small-town Montana works, if the sheriff sympathizes with you, they have a lot of power in just burying everything. So, I quit drinking, and I've put my head down and am working my butt off and now trying to live a better life."

"Well," Trick cuts in. "If you believe shit happens for a reason, maybe it's part of the plan? Maybe something good has come from it. Maybe what happened was exactly what was supposed to happen."

The conversation obviously stirred up a lot of emotions for Rose, and Trick could sense her anxiety being triggered. He pulled her close, and they stared into the fire for what seemed like hours. Every once in a while, he would pull his arm free of Rose's shoulders, reach down to pick up another dead branch, and set it on the fire. They didn't say a word for a long time. The shame from the memories now gripped her and stifled her voice and left her silent.

When the firewood was gone and the flames burned down to just glowing embers, Trick broke the silence. "Hey, let's go to bed."

Rose lay awake for hours that night, wondering what Trick must have thought of her. Did he think less of her for her choices? For putting herself and others in danger? And then the guilt and self-loathing of her own thoughts about what happened with Jake. Rose knew, deep down, she wasn't the one to blame, but she couldn't help feeling somewhat responsible because to not feel that she might have to admit she had no control. And what would be worse?

"Damnit," she thought to herself. "How could I be so stupid? How could I have let that happen?"

Trick woke the next morning to kayakers drifting past their camp. He heard the banging of roto-molded plastic against rocks and the other partnering kayaks.

"Stop!" One of the kids yelled out. "You're gonna flip me!"

"Hey!" Came the shout of a deeper, older voice of a man clearly at the end of his rope and not recognizing the irony. "Keep it down! We're not the only people on the river!"

Trick poked his head out of the tent to see 5 kayaks manned by one gentleman with a fluffy beard, three children who spanned the ages of roughly 12 to 15 years, and a woman desperate to create distance from all of them. The man waved and sheepishly nodded and shrugged, displaying an apologetic gesture of embarrassment for how his children were carrying on.

"Ambitious," Trick yelled out with a little more than a hint of acknowledgement for the man's struggles. "Good for you guys, getting an early start. Have fun!"

Trick looked back to the inside of the tent and saw that Rose was already gone. He scanned the area outside the tent looking for her and Chase, but there was no sign, so he slid out of the tent, pulled a hoodie over his head, and slipped into his Chacos.

The raft was still parked along the bank, now fully out of the water as the river had receded even further through the night. The bear rope and bag were still hanging where they left them a hundred yards downstream. He turned to look back upstream and noticed a figure at the top of a pillar of granite looking out over the river.

Rose was sitting on top of the pillar of rock. She was looking his way, so he waved. She lifted a hand as a sign of acknowledgement.

"I don't think it's deep enough to jump," Trick yells up to her.

"Probably not," she thinks to herself. "But maybe that's the point."

"Let's cook up that bacon," Trick calls back.

Trick stoked the fire with some of the remaining embers from the night before. With a handful of pine duff and fines made of bark fiber from a dead cottonwood, he crumbled it between his hand and his thigh, he balled it all into a nest, and with a little bit of blowing, the embers flared up and danced in his breath. He added finger-sized sticks to build a loose pile on top of the fines that are quickly disintegrating to ash. One by one, the sticks ignite, and Trick adds mini logs until he finally graduates to logs the size of his wrist.

Rose climbed off the pillar and down to the fire pit. Without saying anything, she goes to the bear rope and lowers the food to the ground. She coils the rope and ties it off, and walks the bag and rope back to camp.

"Hey," Trick addresses her, realizing there is a cloud of insecurity hanging over them. "You all right?"

"I don't know," she replies. "I feel like maybe I shouldn't have told you that stuff last night. I'm embarrassed. I feel like a loser."

"I think you're being a little hard on yourself, Rose." He continues, "shit happens. You can't change the past. All we can do is try to be better now and in the future. That's the only thing you have control over."

"You're just saying that because you don't know how to get out of here," she replies with a shy shrug. "But when we get back to town, you're going to run for the hills."

"My feelings haven't changed," he reassures her. "But if you're going to be able to move on, you're going to have to figure out how to forgive yourself and maybe even that guy."

"Fuck that guy," she says.

"Yeah, I get that," Trick answers with some under-standing and empathy. "Maybe it's not so much forgiving him but finding a way to accept the reality that he's probably not going to give you what you want or need. Hating him isn't helping you. So, instead of letting him control your thoughts, how can you get to the point of just being, ok? Tight lines, Fly. Er, sorry. Sex kitten?"

"Let's just go with Rose for now."

Trick and Rose finish up with breakfast and load their gear onto the Maravia. Another raft floats by with a man and two women. The man is in the rower's chair mounted on a half-frame for fun floating. He is sporting cut-off shorts and no shirt. The women who are wearing bikinis that are a little too small to hold back the parts God blessed them with are sitting on the tubes of the raft, one in front and the other in back.

"Asking a lot from those bikini straps," Rose whispers under her breath just loud enough for Trick to hear.

Trick waves to the group, "Hey, dude. Ladies. Sure is looking like a beautiful day."

"Sure is," the man answers back.

Trick turns to Rose and asks quietly, "Lobster bake?"

"Sure hope they've lathered up in sunscreen," she replies.

"I'm thinking butter."

They wait for a few minutes, allowing the raft to get downstream, and then shove off. Rose is feeling a little more confident as she pushes the raft out into the current and straightens it out to follow the path of the main current. Trick turns himself around in his seat, leans over her hands on the oars, and kisses her quickly on the lips. He then turns back to face downstream and grabs his rod. He pulls the stonefly from the guide it was hooked on, rips off about 25 feet of line, and starts aiming at the seams along the bank.

"Hey, Trick!" Rose shouts. "See that rock along the bank at about 10:30 or 11 o'clock? I think I saw a nose come up. Hit that seam and let it drift past the eddy."

Trick grabs the line in his trigger finger on his casting hand and then uses the pinchers of the prosthetic to grab the line and strip in any slack off the water. He rips the line off the water and throws it into his backcast. With a little more line than he wanted to carry, he pauses just a millisecond longer, lets the rod load, and shoots the tip forward towards his target. Another 10 feet of line shoots out the tip of the rod, and the fly drops inches from the boulder and slides past onto the seam.

"That'll get eaten," Rose affirms.

As the bullethead stone drifts along the seam and just as it starts to get sucked into the eddy, the nose of a brown trout slowly emerges from the pool created from the current gouging out the river bottom downstream of the boulder. The brown turns and follows the fly for about a foot, then opens his mouth and clamps down on it.

"Get 'em," Rose yells.

With a firm stroke, Trick lifts his rod up and comes tight. The brown rolls and twists and turns, trying desperately to lose the hook from his mouth. When that doesn't work, he runs out to the middle of the river like a souped-up jet ski in an attempt to wrap the line around another boulder mid-river. Trick lifts his rod tip up high enough to clear the first boulder, but the second one is a little too far out for the angle, and he sees the inevitability of his line wrapping up on it.

Right then, Trick lets a few feet of line slip out the

tip of his rod and pulls the rod back to 2 o'clock over his head. He whips the tip forward, throwing a loop over the boulder, and then yanks his rod violently sideways and downstream, pulling the monster brown out from behind the boulder.

As if the brown knows he's met his match, he relaxes a bit. The trout shakes his head a few times, then rolls a couple of times as a last-ditch effort, but then gives in, and Trick strips him towards the raft.

As Rose nets the brown, she asks, "Where did you learn that?"

"This ain't my first rodeo, Fly," Trick responds.

To that, she doesn't correct him; she just takes it and says, "When you're able to do things like that, you can call me Fly. But don't get cocky, and I better never hear that when we're naked."

"Fair enough," Trick concedes. "Fair enough."

THE CONFLUENCE

It's around 6 o'clock in the evening when Rose pushes the raft into the mainstem of the Missouri River. The canyons they had been drifting through for the past three days are now magnified; much higher and wider, and the river itself turns from gin clear to a copper tinge. The water of the Missouri actually looks a little dirty compared to the Dearborn, which Rose points out, is due to biomass.

"See that scum collecting over along the seam," Rose asks.

"Yeah, looks kind of gross."

"Well," she explains. "It might be gross, but that's why there are so many big fish in this river. It's all food. Dead bugs. And those fish will sit along the seams and chow until they can't eat anymore. They're like pigs in mud and the farmer just keeps dumping scraps to 'em."

"Hmm. Should be like shooting fish in a barrel then, right?" He assumes.

"Yeah, well, it ain't that easy," she explains. "With all those bugs, they don't have to eat if it doesn't look right. Think about it. All that food in the water? They get super keyed in on a particular size and shape and color, and they won't eat anything else. It's what keeps them safe. It keeps them from becoming food themselves. And it's not just the size and color, but it's also the way it's drifting in the water, or on the water if they're eating dries. It's like they're sitting along the seam, which is really just kind of a food trough, and they pick out stuff that looks like food or not just food, but the same food they've been eating for hours, and then something swings by them at a rate and direction that doesn't look right. So, they duck out of the way cuz they know. Up on the Dearborn, or other freestones, there's not as much food. The conditions aren't as favorable to bug life. The water temps and levels are more consistent in a tailwater like the Missouri, so the bugs are happy and have a longer time to develop and reproduce. On the freestones, the conditions are only right for short windows. So, trout have to take advantage of those windows and be more opportunistic when something that looks like it could be food comes along."

"Sounds complicated," Trick says with admiration.

"Yep. That's why we make the big bucks," she lets out a sarcastic chuckle. "You know what's kind of crazy, though? That big 'ole brown you caught? That fish doesn't live in the Dearborn. It must have come up last fall to spawn, or maybe this spring when the rainbows were running to eat their eggs. Throughout his time up there, he had to become more opportunistic. They actually learn. When that fish eventually makes it back to the Mo, it'll adjust its habits back to being less opportunistic and more selective."

"That is pretty crazy," Trick agrees.

"Billy never explained that stuff to you on the healing waters trip?" She asks.

"Nah, all Billy cared about was Billy." Trick answers. "In fact, he often made comments about how our boat was going to be 'top dog'. He really just wanted to put the most fish in the net regardless of what we were getting out of it."

"And you never fished other tailwaters before that trip?"

"No," he explains. "I was supposed to a couple of years ago, but then this."

Trick holds up the prosthetic that was his left arm.

"What do you mean?" She asks.

"My accident," Trick says. "We were supposed to be fishing that day, here on the Mo. It was a bunch of us from the team and a couple of the guys who were helping me through the draft."

"You were pretty good, huh?" She inquires.

"Yeah, I was," Trick continues. "I mean, that's what they were all telling me. It was pretty insane. The whole thing with the combine and all the scouts and teams creeping all over you."

"Combine?" She asks.

"Yeah. It's where they parade all the cattle in front of the GMs and coaches, and they see what you can do," Trick explains. "The NFL is a big fricken business. They don't want to just roll the dice on guys without seeing what they can do, so they get us all together in one place, like in Indianapolis, and put us through all sorts of drills and tests and interviews because they want a better look at what we can do."

"Why Indianapolis?"

"It's centrally located." Trick explains.

"Didn't they see you play in college?" She asks.

"Well, yes and no," Trick continues, understanding she's probably not the biggest football fan but still interested. "Most of the players come from big schools and have plenty of film, but a guy like me? It gives me a chance to compete next to all those guys, and no, most of the GMs and coaches probably didn't see much of me playing because Montana doesn't get a lot of national run. Outside of the play-offs, we're not making it on ESPN."

"Sounds pretty intense," she says.

"It is," and then corrects himself. "It was. I mean, if you have an off day, you might go from a second or third round draftee to a sixth or seventh or even fall off the board altogether. It's a lot of money, or potential money. Even if you make it in the draft, it doesn't mean you're going to make a team. One day, you might be thinking you're going to be a millionaire, and the next, flipping burgers or selling insurance. It's really that big of a deal, and it all comes down to finding a door that's cracked open just enough to plow through. Only there's a hundred other guys that play your position that are trying to plow through the same door at the same time."

"Yeah, I think that would be a lot of stress," Rose admits.

"It was, but I had a great support team," Trick says. "And that's what we were supposed to be doing. The Combine was over, and the draft was coming up. Mike, who was my trainer at the time and my agent, decided we should get away and blow off some steam. So, we came over here. And then it all fell apart."

"So, what happened?" She asks.

Rose picks the oars out of the water, slides the handles under her legs, propping them up, and lets the raft drift aimlessly downstream. She waits for Trick to respond, and when he doesn't, she reaches forward and puts a hand on his shoulder.

"You don't have to tell me, Trick," she says. "Not now anyway, but when you get to a place where you want to share, I'll be here."

"Well, thanks," he says. "My therapist says I probably should, but it's still pretty raw. Besides, it's all kind of a blur. One minute I'm driving down the Rec Road heading back to town to pick up Bret, my agent, and the next minute, I'm waking up in the hospital."

"God, that sucks," Rose consoles.

The raft continues to drift down the Missouri towards Mid-Canon, where Rose's Jeep is waiting. As they round the corner and shoot through riffles where the river braids out, they notice the rafters that passed them earlier that morning. They have just arrived at the take-out point, and the gentleman, still shirtless, is pulling the raft up onto the gravel. One of the women has just fallen into the river, and the other is lying on her back in the weeds, a few feet from the water.

Trick motions to the threesome and says, "Hey, check it out. Looks like they're cooked."

The man is a crispy, shiny pink in color. The two women are a little lighter but sunburnt as well, and too drunk to be of any use to the man packing gear and cleaning up the mess a few dozen White Claws and Natty Ice's have created for him. As he lifts his cooler out of the raft, he falls over, allowing the cooler to tip over. The lid opens, and several empty cans roll out and find their way to the river.

Rose drops anchor, leaps from the rower's chair, and with net in hand, runs through the knee-deep water to rescue the empties. Trick follows, and they round up the empty cans before they get out into the main current. She brings the cans back to the gentleman's cooler and dumps them from the net.

"Oops," the man utters with almost no contrition.

"Come on, man," Rose lets out. "You gotta do better than that."

The man stands, and Trick sizes him up. He's about 5'10 inches tall and weighs roughly 220 pounds. A disproportionate amount of that weight he carries just above his belt line, which he is now propping up as he takes a breath and pushes out his chest.

"Go fuck yourself," the man tells Rose.

"Classy," Rose replies as she points at the two women who are now passed out next to each other on the bank. "Too bad your skanky girlfriend there can't handle her White Claws. Bet you thought you were gonna get laid tonight, but that ain't happening."

"You little…" the man starts toward Rose, and Trick cuts him off.

"Whoa, dude, probably be a good time to cut your losses," Trick assures him.

Trick has lost a considerable amount of the weight he had gained while playing football, but he still towers above the man as he steps in between him and Rose.

"What are you gonna do, freak?" The man says as he looks at Trick's missing arm.

Trick tilts his head forward and leans into the man to look him in the eyes. He stares the man down for a couple of seconds without a hint of emotion.

Trick takes a deep breath and says, "This won't end well for you, dude. Let's just say I'm doing you a favor, and if I were you, I'd think long and hard about your next move."

"What the fuck are you gonna do?" The man asks.

"You don't have to worry about me," Trick responds. "I'm the nice guy. The one you probably should worry about is the little 'lady', as I'm sure that's where you were going a minute ago. She's the one I wouldn't be messing with. I'm just trying to help you out, dude."

"You know what? Fuck you people," the man says as he turns back, retreating towards his raft. "You all think you own the river with your Simms gear and your Sage rods. You think you're better than everyone else? Bet you're a guide too, aren't you?"

"Yeah, I'm a guide," Rose pipes up. "And I spend a hundred and twenty days a year on this river picking up after you drunk fucks. And I know it's the rec floaters cuz we aren't the ones drinking that shitty beer that seems to always find its way into the river. How about you show a tiny bit of respect for the rest of us that don't want to see a bunch of garbage floating downstream?"

"Fuck you," the man yells back over his shoulder as he tosses a few more empties into his cooler.

Trick and Rose unload the Maravia onto the beach. Rose walks to her rig that is parked along the back side of the parking area at the take-out. She jumps in and backs the trailer far enough into the water so that the platform of the trailer is just above the waterline. Jumping out of the Jeep, she then wades back into the water, pulls the raft off the beach, and lines it up with the trailer platform. Trick grabs a handle on the far side of the raft, and they both pull and slide it into place. Then she pulls the Jeep with the trailer in tow, up out of the water along the shoulder of the road, heading out of the parking lot.

The two women are still lying on their backs just off the beach where Rose and Trick pulled the Maravia from. The man has unloaded their raft and is now backing his trailer down towards the water. He spins the steering wheel a little too far, and the trailer jack-knifes and heads off the beach and into the willows. He pulls forward and takes another run, this time over-correcting and backing sideways along the beach, almost running the two women over.

"Whoa!" Trick yells as the man slams on the brakes.

The man jumps out of his late 80s, half-ton Chevy to assess the damage. One of the women on the beach sits up and looks around to see where all the commotion is coming from, and then drops back to the ground.

Just then, Keith Merchant pulls his skiff into the FAS.

"You need some help?" He asks the man.

"I got it," the man grunts at Keith.

The man straightens his rig and trailer and finally is able to back his way down into the river to a point where he can load his raft.

Keith jumps out of his hard boat and helps the man line up the raft with the trailer. The two heave and slide the raft into place.

"You alright, dude?" Keith asks.

"Yeah, it's just that bitch over there," as he gestures towards Rose. "Giving me shit for just trying to enjoy a float."

Keith sees that the man is obviously drunk, and he quickly takes inventory of the situation. Noticing the women passed out, Keith can guess the interactions that must have taken place. Not wanting to pour more gas on the flames, he shrugs it off.

"Yeah?" Keith defuses. "She can be kind of intense. But you're good now, right?"

"Yeah," the man replies. "All good now."

The man pulls the trailer out of the water and drives up away from Rose's Jeep but still close enough to load his gear. He doesn't thank Keith or even acknowledge the help as he pulls away. Keith waves and walks towards Rose and Trick.

"Hey, Fly," he addresses her. "How's it going?"

"It's fine," she replies. "Same 'ole same 'ole. Keith,

this is Trick. Trick, Keith."

"Good to meet you, Keith," Trick says.

"Yeah, you too," Keith replies. "Hey, you guys float the Dearborn today?"

"Yeah," Rose answers. "It was beautiful. We started up above the High Bridge. Three days of floating."

"That's awesome," Keith applauds. "How was the waterfall?"

"No scars," she says. "But we camped at the bottom of the falls and had a visitor that night."

"Oh yeah?" Keith inquires.

"Yeah," she says with excitement. "A fricken griz came down in the middle of the night to check us out."

"No shit?" Keith peaks. "Did you see it?"

"No," she explains. "But his tracks went along the beach to the bear hang. We saw them the next morning, and they weren't there the night before."

"That's cool, or scary…or both, I guess," Keith says.

"Yeah, I'd rather not run into a griz if I'm going to be honest," she concedes.

"So, what happened with this guy?" Keith asks.

"Same shit," she answers. "We saw them up on the Dearborn this morning and let them get out ahead of us. We caught up to them just as they hit the take-out. He dumped a cooler full of empties into the river, and we had to chase them down. They're so drunk they can't even function. The two women are passed out on the bank over there."

"You know the drill, Fly," Keith says. "Best to just get out of their way. You ain't changing anything by saying shit to them."

"I know," she admits. "But somehow we always get a bad rap for screwing up this river, and we're the ones that have to clean up after these pricks."

"Yep," Keith agrees. "And you getting into it with them ain't going to fix it."

"Yeah, I know," she says.

"Well, no harm, no foul," Keith nods to Trick. "Good to meet yah. I'll see you guys back at the ranch."

Keith walks over to his black Suburban, lifts the tailgate so he can see out the back, and backs his way into the river. His clients have gotten out of the boat and are watching as he cranks his boat up onto the trailer. Rose and Trick finish strapping down the Maravia and jump into the Jeep and pull out. The two women are still passed out on the bank of the river.

"You alright?" Trick asks as they slow down to ease over the speed bumps that have been placed across the road, driving out.

"Yeah," Rose replies. "It's just those rec floaters. They can dump trash in the river, leave their toilet paper littered all over the islands, treat people like crap, and somehow, we're the problem. The guides out here are the ones picking up the trash and bringing money to the area, keeping these people employed, and we have to put up with that every day."

"I can tell that would be frustrating," Trick replies.

"Do you know how many times I've been called 'boat nigger' or 'fish whore' or any other insult you can think of? Just because we're out here trying to make a living. And we share. We don't tell people they can't be on the river. We just ask for a little space." Rose is obviously getting a little wound up.

"Hey," Trick tries to change the topic. "You hungry? Is there anything open?"

"Yeah, I know," Rose concedes. "I gotta let it go. We

can go stop by Craig and check out Izaak's? You haven't been there yet, and they have an upscale kind of bar menu?"

"Let's do it."

Rose turns onto the ramp to get to I-15 and steps on the gas. The Jeep accelerates and quickly reaches 70 mph. They cross over the Missouri just below the confluence of the Dearborn and look back up the canyon. A couple more rafts with three kayaks are working their way down the river.

"It is a beautiful river, Rose," Trick says. "Thanks for taking me. Maybe we should do this every year?"

Trick is making one of those gestures, as a sort of test or maybe a confirmation to Rose that he is still thinking long-term about what they have started. It's the thing new couples do to try to get a sense of where things are going, and often employed when one person feels a little insecure. Although Trick knows where he is, he feels a little uneasy about where Rose might be, given some of the conversations and the fact that they just spent three days together, which is much longer than any time they've spent up to this point. Trick is checking in and feeling he needed just a little bit of confirmation, too.

Rose reaches over and places her hand on Trick's neck and massages him. "If you still want me next year."

"As long as you keep putting me on two-foot browns," Trick replies. "I wouldn't want to be with anyone else."

Rose flips on the blinker and merges off the freeway onto the off-ramp to Craig. She turns onto Bridge Street and cruises through town. The parking lot for Izaak's is full and trucks with trailers are lined up along all the side streets in town. Even the railroad tracks, which have been exempt for years, have rigs parked along them.

"This place is hoppin'," Rose observes. "I'm going to run up the road to check messages. Maybe by then, it will clear out a bit."

They pass over the tracks and head over the bridge. They reach the intersection of the Rec Road, and Rose turns right to head upstream. A mile or so later, she flicks on her blinker again and pulls off the road into the parking area that sits above Missouri on the bluff. Turning off the ignition, she grabs her cell phone and turns it on for the first time in three days.

The phone pings and vibrates as messages register, one by one.

"I wonder how many trips I missed out on," she says.

Trick is sitting silently as he stares out the window, looking over the river. An osprey hovers above the river and then falls from the sky, splashing down feet first. The mid-sized bird of prey violently flaps her wings, but looks as though she is stuck in the water. She fights for flight and eventually goes airborne with a 16-inch trout in her talons. Trick doesn't say a word.

"Did you see that?" Rose asks excitedly.

Trick doesn't respond.

"What's the matter, Trick?" Rose pries.

There's a section of jack-fence at the end of the parking area that is a little more yellow than the rest of the fence, which has obviously been weathered longer than the newly constructed section. The skid marks from Trick's Frontier have long been covered over by other tracks from other rigs, and the vegetation lining the fence has had plenty of time to regrow. It's the first time Trick has been back to this place since his accident.

"This is Cell Phone Bluff," he finally says.

"Yeah," she confirms. "It's like the only place where we can get cell service. Even in Craig, High Banks, and Izaak's have a booster, but MRA doesn't, and I'm a little tired of High Banks, so I come here to check messages."

"This is where it all happened," Trick explains. "See that fence?"

"What do you mean, Trick?" She asks.

"The accident," Trick replies. "That morning. We rented out the Fly Fisher Inn by Mountain Palace. I was heading to town to pick up Bret. I decided to drive the Old Highway, which is the Rec Road, I guess. I just wanted to see the river. I could have gotten on the freeway by Mountain Palace or at Craig, but I decided to stay on the Rec Road. This was the place where I lost control and went off into the river. I don't remember it. I have no idea what happened. I wouldn't even know where it was if people hadn't told me about it. I must have gone into the river right there."

Trick points to the newer section of the jack fence.

Rose's heart thumped heavily in her chest. "When was that?"

"April 12th, almost a year and a half ago," Trick reveals.

"Oh my God," Rose starts, but then something deep inside her grabs her words and stuffs them back into her chest.

"What?" Trick asks.

Rose's heart races as she searches for the words. "Shit. I remember that, but I didn't have any idea that it was you."

Rose's fingers start to tremble. Her lips curl down

and quiver as a tear starts to drift down the side of her face. She wipes it dry before Trick looks back at her and sees. He still stares out over the river. Rose now knows, but she also knows that Trick doesn't. How could this be? She wants to scream. She wants to slam her fists into the steering wheel. The person she loves more than anyone in this world, she now realizes that she is the one who ruined his life.

BOB IS A TREAT

Trick wakes up next to Rose the next morning. They decided not to eat at Izaak's as both were exhausted from the weekend, and Rose really didn't have much of an appetite. Instead, they headed back to the cottage and finished the rest of the cheese and crackers, and the elk summer sausage left over from the trip. They went to bed, and as Trick drifted off to sleep, Rose quietly wept to herself, pulling Trick's arm around her like a comforter that can't seem to stay in place or won't provide the warmth she needed.

Hours later, the light of the morning is barely filtering through the drapes that resemble the curtains she remembered from the camper where she lived all of her first season as a guide. She feels Trick pressed against her. Knowing he is awake, she pretends not to be. Trick presses against her harder, and she feels him, erect. He wraps his arm around her, pulling her in, and she feels his hand travel down her belly and between her legs.

Rose's heart races. The anxiety of knowing what she has done, also knowing he doesn't, is like staring down at a rattlesnake at your feet that hasn't noticed you yet. The desire to jump and scream, yet knowing in doing so, you are sure to get bitten, freezes her. If she doesn't say or do anything, maybe it will all just go away. But how can she live with the lie? How, knowing that she was the one who changed his life forever, could she live with herself? And if he knew, would he still choose to be with her? That was such a big *if*.

Rose presses her body back into Trick and lifts her leg up, letting him touch her. He kisses her on the back of her neck, which would normally cause goosebumps to radiate across her body, but with the anxiety, it does little to arouse her. She worries he will be able to feel something is wrong if she doesn't perform, so she reaches behind herself and grabs Trick and massages him until she can hear his breathing quicken. While she strokes him, she wets her fingers and touches herself, artificially moistening her vagina. Rose lets him enter from behind so he can't see the tears falling down her cheek.

Trick is getting close, and Rose senses this, so she moans and pretends to be close to orgasm with him. She feels his body flexing and convulsing as he releases inside her and then relaxes and goes limp. He pulls from her and kisses her shoulder. Rose lies motionless.

"I'm so glad you are in my life," Trick says, not detecting her strife.

Rose quickly wipes the tears from her face, rolls over, and buries her head into Trick's chest. She wraps her arms around his waist and pulls him close, squeezing him as if it will be the last time she touches him.

"I love you," she whispers and then continues in her thoughts to herself. "I will miss you."

"I love you, too," Trick reciprocates. "You're the best thing that's ever happened to me."

"Shit," Rose says. "I gotta get moving. I've got clients at the lodge. Meeting them at eight."

She jumps from the bed, pulls on her underwear, and grabs a clean pair of quick-drying pants and a thin hoodie from the closet. As she steps into her pants, she watches as Trick rolls off the opposite side of the bed and dresses too. She watches him intently while she flips the covers up to halfheartedly make the bed. She looks for any sign that he might know something is wrong.

"I gotta go, Trick," she says as she kisses him on the

lips. "Are you ok with letting yourself out?"

"Yeah," Trick replies. "I've got a coach's meeting this afternoon, so I'll be heading out this morning."

"Ok, drive safe," she tells him, and then rushes out the door.

Rose turns the corner of the historic hotel. While out of sight of Trick, she lets the tears flow and buries her head in her hands. Ross opens the front door to the hotel and sees her.

"Are you ok, Rose?" He asks in his fatherly way.

She nods but can't get words out. Ross sees Trick's 4Runner parked out front.

"Did you guys have a fight?" He asks.

"No," she replies. "No, not at all. I just…it's nothing. I'm just running late. I'll talk to you later, Ross."

She runs out of the gate of the picket fence in front of the hotel, rips open the front door of the Jeep, and launches herself into the driver's seat.

"Damnit," she thinks to herself. "Chase."

Rose runs back through the yard in front of the hotel, rounds the corner, and then back into the yard of the cottage. Flinging the door open, she sees Trick standing in the kitchen. Their eyes meet. Hers are now bloodshot red from crying, and her face, stained from the tears. She looks down to avoid his inquisitive stare.

"Can you feed Chase?" She blurts out. "And then just leave him in the yard. Make sure you latch the gate?"

"Of course," he answers, tilting his head, brows furrowed. "What's wrong?"

"Nothing. I've gotta go," she says as she steps towards him and gives him a quick kiss on the mouth.

Rose runs back out into the yard and around the corner of the hotel. Ross's head turns to track her as if he's watching a tennis or soccer match. He opens his mouth and begins to ask Rose if she's alright again, but knows better. He's had plenty of discussions with her to know, when she's ready, she'll open up to him, but prying won't bring anything out of her.

Rose pulls into the parking lot of MRA, hooks her boat trailer to her hitch, plugs the wiring harness into her Jeep, and jumps back into the driver's seat. She's got eight minutes to be at the lodge, which is a few miles downstream from Craig along the Rec Road. She sees Keith standing next to his skiff, Suburban hatch open, smoking a cigarette. He waves as she pulls her rig around and heads out of the driveway onto Bridge Street. She doesn't want him to see her, still showing signs of crying, so she drops her chin to her chest and pretends to be reaching down for something that might have dropped onto the floorboards of the Jeep.

Speeding through town, though Rose has been reprimanded by Kim for speeding in the past, she makes her way across the bridge. She rolls to a stop at the Rec Road and looks to the right, then her left, and then back upstream to the right. Although she can't see Cell Phone Bluff from the intersection, she knows it's there, and all she can think about is that morning of April 12th, a little over a year ago.

She pulls out onto the road, turning downstream towards the lodge. She'll get to the lodge just in time, but at this point, that's not even entering her thoughts. All she can think about is Trick and what she did to him. The guilt and shame she feels and the fear of what will happen when she tells him are crippling. Or maybe she won't tell him? Maybe it would be best if he didn't know. Why tell him? He's been hurt enough. If she tells him, she'll just hurt him even more, and then they won't be together. Or maybe he will forgive her? Maybe they can survive this?

"Damnit," she says out loud as she pounds the steering wheel. "Ahhh!"

Rose pulls into the driveway of the lodge and parks her Jeep and boat in a manner that she can pull straight out without having to maneuver around the other rigs that are already there. She also makes sure not to box anyone else in, as she's aware that they would have met their clients already and are probably champing at the bit to get out on the water before the rush of other guides and anglers clog up the boat ramps.

As Rose opens the door to the Jeep, she sees Billy coming down the stairs from the lodge. He's carrying his clients' gear, and as he reaches his truck, he tosses it in the bed with little regard. Rose begins her ascent, trying hard not to acknowledge him.

"Hey, Fly!" Billy waves.

"Billy," she gives in.

"Wait," Billy stops her. "Where you heading today?"

"Not sure," she responds. "I haven't talked to the clients yet. I'll see what they want."

"Well," Billy informs Rose. "I fished with them yesterday, if you have Bob and Sue, and did pretty well."

"Awesome," Rose responds with more than a hint of sarcasm.

Since Billy and Rose both worked for High Banks for a summer while getting into guiding full-time, they established relationships with many of the same outfitters, which meant they were often working together. Billy's competitive nature and arrogance always rubbed her the wrong way, but she had found a way to suppress the things she really wanted to say to him and just let things be.

"I'm just saying," Billy rationalizes while trying to show some humility. "It's a pretty competitive group. Bob's a treat. I'll probably just head back up to the dam. All they care about are bent rods."

"My kind of anglers," again with sarcasm.

"Hey," Billy says, trying to soften things up. "I know I can come off a little cocky, and I probably wasn't the easiest person to be around, but I'm working on it. I hope you can give me another shot and not write me off as one of the bro-bras just yet. Maybe I can buy you a drink later."

"I haven't had a drink in over a year, Billy," she informs him.

"Shit, I'm sorry," he says. "I hadn't seen you around for a while, but I didn't know you went cold turkey. Maybe a Coke then?"

"I'm good, Billy," she deflates him. "Besides, aren't you dating that Hannah chick from Bozeman?"

"First of all," Billy tries to preserve some dignity, "I wasn't asking you on a date. Geeze. Us guides gotta stick together. I was just asking as a friendly gesture. But yeah, Hannah and I are no longer. We got into a fight, and she tried to run me over with my own truck. She took off towards Helena, and I called the cops. We were pretty drunk, so…she got all the way down to the Grub Stake before they caught up with her. She spent the weekend in jail. Her brother had to come up from Bozeman to bail her out. I had to get a ride down from Josh to get my truck. It was a shit-show, so no, I'm not seeing Hannah."

"Well, at least not this week," she stings him with a barb. "I'm late, Billy. I gotta get my folks and get loaded up. Good luck on the water."

Rose runs up the steps to the lodge, gliding through

sliding doors on the deck that have been opened to let the fresh morning air in. The smell of bacon still lingers from breakfast. Leslie, the wife of the lodge owner, is cleaning up the breakfast dishes and greets Rose.

"Hey, Rose," she says and walks around to give her a hug. "Good morning. How've you been?"

Leslie is one of the few people in the fly-fishing community who calls Rose by her first name out of respect. 'Fly' is what the guides call her, and she likes to see Rose as more of a friend and a fellow woman in an industry where women need to stick together.

Ken Jorgenson, Leslie's husband and owner of the lodge, enters the dining area and greets Rose. He's a large man, standing roughly 6'3" and has the body of an aging linebacker who suffered the wear and tear of playing in a Big Ten football program. The limited knowledge Rose had of football life, which made it easier to relate to Trick, was because of all the stories she had heard from Ken as he boasted to his clients. Ken was a proud man and always wanted everyone to understand he was the top dog, both in storytelling and on the river. Ken's clients always wanted to fish with him because he made them feel like they were catching the most fish, whether they did or not.

Max capacity at the lodge is 14 anglers. With the lodge full, that would mean Ken would have to contract out six other guides, not including himself. On this particular day, they had 10 guests, so Rose was one of the four guides Ken hired. Although she didn't necessarily fit the profile of the guide Ken was, she felt good knowing he contacted her to help out with trips before some of the other guides.

"Hey, Fly," Ken greets her. "You've got Bob and Sue

Cromwell. They're downstairs getting their gear ready."

Ken didn't talk much unless he was talking about himself. Rose thought she recognized the name from a trip she was on last year, but couldn't be sure.

"Did I guide them last year?" Rose asks.

"Not sure," Ken responds.

As Bob and Sue came up the steps carrying their rods in tubes, rain jackets, and a duffel bag, Rose was sure she recognized them. They make eye contact, and Sue holds out her arms to hug Rose.

"Hey, Rose. It's so good to see you again," Sue says. "We had such a great time last year, we wanted to fish with you again. Hope that's alright with you?"

That was another thing about Ken. He hated the idea of his clients wanting to fish with anyone but him. So, when the Cromwells requested her, he facilitated the ask, but he wasn't going to let on to Rose that they had requested her.

"Absolutely!" Rose is trying her best to show enthusiasm. "We're going to have a blast."

Rose takes the bag from Bob's hand that has their reels, sunscreen, and a few other comfort items, and waves to Leslie, gives Ken a nod, and motions towards the door.

"Let's get after 'em," she says.

Rose had an uncanny ability to flip the switch when she was with clients. No matter what the circumstances, she never let on that there was anything else going on except being with her clients and entertaining them. She made every client feel as if they were the only thing in her life at that moment. On this day, keeping up with the facade was going to be a challenge. Even as they walked down the steps to the lower parking lot, her mind drifted off to the realization that she was the one who caused Trick so much pain. Rose knew it wouldn't be fair to keep him from that truth, but it also wouldn't be fair to either of them not to have each other.

"So, where are we going today, Rose?" Bob asks.

"Well," she begins. "We have options. The entire river is fishing. It depends on whether you want to catch a bunch of fish while you play bumper boats with the other guides or if you want to roll the dice and have a little room to breathe."

"I think we caught 35 fish with Billy yesterday," Bob brags. "We had a blast."

"Did you fish the dam?" Rose asks.

"Yeah," Bob says. "We did. God, there are a lot of fish up there."

"Yeah, and a lot of boats," She admits. "Do you want to see some more river? Maybe go downstream through the canyon?"

Rose looks at Sue, and she gives the look as if to say, "Don't ask me. I'm just along for the ride."

"Are we going to catch 35 fish if we go downstream?" Bob asks.

"I can't guarantee the fish will cooperate, but I know you'll see a cool part of the river, and we can avoid the crowds. You'll get your chances," Rose assures.

"I'd rather just fish where we have the best chance at catching a bunch of fish," Bob tells Rose.

"You're the boss," Rose acknowledges. "The dam it is and today; you'll catch thirty-six."

"Really?" Bob gives her a look of contempt for her cockiness.

The three load the gear and themselves into the Jeep, and Rose drives to Craig, stops at the shop to set up a shuttle, and then takes I-15 south to Wolf Creek. She opts to take the freeway and not the Rec Road because she doesn't want to drive past Cell Phone Bluff and be reminded of the inevitable. They pull off the freeway and drive through Wolf Creek, passing by the cottage and the historic hotel. Ross is patching the picket fence where a couple of rungs were busted from one of their guests backing into it after a few drinks. He sees Rose and waves. She waves back.

Rose turns her rig to cross under I-15 and then over the Little Prickly Pear Creek and heads back to the east, towards the Missouri River. There's a road that crosses through the Oxbow Ranch before you get to the Wolf Creek Bridge that is essentially an alternative route heading to the dam. It's scenic and less traveled than the main road, so she turns onto it and heads over the foothills towards Holter Reservoir. As they crest the foothills, before descending back down towards the river, they look out over the reservoir and can see the entirety of the dam spanning the width of the river. From that distance, the dam looks impressive but somehow incredibly modest given the size of the body of water it is charged with holding back.

"That's so cool," Sue declares.

"Yeah," Rose agrees. "And what you're looking at is about half of Holter Lake. There's another ten or twelve miles that you can't see that goes through the canyon and opens up to the upper part of the reservoir. It's the spot Lewis and Clark named the Gates of the Mountains."

"Why is that?" Sue asks.

"Because as you follow the contour of the canyon," Rose explains, "there's a pinch point where the canyon walls come together. As you get closer, they look like they are separating or opening up like a huge gate. It's an optical illusion. It's pretty cool though if you've never seen it."

"That sounds amazing," Sue says. "How does a person get to see that?"

"Well," Rose tells her. "You can either take a tour boat from the marina on the upper end of the lake, or when you fish with Ken up there at the Land of the Giants, which is the stretch of river above the lake, you can have him take you across with the jet boat. If you ask nicely, I'm sure he'd love to show you."

The stretch of river, deemed the Land of the Giants, gets its name from producing huge trout that resemble hatchery steelhead more than wild trout. In fact, most of the trout in that stretch are a hybrid of rainbow trout, either Arlee or Eagle Lake trout, which have some steelhead DNA introduced to them. FWP stocks these fish in the reservoirs because they grow faster and larger than the wild trout in the lower stretch, so people can fish for them and take them home to eat. Ken has capitalized on these fish by being one of the few outfitters with the jet boat and the Captain's License to run commercial trips up there. The fishing itself is less like fly-fishing and more like dredging the riverbed with bottom bouncers and egg patterns, but anglers and guides do look like heroes with grip and grins of 25-inch rainbows that weigh upwards of seven or eight pounds.

"We're here to catch fish, Rose," Bob cuts in. "We're not here for the sightseeing."

Feeling like a puppy that's just felt the slap of a rolled-up newspaper, Rose capitulates, "alrighty then. Let's go fishing."

Rose feels herself tense up, and the desire to lecture

Bob on what fly-fishing is, or ought to be, almost gets the best of her. Having had this conversation with other guides multiple times over the past couple of years, she is just beginning to find her niche.

"If it were just about catching numbers of fish," she would hear other guides say, "then there are easier ways to do it. Bring a spinning rod and some worms or spinning baits, and you'll catch as many fish as you want. But if you're going to learn how to fly-fish, then put the work in and actually learn to fly-fish."

A parallel to archery hunting versus rifle hunting for elk is often made during these discussions. Catching fish on a fly is not supposed to be easy. The purpose is supposed to challenge a person to learn how to cast and present a fly to spooky fish that don't always cooperate. But tricking them to eat an imitation that represents natural food with rudimentary gear and sophisticated techniques is the pinnacle of fly-fishing, much like calling in an elk to a distance that a person can kill by launching a stick with a bow. Obviously, the gear has advanced over the years, but the traditions remain.

Rose likes this perspective and often finds herself on that side of the argument, which sometimes leads her to a path of contempt for folks that just want to go after the less savvy hatchery fish through methods that don't include casting or managing their drift or even recognizing the food the trout are keying in on. And the Land of the Giants is just perpetuating a discipline that strays further and further from fly-fishing, where the only thing that seems to matter is the Instagram post, regardless of the methodology or consideration for the prey. This type of fishing just feels so contrived and cheap to her.

THE DAMN DAM

Suppressing those thoughts for the time being, Rose drives the winding road down to the parking lot at the BLM access below Holter Dam. At least twenty-five rigs have pulled into parking spots nose-in, with the stern of their boats pointing towards the double-wide, concrete ramp that ramps down to the river. A ritual that every guide engages in, they park their trucks and sit in the rower's chair of their boats, still trailered, while rigging up their client's fly rods. After finishing tying on flies and adjusting sinkers and bobbers, they check in with the other guides to see who's ready to head back in. Head nodding, waving, and the occasional conversation of, "nope, it's all you. Still got another rod to rig," ensues as guides do their best to be viewed as accommodating to their guide cohorts.

Some guides purposefully drag their heels while rigging rods because they know the longer it takes to get on the river, the less time they spend watching clients flail around trying to get their line out of the boat. Many guides even spend a good half an hour or more going through the finer points of casting and landing fish on shore before getting into their boats, eating up more time before lining up with all the other boats to do the row-arounds, taking turns cycling through the good runs.

Rose pulls into a parking spot that another guide just backed out of. She feels like she is getting claustrophobic. Her heart beats a little quicker as she breathes, trying hard to get a hold of the anxiety she's feeling. The feeling is like a mild form of PTSD since she's had confrontations with guides up here in the past. They haven't always given her the respect other male guides are afforded. They often cut her off because they know she won't say anything for fear of being ostracized as the entire guiding community watches. But with a little help from her friend, Keith, who just happens to be parked in the adjacent stall, she's overcome most of the disrespect and the guides that have had the misfortune to cross her, and now understands she's a real player who can't be pushed around.

"You gotta stand up for yourself every once in a while, Fly," Keith would tell her. "Don't let those assholes push you around. But don't forget, you'll be guiding with all of them from time to time, so don't push so hard that nobody wants to work with you. And don't be a bitch. I'm sorry, but that's how it is. You gotta be confident, but dudes don't like chicks that knock them down to their knees. You'll only make things worse. Nope, you can't just bend over and take it, or they'll always be taking from you, but you can't be kickin' 'em in the balls all the time either."

Rose jumps from the Jeep and gives Keith a "hey, dude."

"Fly!" Keith announces for the entire parking lot to hear. "What brings you up this way on this fine summer morning?"

"Just looking for a few bent rods," Rose replies. "Bob and Sue here want me to wear them out, so here we are."

Bob likes the sound of that. Sue isn't as sure.

"So, what 'er they eatin for you up here?" Rose inquires.

"Oh, the usual," Keith replies. "Sow bug and a zebra midge below it—the split shot, the tip of your finger to your left nipple."

Keith reaches his hand out as a ruler to show Rose how deep he is setting his rig.

"What I figured," Rose says.

"Hey, is that your new boyfriend I saw you with yesterday?" Keith asks.

"Yeah," she sheepishly admits. She doesn't like that kind of attention from the other guides, so she downplays. "He's a good guy."

"What happened to his arm?" Dancing around things was never a strong suit for Keith.

Rose's heart thumps and she feels her head getting lighter, but oddly, her legs feel like they are strapped to concrete abutments.

"It's a long story," she says. "Someday I'll tell ya."

"Fair enough," Keith lets her off the hook. "Well, I'm ready to splash this thing. You dropping in?"

"You're good," she tells him. "We've still got to rig up."

Sensing Bob growing a little impatient as he watches other boats on the river catching fish already, she expedites the process and quickly drops her boat in. She drives the Jeep with an empty trailer to the road to make it easier for the shuttle drivers and heads back down to the boat.

"Let's do this," she says and helps Sue into the bow and then gives Bob a hand as he steps into the back of the Clackacraft, behind the rower's seat. "We're off."

Rose takes Bob and Sue to the far side of the river and instructs them to cast to the left. They've been fishing the Missouri several times a year for the past few years, so they know the drill. Just get it out there and mend your line upstream from your indicator and let it drift. If it twitches, hit it hard and hit it often. If there's nothing there, you'll be into your back cast, then throw it back out and get a drift. It's not the most technical means of fly-fishing, but it is effective. The rower does most of the work, keeping up with the indicators as they drift downstream, slowing the boat down when needed, and crabbing side to side so that the indicator doesn't get too close or too far away. If the rower is good, the angler shouldn't have to do much until the bobber gets pulled under.

"Let it drift," Rose tells Bob. "Fish live in the water. They can't eat the fly if it ain't wet."

Nervous anglers have nervous habits. If they aren't getting action right away, they feel like they need to be doing something, so they tend to cast more often or mend their line too much. The more they cast, the less the fly is in front of fish, and if they mend too much, they never get a natural presentation.

On the first run, neither Bob nor Sue touches a fish. Rose pulls the boat over and asks Bob for his rig.

"We have to get deeper," she explains. "We're not even ticking bottom, and you gotta get down to them. Apparently, Keith's tip of the finger to his nipple is further than mine."

She adjusts Bob's rig and then Sue's and begins the arduous task of rowing the boat back up to the top of the run, which started about 150 yards upstream. Three boats wait at the top of the run for their turn to pull out and drift. When it's Rose's turn, she slides the boat out further from the bank and instructs them to cast to the left again and mend their line. This time, they both hook up ten yards downstream.

"There you go," Rose congratulates. "Keep pressure on them but don't horse 'em.".

Sue's fish takes a run across the river. She grips her rod and line with the strength of an alligator on a death roll, and as the hot rainbow pulls away, the rod tip goes straight down to the water and smacks against the gunwale of the boat. Sue tugs back, and the rod tip snaps up as her line goes limp.

Bob's fish is a little less unruly and, after taking a more modest run, decides to give up the fight and settles in. He brings the 16-inch rainbow to the net. Rose scoops it up as the boat continues to drift downstream. She cradles the trout in her hand and holds it up for them all to get a good look.

"That's a good start," Rose congratulates Bob. "We'll get bigger ones."

Rose slides the rainbow back into the river and, with a kick of the tail, splashes her in the face with a few drops of the Missouri. She always appreciated it when fish showed some attitude.

Rose pulls the boat over to the bank and starts re-rigging Sue's rod.

"Got to get used to these fish again," Sue says.

"Yeah, they've got some shoulders, huh?" Rose shares, trying not to show any letdown or condemnation.

"The trick is," she coaches, "to keep just enough pressure on them to keep the hook in their mouth but not so much that you pull it out or break 'em off. And when they run, just let 'em run. It's easy to get into the trap of punching back when they punch first, but just let them do their thing. All you can do is control the bend in the rod by keeping just enough pressure on it. If the rod tip comes down and straightens out, you need to loosen up your grip. If the rod tip is up and straightens out, you need to put more pressure on it. And I promise you'll get more chances, so if you lose her, it's no big deal. We'll get another."

Rose drug the boat back to the top of that first run four more times. Bob landed a fish each time they drifted through the run. Sue finally landed her first fish on the last.

"There you go, Sue," Rose pats her on the back.

Rose holds the fish up in front of Sue so that Bob can take a photo. Sue is draping her arms around Rose, grinning ear to ear.

"Nice work," Rose says again. "That's how you show them who's boss. Let's head down around the corner to the grass flats."

As they round the corner, they see roughly two dozen boats spanning the width of the river, fishing the grass beds that run about two hundred yards down the middle. Rose never understood why people would want to come all the way out to Montana from the cities where they wait in traffic all day to sit in traffic just to catch trout. But it's their money, so she lines her boat up on a path that will put her anglers' casts along the edge of the grass and tells them to throw it to the left again.

As they drift along the grass beds, Sue's indicator bobs and then darts horizontally across the river.

"Hit it!" Rose shouts.

Sue jerks her rod tip straight up and comes tight on another hot rainbow. The trout runs a few feet of line off of Sue's reel and then turns back to the boat. Sue cranks on her reel desperately, trying to keep up with the trout and keep pressure on it. The fish then turns back to run away from her, and as it reaches the end of the slackened line, the force of the fish running out pulls the rod down to the water, and her leader snaps again.

Before Rose can say anything, Bob yells, "Let 'em run, Sue!" And as her rod tip pops back up and the line goes limp again, he adds, "Jesus, Sue. Don't horse 'em!"

"Well, I was trying, but," Sue defends.

Bob cuts her off, "That would have been number six. Come on, Sue. Did you get him on the reel?"

The entire exchange was loud enough for most of the anglers in the surrounding boats to hear. Guides and clients alike looked over their shoulders to check out the person the aggressive attack was coming from. Embarrassed, Sue pops herself down in the front seat and looks down at her knees.

"Can't let these bastards win," Bob continues.

"What do you mean?" Rose asks. "The fish?"

"No," Bob says. "The other couples at the lodge. We've got fifty bucks on this."

It was this exact moment when Rose realized her growing disdain for the industry. This wasn't at all the reason she got into fly-fishing or guiding. She also realized she had contributed to the pressure they were all feeling when she declared they would catch 36 fish earlier at the lodge. And now Sue is sitting in the front of the boat, embarrassed and ashamed, just because she lost a fish.

Rose pulls the boat towards the bank and drops anchor. She grabs Sue's leader and starts to tie on her flies.

"Well," Rose starts, "I have to be honest, Bob. That reel Sue's using isn't doing her any favors. It's got too small of an arbor, and you're telling her to use the reel instead of stripping line in, and the reel isn't built for that. It's like 30 years old."

"The reel's fine, Rose." Bob lets out. "She's caught plenty of fish with it."

"Ok," Rose yields. "We'll figure it out."

Rose turns to Sue, "I like to strip them in—at first anyway. Get that line in your trigger finger on your rod-hand and grab the line with your left, below your rod-hand and strip."

Rose demonstrates using Sue's rod. "Like this. That way, you're gaining a few feet with every pull versus a few inches with every crank on your reel. Once the fish settles down, then you can use the reel."

It took Sue three or four more fish to figure out the new technique, but once she mastered it, she was landing more than she lost. By lunch, they had 17 fish in the net, which Bob had made everyone very aware of, especially the couple that were fishing out of Billy's boat. Every time he would hook up, he would yell out the number, making sure they were in earshot. When Sue hooked a fish, he waited until it was in the net to declare another notch.

Most of the boats that were fishing at the dam that morning had made their way downstream by lunchtime. Rose had decided to shorten up their float, given how important it was to Bob to just land a bunch of fish. Her shuttle was taken down to the Wolf Creek Bridge, which was only a couple of miles downstream. The other boats, including Billy, were going all the way to Craig, which was 5 miles further.

By 4:30 in the afternoon, Bob and Sue had landed 35 trout. Bob was proud of himself, but wasn't giving any props to his partner.

"Great day of fishing, Rose," was about all the acknowledgement he would give.

Rose dragged the boat up to the top of the grass flats for one more run and dropped anchor. "Ok, now we're going to do something different."

"What's that?" Sue asks.

"I'm seeing a few crane flies buzzing around. Some people call them mosquito hawks," she explains. "They are big, awkward bugs that look like giant mosquitoes.

I've also seen some big rises out there, so let's see if they eat something on top."

Rose grabs Sue's rod first, changes up the leader and tippet material, and ties on a big water-walker. She does the same with Bob's and then pulls out towards the grass.

"Throw that right on top of the grass beds," she tells Sue.

Sue takes her first cast. The fly drifts for about 10 feet, and a huge rainbow crashes the surface to inhale it down. Screaming, she lifts the rod up, and an 18-inch rainbow goes airborne. Her fly pops out of the trout's mouth and drops to the surface of the river.

"Throw it again," Rose instructs.

As the fly settles onto the surface, another trout smashes it, and again, Sue hooks it but can't seal the deal.

"Do it again."

By this point, Sue is laughing and screaming like a little girl.

"Holy shit! Are you seeing this?" She yells back to Bob.

Bob doesn't say a word, and Sue takes another cast. With all the excitement, however, she loses the tension on her fly line in the middle of the cast, and her loop collapses, wrapping around Bob's head.

"God Damnit, Sue!" Bob yells.

"I'm sorry," Sue says with genuine contrition.

She sits down again and reels her line in, hooking her fly on the hook keeper at the top of the handle of her rod.

Stunned at the outburst, Rose has nothing to say.

They continue to float for about half a mile. Sue stays seated, and Bob casts from the back of the boat with little success. Rose hears him sigh.

"You alright back there?" she asks.

"Well, we're not catching anything," he says disappointedly.

"You put 35 fish in the net," Rose argues.

"Yeah, back there," he argues back.

"You know what, Bob?" Rose stops herself and then changes direction on what she was going to say. "You see that rock sticking up over there? Throw your fly as close to that rock as you can."

As the fly drifts along the seam, a 15-inch, snaky-looking rainbow sucks it down, and with little fight, Bob brings it to the net, and Rose scoops it up.

Letting the trout slide back into the water, she looks back at Bob and declares, "There, that's 36. We're done."

They were about a half mile from the bridge. Rose sits back down in the rower's chair, spins the boat around, and pulls downstream. She can't make the boat move fast enough. All she wants is to get off the water and get rid of Bob.

As she pulls, the boat becomes awkwardly quiet, giving her time to think. Her mind is back with Trick. She feels a pit forming in her stomach and a tear swelling in both eyes. Rose wants to run and hide. She wants to grab Chase, jump in the Jeep, and drive. And then she feels the craving to go have a drink.

OFF THE WAGON

Rose dropped Bob and Sue off at the lodge, and as she helped Sue with their gear, Bob checked in with the other couples. Sue hugged Rose and looked into her eyes with sympathy and understanding as someone who's also gone through some things in her life.

"Are you ok, Rose?" Sue asked her.

"Yeah," Rose told her. "Just a little frazzled. I'll be ok."

Bob came back from the lodge and met Rose on the landing at the bottom of the stairs and handed her a twenty-dollar bill.

"Well," he said. "We were the top boat today."

He looked her in the eyes and leaned in.

"But I don't appreciate your attitude out there, Rose." He continued, "I pay to catch fish. I don't need some guide trying to show me up or lecturing me about my gear in front of my wife, especially not some second-year guide like you."

He turned and walked back up the stairs without waiting for a response. Rose jumped back into her Jeep and pulled out on the Rec Road, letting her tires bust loose, spraying gravel across the road.

Now driving back to Craig, she relives the conversation, or lecture, from Bob.

"Second year guide?" she says out loud. "It's my third, you asshole. And maybe if you weren't such a dick, your wife would have caught fifty. And what do you mean, a guide like me? Because I'm a woman? Such an a-hole."

She speeds back towards Craig and pulls into MRA's parking lot, backs into a spot, and turns off the ignition. She jumps out and unhitches the trailer, and lets the tongue bounce off the ground. She then slams the door of the Jeep and storms off across the parking lot in the direction of Izaak's.

"Yo, Fly!" She hears from a circle of guides hanging out in the parking lot. "Where you heading?"

It's Keith. He steps through the gallery of guides and jogs towards her.

"I need a drink," she tells Keith.

"Hold on," Keith says. "What's going on?"

"Fuckin assholes," she says. "This guy gave me a twenty-dollar tip and then lectured me about my attitude. He was such a dick to his wife. I had had enough of him."

"Really?" Keith asks. "This is the first asshole you've guided?"

Shaking her head, she lets her chin drop and shuffles the gravel with Chacos. She feels the tears forming and doesn't want Keith to see.

"Ok," Keith says. "If you're going to have a drink, you're not going alone. Let me lock up my shit, and I'll be right there."

"You don't have to babysit me, Keith."

"Babysit?" He asks. "Nah, I'm just looking for some comic relief from this place. I'm going to enjoy this. And tomorrow when I see you on the river, I'm going to enjoy watching you suffer through the hangover."

Keith and Rose walk the ramp to the front door of Izaak's, and they make their entrance. Keith calls across the bar, "Set 'em up, Scotty."

"Sin Fire?" Scotty asks.

"You know me too well, Scotty," Keith responds.

As Scotty pours two shots, he asks, "Anything else?"

Keith returns, "I'll do a Tito's and soda. Fly? I'll get these."

"Just a Bud Light," she answers.

She watches Keith reach for one of the shot glasses and slide it in her direction. He grabs the second and lifts it towards her and says, "Cheers."

Rose grabs the shot and lifts it, clinking it with Keith's, and says, "Prost."

They tip the shots to their lips and gulp them down. Keith grimaces, and Rose clears her throat. She lets her head drop as the shot warms her belly. Guilt radiates throughout her body. What she thought would be a familiar, calming feeling is now polluting her veins with shame. She grabs her bottle of beer and takes a pull, and although the cool beer settles the burn, it does nothing to calm her nerves.

"Let's go smoke," Keith suggests.

Sitting on the deck outside of Izaak's, Rose takes a drag off the Camel Light she's bummed from Keith. She hasn't smoked a cigarette since the last drink she had over a year ago.

"Hmm…" She utters as she looks at the burning cherry on the cigarette. "These things taste like shit."

Then she takes another drag.

"So, what's going on?" Keith asks Rose while letting out a stream of smoke.

"Just had enough of these guys," she responds.

"Well, fuck, Fly. It's only July," he tells her.

"Yeah," she concedes. "I'll get over it. Just one of those days, I guess."

"What else, Fly?" Keith asks.

"What do you mean?" She asks back.

"Fly," he begins as he tilts his head down and raises an eyebrow. "You've been here before. You've fished with these kinds of guys. Some days it's just work. Drop 'em off at the end of the day, kick 'em down the road, and saddle up for another ride in the morning."

Rose's phone dings. They are just close enough to the cell phone booster inside of Izaak's to get incoming text messages. She looks down to see a notification from Trick. Her heart sinks. She feels anxiety now, replacing the numbing effect of the Sin Fire and Bud Light.

"Shit," she whispers.

"What's that?" Keith inquires. "That's your boy I saw you with yesterday?"

"I fucked up, Keith," Rose opens up.

"What do you mean?" He asks.

"Trick," now with tears streaming down her face. "We were parked at Cell Phone Bluff after we got off the river yesterday, checking messages. I had no idea. He got quiet, and I asked him what was going on, and he told me about his accident. How he lost his arm. How his life was taken from him. It was me!"

"What?" Keith asked. "What are you talking about?"

"Remember the truck that went off into the river last spring?" She continues. "That was Trick's truck. He was the one who went off the cliff at Cell Phone Bluff!"

"So, what does that have to do with you?" He asks. "I mean, you knew he had been in an accident. That's what happened to his arm, right? Isn't that how you guys met? Through the healing waters program?"

"Yeah, but listen," she demands. "Remember that night last spring? I stayed in the Sutton Place after getting shit-faced at Izaak's? I never told anyone except the sheriff and my landlord, but I woke up that next morning with Jake in bed with me."

"What?!" Keith blurted out. "Jake? You slept with Jake Trapper?"

"Keith!" Rose defends. "I was fucking passed out. I

didn't really have a choice. And when I woke up in the morning, I got my shit and ran out of there. I drove over to the bluff to call my friend, Beth, in Missoula. I didn't know what to do. But she didn't pick up, and I didn't have anyone else to call. I was freaking out!"

"So, what does that have to do with Trick?"

"Just listen, Keith," she pleads. "I couldn't get a hold of anyone, and I remembered Chase was in the cottage all night. I felt horrible and just needed to get home, so I threw my phone down and punched the gas to get back out onto the Rec Road. I didn't look. I heard the tires squealing and looked in my rearview mirror and saw this truck coming at me. I closed my eyes, bracing for impact, but it didn't come. I mean, I felt a little nudge because he grazed me, but not enough to knock me off the road, so I kept going. I didn't even look back. I knew he was probably going off the cliff, and I knew it was going to be bad, but I was fucking terrified. There was an SUV coming from the other direction, and I saw him go into the ditch and thought I just had to get out of there, and I knew there was someone else there, so I just fucking left."

"You just left?" Keith asks, horrified.

"I had to," Rose defends herself. "I didn't even know if I was still technically drunk. And all this shit was going through my head. I was scared and so fucking pissed off and fucking sad. I just wanted to get out of there. And then I saw Jeff coming up from Wolf Creek and knew he was going to take care of it, so I just kept going and didn't call anyone. But Jeff must have seen me, and later that afternoon, the sheriff showed up at my door."

"So, what happened?" Keith asks.

"To me?" She asks. "Or Trick?"

"Both, I guess," Keith answers.

"Nothing to me," she tells him. "Given the circumstances, the sheriff didn't charge me with anything! And because he couldn't prove I was drunk, he couldn't charge me with a DUI. He kept it all on the down-low and as long as I quit drinking and volunteered with the healing waters program, he said he would leave it at that."

"And Trick?" Keith asks.

"Well," tears are now streaming down her face, and her nose is running profusely. "He lost his arm. He was supposed to be drafted into the NFL, but he lost his fucking arm. I took it from him!"

"You didn't take it, Fly," Keith argues.

"The fuck I didn't!" Rose answers back. "I took everything from him. His arm. His career. Everything! He almost died, and I just drove away, and in the grand scheme of things, I got away Scott-free. And I don't know how I can tell him. Fuck!"

"Shit, Rose," Keith puts his arm around her and pulls her in. "I don't know what to say."

Rose lets her cheek rest on Keith's chest. "I don't know what to do, Keith. I haven't felt this way about anyone, ever. I don't want to lose him, but I know I've hurt him, and he'll never forgive me. How could he?"

"If you don't tell him, he doesn't get that choice," Keith reasons. "That's not fair, and you'd never be able to live with that lie. The one thing you can't do, Rose, is you can't run from it or hide in this bottle of Bud. How about we get you home, and we can talk about it? I'll call Kelly."

Rose sets down her beer and reaches for her phone, and answers Trick's text, "Hey, Babe. Rough day today. I'll call you later." And then she hits send.

That night at the cottage, Kelly and Keith hung out until they thought Rose had settled down enough to where she would stay home and not run next door to the Frenchman to drink away the pain. As Keith and Kelly walked out the door, Rose reached for her phone. She had to call Trick. If she didn't, he would know something was wrong. She just wanted to get through the next few days of guiding until she could see him, face to face, and tell him she was the one who ruined his life.

"Maybe he will forgive me," she told herself. "Maybe he will understand and believe everything happens for a reason and that we being together is all that matters…"

Then her brain flipped, and the self-loathing demon reared up and dominated her thoughts.

"He'll hate me. He should hate me," as she continued beating herself up. "How could anyone be forgiven for this? I fucking destroyed his life."

"Fuck!" She called out.

Chase jumps on the bed and crawls to her side. He doesn't lick her face. He leans in and pushes his nose into her shoulder, nudging her to pet him. She lifts the phone to dial Trick's number and sends it.

"Hey Rose, what's going on?" Trick answers his phone. "Tough fishing today?"

"Nah," she answers. "The fishing was fine. That catching was a little tougher. But the company was the problem."

Rose fought back the tears as she told him about her day and how Bob was treating her and his wife and all the things she hated about guiding. The story was like a ghillie suit, though, camouflaging what she was really feeling and what she didn't want to reveal to Trick over the phone. And when she was done venting, she listened as Trick reassured her that she was a really good guide who didn't deserve the treatment and that there is no perfect job or profession that doesn't come with challenges. She listened as he said all the right things and showed sympathy and compassion, and it made her hate herself even more.

"Thanks for listening," she ends the conversation. "I'm sorry. I'm not much fun tonight."

"Hey," Trick responds. "Life's hard sometimes. I'm here for ya."

The pit in her stomach grew, and her eyes burned as she contemplated telling him right then. "No," she thought. She has to do this in person. If there is any chance of forgiveness, he has to see how much she is hurting when she tells him. Trick has to see the guilt and shame and has to know how much she loves him.

"I'm on the water for the next few days," she averts. "Can we get together Friday?"

"The team's got conditioning at 6 am, Friday morning, and then on the field until about noon," he tells her. "I can leave from there and be in Wolf Creek by two?"

"That would be amazing," she does her best to cover. "I just want to be with you."

"Alrighty, then," he does his best Jim Carrey impression as Ace Ventura. "Can't wait."

"I love you, Trick," she tells him.

"Love you too, babe." He reciprocates. "Get some sleep. Tomorrow will be a better day with better clients."

"Thanks," she replies and thinks to herself. "If you only knew…"

SHARKS ON A CHUM LINE

The next three days dragged on for Rose as she played out every possible conversation with every outcome in her head. She'd been working on the river, which was a welcome distraction. The nights, however, were long and restless, filled with constant rolling over and punching pillows and staring at the clock. She didn't know what was worse, living with the anxiety of having the conversation with Trick, or finally seeing the look on his face when she told him.

The sun rose Friday morning without a cloud in the sky, burning off the cooler pockets of air that were trapped in lower valleys between the ridges of the Big Belt Mountains. The fog banks resemble cotton bats, floating gently to the ground, smoothing and filling in the rough edges of the mountains, inviting thoughts of climbing back into bed for a few more minutes of sleep. As the sun warms the valley walls, updrafts pull the cotton from its resting place, and it ascends towards the peaks and eventually disappears, leaving the ruggedness of the mountains behind.

July days in Montana often begin this way, with temperatures in the 40s, rapidly accelerating into the 90s by early afternoon as the sun fuels the volatility of the weather patterns in early summer. As the warm air rises rapidly, it cools and condenses and generates clouds filled with much-needed moisture, but also produces the energy for massive storms with dangerous electricity. It's a cruel paradox and as these fronts move across the plains and slam into the mountains, they rise even faster, spilling their loads on the land like dump trucks and releasing energy by way of massive streaks of lightening that often reach the dead snags that stain the lush ridges that have become more prevalent in recent years due to the beetles that have killed off millions of pines.

Rose walks through the gate from her yard and sees Ross tinkering in one of the sheds. He looks out the door of the shed and waves.

"Morning, Ross," she greets him

"Morning, Rose," he responds. "Working today?"

"Yeah," she answers. "Not sure what this weather is gonna do."

"Well," he advises. "Could be some afternoon storms, so be careful."

"I'll be off early. Hopefully, we'll be off before it gets too bad," she tells him.

A group of ladies is huddled together in the parking lot in front of the porch at MRA with that look of the first day of school, just waiting for an adult to give them instructions on where they should be going. All of them, with the exception of one, have crisp button-up shirts and clean wide-brimmed Tilly hats. They're all holding their packs and rod tubes close to their chests as they nervously pivot and question each other if anyone knows who their contact person is.

As Rose approached the group, one of the ladies, who may or may not be in charge but is definitely motivated to figure this pressing concern out, asked, "Are you with us?"

The question is almost rhetorical, as Rose is one of fifteen guides who are also standing around with a lost look on their face, looking for their clients as desperately as their clients are looking for them. Out of the fifteen guides that are standing there, these women will be fishing with three of them, and as the question comes to Rose, she detects a hint of wishful thinking. She is the only female guide doing this dance, and oftentimes, women would just rather be guided by other women. For some, it's less intimidating, although they have no idea who Rose is or how much of a hard ass she might be with them. But, because she is a woman, they assume she will be softer in her delivery if they need coaching. The question does begin the conversation, however, and movement toward a resolution of the conundrum, "Who the hell are our guides for the day?"

"I'm not sure," Rose answers. "But I can find out. Give me two minutes."

Rose enters the shop, and Mike calls out to her, "Hey, Fly! It's a great morning here in the fly-fishing mecca, and the shit-show has begun. Your clients are all standing out front—the group of ladies." Mike points in the direction of the huddle of women. "I'll let you introduce yourself. It's you, Clint, and Rich. I just saw them both walk through, so they should be around. Don't forget to have them all sign in."

"Got it," Rose assures him. "Thanks, Mike."

As Rose walks out the front door of the shop, she scans the parking lot and sees Clint and Rich standing next to their rigs, chatting with a couple of the other guides and pulling hard off their cigarettes. Rose whistles and waves them over.

"Hey, Fly," Rich says. "It's the three of us today?"

"Yep," and as she corals the two other guides towards the group of women, she introduces them. "Ladies. I am one of your guides for the day. These two gentlemen are also going to be on the trip. This is Rich and Clint."

The three guides reach their hands out to the group, and they alternate from guide to client, each introducing themselves, which is all about formality because, minus each guide's own clients they are paired with, they won't remember any of the other ladies' names. It may even take them half the morning to remember their own clients' names.

Rose steps up, "Who's with me?"

The leader of the group, Jane Dickson, is a petite woman in her sixties. Her rod tube is generously worn, and her shirt wears the holes of the errant casts of previous fishing companions she has led throughout the years while putting these groups together. The sun has not been kind to her skin as she shows the dark patches of damaging rays on her hands and face, but she is in immaculate shape for a mother with grown children and has the features of someone who must have attracted her share of potential suitors in her younger years. Rose figures she must have picked well in a partner and shows the confidence of a woman who was more than just a mother to her husband's children. Although not necessarily the breadwinner, she was an equal partner in a relationship that now affords her these fishing opportunities. Her husband, who was a successful entertainment lawyer out of Nashville, succumbed to cancer two years prior. After his death, she decided to live out their dreams with her husband riding along in spirit while she fished her ass off.

"Rose," she holds out her hand. "I'm Jane. This is Carolyn. She has never fly-fished before, so we're going to go with you today. She'll be up front and I'll fish out of the back."

The assumption here is that Carolyn is going to need a lot of help, and Rose should focus all her attention on her. The other assumption is that again, because Rose is a woman, she will be better at teaching another woman, so she will be with the one lady who has never fly-fished.

"Perfect," Rose declares and holds her hand out.

Carolyn reaches out and takes Rose's hand. Her grip is much softer than Jane's. Her eyes are gentle and reserved. She is in her mid-forties and with a diamond on her left ring finger that could make the sun blush, has also appeared to have done well in the marrying department.

"So, what brings you to the Missouri?" Rose asks Carolyn.

"Oh," she begins in a sweet southern way. "My husband bought me the trip. He used to fish with Jane's husband before he passed. They took trips all around the world. Sometimes I would tag along, but I was more into hanging out at the spa with a mimosa than fishing. When Jane's husband, Ronnie, died, I think he decided he needed a new fishing partner, and he's very aware of the challenges a spouse has teaching their wife to fish."

"That's very intuitive," Rose admits. "Where's your husband now?"

"He's on the porch," she motions over to a gentleman trying desperately to find a cell signal. "He's in the music business in Nashville. He's probably trying to talk a tour manager off the ledge. It's how he and Ronnie got to be friends."

"Is he fishing today?" Rose asks.

"Yeah," Jane cuts in. "The boys are renting a boat and doing the DIY thing. I like to catch fish, which is why I hire a guide."

"Smart," Rose agrees. "Speaking of which, let's get on the river."

"Hey, Fly!" Clint yells from his rig. "Where you guys heading?"

"I think we're going to splash the boat at the Wolf

Creek Bridge and take out at Stickney." She informs him.

"Right on," Clint approves. "We'll probably do the same, but take out here. Off by one?"

She gives Clint a thumbs up and reaffirms with Jane, "We are doing a half day, right?"

"Yeah," Jane responds as she points a thumb towards Carolyn. "Don't want to wear anyone out."

Rose spends about 15 minutes with Carolyn in an abbreviated, 101 fly-fishing class, showing her the basics in casting, mending, and landing fish. She does all of it in the grass along the parking lot at the Wolf Creek Bridge. As she instructs, others listen in and pick up pointers as she does her thing. In this role, Rose finds self-worth, sharing knowledge with others, and helping anglers find success regardless of whether they are in her boat or someone else's. She loses track of all the other things that have been occupying her mind since she realized her involvement in Trick's accident.

After the mini-course, Rose rigs up Carolyn's rod with a double nymph rig consisting of a purple weight fly and a split cased PMD nymph.

She explains, "The purple weight fly will help get your bugs down a little bit, and the PMD is the flavor of the day. They should start popping later in the morning if this sun sticks around for a bit. And the weight flies? Well, I'm not exactly sure why they eat it, but they do. I guess it kind of looks like a cased caddis."

Jane pipes up, "Do you mind if I don't chase the bobber?"

"Not at all," Rose answers. "We'll set you up with the Labrador and a split case with a tungsten bead, and we'll look for heads to throw at. You'll get some chances, and we'll find some fish feeding on the flats."

Rose helps the ladies load up into the boat, pulls up her anchor with the rope she has run through pullies along the side of the hull, drops the rope into the cleat to keep the anchor suspended off the stern, and pushes off.

"Interesting anchor system," Jane admires.

"Yeah," Rose responds. "I'm not big on the center pull system. The floor pedal gets in the way, and the rope keeps wrapping around your feet. Plus, when you get up on rising fish, it's a lot quieter dropping anchor with the side pull versus the pedal. We've got some river to cover, so let's push down a bit before getting those flies wet."

At around 10 am, Rose pulls into Peter's Channel, about a mile downstream from the bridge. She points up to the house on the bluff and informs the ladies, "That's old man Peter's place up there. He pumped about a million dollars into that house and then died. Poor guy."

"Anyone live there now?" Carolyn asks.

"Nah," Rose responds. "It's been sitting there for a few years now. I guess the owners of Orvis are looking at buying it. By now, though, I would imagine the pack rats have taken over, and they'll have to do a ton of work on it."

As Rose guides her drift boat into the channel following the riffle that pinches in towards the bank on the left and then straightens out to dump down into a pool mid-channel, she looks along the cut bank caused by the swollen current for rising fish.

She slowly lowers the anchor, hand-lining it to the riverbed and tells Jane, "Hey Jane, look along the bank right there. Do you see that nose coming up? She's right on that seam coming off the tuft of grass about 20 feet downstream."

"Got it," Jane assures Rose.

"How's your reach cast?" Rose asks.

"Serviceable," Jane answers.

"Do you want to come up front?" Carolyn asks.

"I'm good," Jane responds and rips off about 30 feet of line from her reel.

"Hold on," Rose instructs. "Let me see that fly."

Jane drops the rod tip towards Rose so that she can grab the line. Rose slides the rig to her and snips off the dropper nymph so that Jane is just throwing the Labrador.

"Alright," Rose tells her. "If you can drop that about six feet upstream from the seam and stack a little line, you should be able to feed it down to that fish. When she eats it, she's not going to be happy, so be prepared. It looks like a good one."

Jane does as she's instructed and, with her first cast, drops the fly perfectly along the bank, reaches her rod tip upstream as the fly settles in order to get the fly-line set to get the optimal drift, then drops the rod tip and shuffles out a few more feet of line, stacking it on the water. The fly drifts drag-free, heading directly into the seam.

"That's gonna get eaten," Rose predicts.

As the fly drifts into the seam, the nose of the 21-inch hen, brown trout slowly rises up from her resting spot inside the eddy adjacent to the seam and turns on the Labrador. Her mouth opens and angrily smacks the fly down, and Jane lifts her rod tip.

"Got her," Jane declares as she puts just enough pressure on the massive brown to double the rod over.

Rose pulls on the anchor rope and lets the boat drift downstream, aiding Jane with fighting the beautiful hen brown, and when the old girl finally decides to succumb, Rose scoops it up with the net.

"That was pretty much textbook," Rose admires. "I'm

not sure what I'm doing here."

"Well," Jane says, giving Rose some credit. "You picked the fly, and she really wanted it. You call it the Labrador?"

"Yeah," Rose explains. "It's really just an elk-hair caddis, but I use some of my chocolate lab's undercoat for dubbing. It's just the right color, and it floats. There's some palmered hackle, with a little longer barbs than what's normal, just to make it look a little buggier, and some green crystal flash for the butt. The guard hairs from the undercoat also add to the sexiness. Pretty deadly."

"Indeed," Jane agrees.

"That was impressive," Carolyn says with complete admiration. "I can see what could be so addicting to this."

The three ladies fish their way downstream for the next couple of hours, with a few fish coming up to the Labrador and a few more taking Carolyn's nymph rig. Carloyn lands her first fish after hooking a few and losing them, and is elated. She can't believe it took so long to pick up a rod and start fishing herself. The whole time, she marvels over Jane's ability to cast and Rose's ability to push her drift boat around, putting both of them in the perfect position to fish the seams along the banks.

"It's a lot like skiing," Rose admits. "Work smarter, not harder. You let the current do the work, kind of like gravity, and use your skis to ride the momentum. And when you're on the right line, it's like driving a car. Make minor adjustments and don't overcorrect, and you're golden."

"Well, it's still impressive," she compliments.

"Hey, Rose," Jane gets her attention. "You see that cloud?"

Rose looks to the southwest.

"Yeah," she says. "That one is going to dump on us. I'd say we have about an hour before it gets nasty out here."

"How much further do we have to go?" Carolyn asks.

"To the take-out?" Rose asks. "We're supposed to be going to Stickney Creek, which is a few miles downstream from Craig. We could hustle and be down there right about when the storm hits? Or, if you want to see something cool, there's a pool just around the corner, and we can wait it out. When that cloud gets closer, the barometer will drop out, and every fish in that pool will be up eating. You'll get an idea of how many fish there are in this river. And then we jet on down to Craig, which is only about a half mile. I'll find a ride to my Jeep and pick up my boat in Craig and meet you at the bar?"

"I wouldn't mind seeing that," Jane admits.

Rose instructs the ladies to reel in their lines and have a seat, as they will be heading downstream for a bit.

They see the cliff wall jutting out into the river, towering over the pool Rose was talking about. The wall rises up above the river and flattens out, creating Cell Phone Bluff. They see the ponderosa pine hanging out over the cliff wall and the jack fence. Rose feels the pit in her stomach grow. When she talked about this eddy, her mind had been on a reprieve from thinking about Trick. While in her zone, it was like she was on stage, and when she is in this place, the rest of the world and all her problems somehow get stowed away in the corner of her mind, much like the life jackets and extra rain gear under the seats of her boat that rarely see the sun. Sometimes she remembers to let her clients know they have PFDs under the seats, but with how benign the Missouri is, she rarely thinks of it.

"If you need those life jackets," she would joke with

clients when she did remember, "I've done something seriously wrong."

Now approaching the eddy in the shadow of Cell Phone Bluff, thoughts of Trick and guilt she has purposefully suppressed for the bulk of the day have reared up like that big hen brown, but instead of the excitement and pride triggered by Jane hooking that fish, all she feels is anxiety and shame. The pit grows larger, and she feels like she might get sick.

Rose does her best to suppress her emotions and crawls back into her instructor role.

"See how the current runs along the eddy there?" She asks the ladies. "We have the perfect amount of water to have the current split as it hits the wall there. Half the current slides along the cliff heading downstream, and half circles back, creating the eddy. We can get into the eddy and fish from the inside, out to the seam, and let the current cycle us back. You'll see fish up on the seam and along the scum-line there. As that cloud gets closer, more and more fish will come up."

Just upstream from the eddy, a point of gravel and sediment that was deposited over years of spring run-off and high water has formed, helping to set the seam. The distance between the head of the seam and the cliff wall, diverting the current back upstream, runs about 50 yards with the churning water and a scum-line about 5 or 6 feet wide. Rose pulls the boat inside the eddy and stands up to look down into the seam.

"You see all those trout down there?" She asks as the ladies lean out over the gunwales and look down. "They're like sharks on a chum line, picking off dead bugs as they get swept into the eddy. Just wait until that cloud comes over. All those fish and all the ones you can't see yet will be up on the surface."

"So, what's the plan?" Carolyn asks excitedly.

"I'll bring the boat back up to the top of the seam from the inside. When I say go, you'll cast a little downstream and out to the seam, get a good mend in your line, and let it drift. Any movement on the indicator and that's a fish. Hit it hard and hit it often, and when you hook up, I'll spin the boat so that you're inside the eddy and it will put Jane in position to cast that dry fly on the seam."

"Sounds good," Jane approves.

The first time through, the plan works to perfection. Carolyn hooks up first, and while she's fighting her fish, Jane also hooks up. They land both fish, and as Rose unhooks the second, she allows her boat to follow the current around the eddy and back up to the top of the seam.

"Let's get a couple more," Rose tells them, and they do.

They continue to cycle in the eddy five times and hook fish every time. Rose keeps one eye on the storm coming and the other on the increasing number of fish showing themselves on the surface. Eventually, dozens of fish are up eating bugs. With each gulp, they break water, and as their mouths close on the bugs, air is trapped and released, making popping sounds. As more and more fish come up, the popping sounds more like the gurgling of an aerator in a fish tank. At some point, there are so many fish coming up that the woman can't pick a single target to fish to.

"It's like a kiddy pond," Jane giggles. "I can't even pick one out."

"Just throw it out there and it will get eaten," Rose tells her. "You too, Carolyn. Just get it in there."

The skies get darker and darker as the storm cloud

moves in. The light turns flat, making it impossible for Jane to see her fly and nearly impossible to even see the strike indicator on Carolyn's leader. But it doesn't matter. As their flies hit the water, they are immediately eaten by one of the cookie-cutter rainbows that are devouring bugs in the seam. For about ten minutes, it's a feeding frenzy that might put to shame a pack of hyenas on a fresh kill.

A bolt of lightning cracks and booms as it strikes a snag on the ridge just outside of Craig.

"Ladies," Rose yells out. "Bring 'em in and get those rod-tips down. We are out of here!"

Rose pulls her drift boat out into the main current of the river, spins the boat around so that the stern is facing downstream, and starts pulling hard on the oars. She leans into each stroke, reaching as far as she can and with her feet braced against the front seat compartment, heaves back on the sticks. She digs deep and pulls hard, finishing every stroke by rolling the blades of the oars to get every ounce of energy out of every stroke.

Drops of rain the size of pennies splash off their heads and rain gear. Soon, the rain turns to ice as the sting of hail peppers their backsides.

"Cover up, ladies," Rose instructs. "This might hurt a little bit."

Another bolt of lightning, another crack and a boom, and Rose wonders if these strikes are going to touch off a fire, if they haven't already.

"Almost there!" Rose yells as the Craig Bridge comes into view.

Rose pulls into the boat ramp, bow first, and runs it up onto the gravel. The rain and hail are coming down so hard, it's almost like a white-out blizzard.

"Go ahead, Carolyn!" She yells. "Just leave your gear here and we'll get it later! Head on up to Izaak's! It's just up past the tracks!"

Carolyn jumps out of the boat onto the gravel bank and runs up the boat ramp. Rose spins the boat around so that Jane can jump out of the stern and follow Carolyn up the ramp. Rose drops anchor and lets out an extra six feet of rope, jumps from the boat, picks up the anchor, and wedges it into the rocks. She then drags the boat so that it's firmly beached and tightens up the rope to give no leeway. She takes one last look to make sure all their gear is secured and not able to blow out of the boat, and then runs up the ramp, catching up to Jane and Carolyn.

As the three ladies enter Izaak's, they are met with Scotty's smiling face from behind the bar.

"Hey, Fly. Looks like you ladies were ten minutes late," Scotty says sympathetically. "What can I get you?

"How're your martinis?" Carolyn asks.

"My specialty," Scotty replies.

"Makers on the rocks," Jane orders.

"Just a lemon water for me," Rose tells Scotty.

"Fly?" Carolyn asks.

"Long story," Rose responds. "Everyone in Craig calls me Fly after some miscommunication with the owner here. It was 'that fly-bitch' or something like that, then shortened to 'Fly' after they got to know me."

Just then, Rose's phone dings as a text message comes through. She pulls the phone from the breast pocket of her rain jacket with an obvious sense of urgency and looks at the notification.

"Crap," she says. "I'm late."

"Late for what?" Carolyn asks.

"Another long story…"

It was already past 2 o'clock, and Rose still hadn't hitch-hiked to her Jeep, and her boat was still beached at the Craig ramp.

"Hold on, ladies," she says. "I'm going to make a call. I'll be right back."

Rose walks out the front door of Izaak's and huddles under the eaves of the porch to stay out of the rain and dials Trick's number.

"Hey, babe," he answers. "Where you at?"

Rose tells Trick about cutting their trip short and how her Jeep was still at Stickney Creek.

"No problem," he says. "I'll grab Chase, and I'll come give you a ride. I'll be there in fifteen minutes."

Rose heads back into the bar and sits down with Carolyn and Jane. She draws on the straw that hangs in her lemon water and wishes it were something stronger.

"Everything alright?" Carolyn asks.

"Well," she sheepishly tips her toe into the conversation. "That was Trick. He drove up from Missoula."

"Boyfriend?" Carolyn asks.

"He was, but after tonight, I'm not sure what he'll be," Rose responds as tears start to swell.

"Is it going to be a break-up talk?" Carolyn asks. "I'm sorry. I shouldn't pry."

"No, I just really messed up and I'm not sure I can be forgiven," Rose reveals.

"Rose," Carolyn touches her arm. "We all deserve forgiveness from time to time."

"I'm not sure I do," Rose responds. "He'll be here in a few minutes and can give me a ride. Looks like the rain is letting up. If you would like, I can drive you back to the shop after getting my boat on the trailer."

"Rose," Jane starts with a bit of contempt. "The shop

is only a block and a half away. We can manage. But we also have to take care of you."

Jane pulls some cash from her pocket and hands Rose two fifty-dollar bills and says, "I had such a great time with you, Rose. The first fifty is for working so hard and knowing your shit. The second is for that hen brown."

Carolyn pulls another fifty from her pocket and hands it to Rose. She then hugs Rose and looks her in the eyes.

"It will all work out, hun," she tells Rose. "I don't know what you did, but you're a special lady, and any man would be crazy to let you go."

"Thanks," Rose replies. "But I'm not sure I'll ever forgive myself."

ALL OUT ON THE TABLE

Rose walks out of Izaak's and waits for Trick on the front deck. Imagining the conversation with Trick over and over again, she thinks of ways she can justify her decisions on that night and the next morning. She thinks of details she can withhold that might soften the blow. Clasping her hands together, Rose begs for help from a God she doesn't really know if she believes in.

Trick's 4Runner crossed the bridge heading into Craig. As he rolls across the railroad tracks, Rose hears the familiar sound of b'bump, b'bump as the tires slap the rails. Her heart races, and she finds it difficult to control her breathing. She waves at Trick as he pulls into a parking spot in front of Izaak's.

As Trick turns off the ignition and opens the door, Rose lets her hand glide down the rail going down the handicapped ramp to the parking lot. She swings around the railing and tries her best to walk normally as if nothing was wrong, but she's having a hard time moving her feet without feeling like she's walking through two feet of mud. Finally, when she meets Trick at the front bumper, she gives him a hug and a peck on his lips.

Trick wraps his arm around Rose, slides his hand up her back to her neck, gently squeezes and pulls her in, and gives her a proper kiss. Rose melts. Her legs tingle and go numb. Her stomach churns, and she feels paralyzed from the heart down. She feels the tickle of mucus running from her nose and the burning in her eyes as she tries desperately to hold back the tears. She pulls away and drops her chin to her chest.

"Let's get my Jeep," Rose says as she turns to round the truck to the passenger side, hiding her face.

"You ok, babe?" Trick asks as she jumps into the 4Runner.

"I'm fine," she quickly responds, and as Trick grabs the handle to lift himself into the driver's seat, she explains, "just a little rough out there with that storm, and I need to get my boat off the ramp before it gets too busy."

"Ok, let's do this," Trick tries to help.

"Ah shit," she remembers. "My ladies' gear is all still in the boat. Can we grab it really quick?"

"Of course," Trick responds.

Trick pulls into the FAS, Rose puts the gear in the back hatch of the 4Runner, threading the rods all the way to the windshield between the front seats, and jumps back into the rig. They drive downstream to Stickney Creek. Rose stares out the window the entire way. The trip takes about ten minutes. In that time, Trick asks Rose about her clients, how the fishing was, what bugs were hatching, and how much rain they got. Rose answered all the questions in just a few words each, knowing she was giving signals that something was wrong. She knows he's starting to feel anxious, too. It's a semi-conscious way of preparing him for what she will be telling him when the anxiety for both is too much, and she just has to get it out.

Like she's in a covey of Hungarian partridge, hunkered down in the grass along the rim of a coulee, Rose nervously anticipates the moment she reveals her secret. The birds hear the dogs coming and they do their best to hide, running into thicker grass and crouching as if they can avert the danger. As the dogs get closer and they get more nervous, they crouch into the grass even further, but not to hide. They crouch, preparing themselves to bust up out of the grass to take flight. Rose feels that tension. She wants to bust out. She wants to just get it all out on the table and then fly away as fast as she can, avoiding the shots she knows will come.

Trick lets the 4Runner coast into a spot next to Rose's Jeep. The 4Runner's brakes squeal with oppositional defiance as if they would rather the rig keep rolling. Rose quickly jumps from the rig and turns back to Trick through the passenger door.

"I'm going to grab my boat," she says. "Can you meet me back at the shop so I can drop off the ladies' gear?"

"Yeah, but hey," Trick impatiently inquires. "What's going on?"

Rose lifts her head so that Trick can see her bloodshot eyes she's been hiding, and responds, "I need to tell you something, but not here. Just know, Trick, that I love you. I love you more than anything in this world. And I am sorry."

Feeling his anxiety now reaching a fight level, Trick responds, "What? Did you meet someone?"

"No!" Rose responds emphatically. "It's not that at all. There's no one I'd rather be with. Just please, let's take care of the gear and we'll talk."

Rose swings the passenger door shut and turns from Trick's rig to unlock the door to the Jeep. She turns back to watch as Trick backs out of the parking spot, puts his 4Runner into drive, and heads out towards the Rec Road.

Now it's Trick's turn to run through every conversation that might be coming. He wonders what could be causing Rose to act this way. What could she be thinking? She told him she hadn't met anyone, and he trusted her, so he chased that from his mind. Did she decide she didn't want to date a gimped-up guy anymore? Did he do something wrong? All the different scenarios run through Trick's head as he drives back to Craig to meet

Rose at the shop.

Rose pulls into the Craig ramp, backs down, and brings the boat around to hook it up to the strap and cranks the boat up onto the trailer. Strapping the boat down, she leaves the anchor dangling from the bracket off the stern and pulls out of the FAS and then turns out onto Bridge Street heading towards the shop.

She backs her boat into a parking spot alongside Trick's 4Runner, turns off the ignition, and jumps out. Head down, not making eye contact, she finishes her ritual of stowing her anchor and her gear bag into the back of the Jeep, unhooking the boat and tipping it up to drain the water from the hull. Trick watches and patiently waits while he leans against his rig.

"What do you want with this stuff?" He asks.

"The ladies should be here in a minute," she responds. "I'll just bring it up to the deck."

Carolyn and Jane finished their drinks at Izaak's. They have walked up the road and into the parking lot, and as Rose is taking gear from Trick's rig, they come up behind her.

"We can grab that stuff," Jane says.

"Ok," Rose responds. "Your rod tubes are in the back of the Jeep. Let me grab them for you."

The three women collect all the gear, rods, and rod tubes and hastily walk them to the deck of the shop, where Carolyn and Jane pull their rods apart and slide them into their tubes.

As they pack their rods up, Rose apologizes, "I'm sorry. I'm kind of just rushing you guys away. I'm being rude. Let me help you with those."

"Rose," Carolyn stops her. "It looks like you have more important things to take care of. We'll be here if you need us."

"Thanks," Rose responds and then turns to walk back across the parking lot to where Trick is waiting.

As Rose approaches, Trick meets her a few steps from their vehicles and holds out his hand. She takes it. He looks at her nervously. It's as if he's trying to peer into her soul for some kind of tell for what he's about to hear.

"Can we just go back to the cottage?" Rose asks.

"Rose, come on," Trick pleads. "Just tell me what's going on."

Rose drops her head to look at the gravel topping of the parking lot. The corners of her lips curl down uncontrollably, and she begins to sob.

"I didn't know it was you," she blurts out while trying to catch her breath. Her chest convulses. Her breathing stutters like a hyperventilating child.

All the things she wanted to say—the way she was going to soften the blow. The way she was going to set him up to hear her so that maybe she would have a chance. All of it, gone and all she could do was verbally puke everything out she had been keeping inside.

"I didn't see you," she continues. "I was scared and angry, and I didn't look. I didn't see you."

"What are you talking about?" Trick demands.

"It was me!" She cries. "I did this to you! It was me!"

"You did what to me?"

Rose tells him, taking all the blame as if she's so hard on herself, that he will show mercy.

"When we were at Cell Phone Bluff the other day," Rose finally gained some composure. "You were telling me about your accident. It was me, Trick. April 12th? When you went off into the river? It was me. I was the one who pulled out in front of you. I was the one you hit and caused you to go off the cliff."

Trick's mind goes to the broken taillight of Rose's Jeep.

"So, the tape on your taillight?" He asks.

"Yes," she explains. "That was from the accident. I never had it fixed. I'm so sorry, Trick. I took everything from you. I'm so sorry. I was drinking and…"

Trick cuts her off before she can explain. "You were drinking?"

"No, wait," she pleads.

"You were drunk?" Trick responds with disdain. "And you ruined my life?"

"Please, Trick," she responds desperately. "We were at Izaak's the night before, and I drank too much, so I stayed at the Sutton Place. I woke up that morning with Jake Trapper in my bed…"

"So, you go out partying all night, fuck Jake, and ruin my fucking life?"

"NO! Please!" She pleads. "I told you…"

Trick turns back to his rig, cutting her off, "I gotta go."

Chase had been sitting in the back seat of the 4Runner since Trick picked him up at the cottage. Trick opened the back door, and Chase tumbled out. He then slammed the door, jumped back into the driver's seat, and sped off.

Carolyn and Jane were sitting on the deck of the shop, trying not to be obvious but watching the exchange. With Trick now gone, the two ladies stood up and slowly walked towards Rose. Chase trotted off to greet them. Jane put her hand out and scratched his chin, and continued toward her.

"Well, that didn't look like it went well," Jane consoles.

"Honey," Carolyn adds. "Do you want to talk?"

Rose breaks down, and Carolyn holds out her arms and embraces her. The two ladies help Rose to the deck and sit down with her as far from the shop doors as space will allow. Rose cries for a few minutes while Carolyn strokes her arm. When she's ready, Rose tells the two ladies the entire story. She knows these two ladies are the only two women she can talk to. She confides in them and trusts them, and they listen.

It's getting late in the day, and guides are beginning to pull into the parking lot to drop off boats, clean up their gear, order lunches for the next day, and shoot the shit with their cohorts. As more and more guides pull in, Carolyn and Jane recognize the need for Rose not to be seen by the guide community in this condition.

"Baby," Carolyn asks. "Would you like some company tonight? There's an extra bed at the house where we are staying if you'd like."

"I appreciate that, Carolyn," Rose answers. "But I've got to get Chase some food and take care of my gear. I'll be ok."

Keith pulls into the parking lot at MRA, flips the latch, allowing the hatch of the Suburban to pop, and backs into his designated parking spot next to the driveway that no other guide seems to have been able to commandeer. As Rose quickly walks across the parking lot with her head down, purposefully not making eye contact with any of the other guides, Keith calls out to her.

"Hey, Fly," he yells. "Hold up."

Rose stops halfway to her Jeep, and Keith catches up with her.

"Hey," he tells her. "I thought I saw Trick heading back up towards Wolf Creek. That's him in the 4Runner, right?"

"Yeah," she says. "He was here for a minute."

"What happened?" Keith asks. "Did you tell him?"

"Yeah. It didn't go so well," she says. "God, I'm a fuck-up."

"Hold on, Rose," he reaches out to grab her arm. "You can't carry all this weight on your shoulders. Shit happens. People make mistakes. People also deserve forgiveness. Give him a couple of days."

"Yeah, I don't know," she tells him. "He was pretty torn up."

"Maybe I could talk to him?" Keith suggests.

"I don't know," Rose replies. "He doesn't really know you. I'm not sure how much it would help."

"Rose," Keith shares. "You're like my little sister. I know it's a little awkward, but let me put a good word in for you. Maybe hearing it from someone who was there will give him a better perspective?"

With nothing else to lose, Rose gives Keith Trick's cell phone number and then calls for Chase to load up. She jumps in her truck and doesn't notice the guides waving to her as she pulls out onto Bridge Street and heads over the bridge. As she reaches the Rec Road and turns right to head back towards Wolf Creek, she sobs and slams her fists on the steering wheel.

THE OLD WOODSMAN SPEAKS

Rose parked her Jeep in front of the historic hotel, let Chase out through the front passenger door, and made her way towards the cottage. As the gate of the picket fence swung shut, she noticed Ross sitting in his chair next to the window, looking out into the yard. Knowing Ross would want to comfort her if he saw she had just been crying, she did her best to hide her face from his view. Before she could make her way to the back yard and into the cottage, Ross opened the door of the hotel and called out to her.

"Hey, Rose," getting her attention.

"Hey Ross," she answers back.

As he walks around the corner of the hotel, he continues, "I saw Trick come in. I assumed he was coming to meet up with you, but you weren't home."

"Yeah," she acknowledges. "He grabbed Chase and came up to Craig."

"Oh, well," he continues. "Then I saw him drive by and turn back up 434, back towards Missoula. He looked like he was in a hurry. Everything ok?"

A hint of resentment stirred in Rose, "Why are you so damn nosy?" She thought to herself.

It wasn't really how she felt. She loved how Ross and Karen looked after her as if she were their daughter. They had stood behind her and helped her out in those dark days right after the incident. Ross even talked to the sheriff after he interviewed Rose the day of the accident, letting him know he would be watching out for her.

"Not really, Ross," she admits. "That truck that swerved to miss me and went off into the river last spring? That was Trick. I had no idea until a few days ago."

"No way," Ross states ironically. "What are the chances, Rose?"

"Yeah," Rose agrees. "And what are the chances I would fall in love with the person whose life I had just ruined?"

"I guess he didn't take the news all that well?" he asks.

"No. He pretty much hates me, and I don't blame him." She turns to keep Ross from seeing the tears that are again running down her cheek.

"Give him time, Rose. I've seen you two together. I know how much he loves you," Ross tells her in his fatherly voice.

"I don't know," Rose responds. "I ruined his life. I can't imagine he would ever forgive me."

"He may or may not, Rose. But at least you gave him the choice," Ross continues. "You can't control that, but you can work on forgiving yourself. Knowing you, I know how guilty you feel. I know you would hit the rewind button and take all this back if you could, even if that meant you would never have met Trick, just so he would have had the life he was working towards. But you can't, Rose."

Rose turns back and looks him in the eyes, "I'll never forgive myself."

"Rose," he reaches out to her.

Rose turns and calls Chase and disappears into the cottage.

In all that has happened in the past year and a half, Ross had never seen that look on her face. Like a father standing over his son's grave, unable to protect him from the worst thing a parent could endure, he felt helpless. The pain. The look of despair, shame, and complete loss; she looked defeated, and it scared him.

Mike and Sara had just finished dinner. It was Mike's turn to cook, so Sara was cleaning up dishes in the kitchen and noticed Trick pull into the alley driveway, jump from his 4Runner, and climb the stairs, skipping every other step.

"Hey Mike," she calls out. "Wasn't Trick heading to Wolf Creek?"

"Yeah," Mike answers back from the old, tattered recliner in the living room. "He left a few hours ago."

"He just pulled in," she informs. "He didn't text you, did he?"

"I haven't heard anything," Mike answers.

Sara dried her hands on the towel that hung from the cabinet under the sink, pushed the start button on the dishwasher, and headed out the back door to the stairs leading up to Trick's apartment. She didn't feel right about seeing him, knowing he was going to see Rose and knowing how excited he always was when he knew he would be with her.

She knocks on the door and asks, "Trick? Are you in there?"

The door slowly swings inward, and Sara peeks through. Trick has opened the door and is slowly walking back across the living room floor. He plops down on the vinyl-covered barrel chair in the corner of the room. He stares at the TV, which hasn't been turned on. He's slumped into the chair with his legs sprawled out, his right arm draped over the arm of the chair. His prosthetic lies on the floor.

"You ok?" She asks.

Trick stares forward for what seems to be minutes and then musters up a "not really."

"What's the matter?" Sara asks.

"It was her," he says, barely audible. "She did this."

"What do you mean, Trick?"

"Rose!" His voice cracks, gaining intensity. "It was Rose who did this."

Trick gestures to his left shoulder with his right hand and then waves back to the prosthetic lying on the floor.

"Trick," wanting an explanation. "What did Rose have to do with it?"

"She was in the car that sent me off the cliff into the river!" Trick blurts out. "She took everything from me!"

Trick's phone ringer chimes. He picks it up, looks at the name on the caller ID and dismisses the call. His chest rises and falls as he breathes in deep breaths and then forces the air out through his nose. His lips are pursed, and his brows furrow as he clenches his jaw, the muscles in his face along his jawline flexing. The rest of him appears to be relaxed as if he is no longer in his own body.

"I don't understand, Trick."

"The morning of my accident," he explains. "She had been partying all night. She woke up with one of the guides up there and took off in her car and fucking ruined me."

"Trick," Sara responds with some skepticism. "Did she explain what happened? What was going on? There had to have been something, right?"

"She pulled out in front of me and then left me there to fucking die!" Trick is furious. "What fucking else is there to understand?"

"Wait, when did she find out it was you? When did you find out?"

"I guess last week," Trick explains. "When we were at the bluff. I told her that my accident happened right there, and she put two and two together and realized it was us. OR me, she pulled out in front of. She just told me today."

Right then, Mike pokes his head through the door

and asks, "Everything alright up here?"

Sara turns and says, "You're going to have to help with this one, Mike."

"There's nothing you can do," Trick shouts as he sits up in the chair and lunges forward. "There's nothing anyone can do! I'm fucked for life because of some irresponsible bitch that decided to get drunk and ruin my life, and it just so happens that now I'm fucking her. Or at least I was…"

The verbal onslaught surprises Mike like busting a goose off her nest as he wades along the riverbank. His head pulls back as if he's protecting himself from the wings of that goose, but stands his ground, knowing the fury isn't specifically directed towards him. He gives it a second to set in and then walks further into the living room of the apartment, letting the door close behind him.

"So let me get this straight," Mike clarifies. "You're saying Rose caused your accident?"

Trick leans back into the chair and stares back at the blank TV.

"And she did it because either she wanted to hurt you, at worst, or that she just didn't care enough and was too irresponsible to not hurt you?" Mike asks rhetorically.

Trick doesn't respond; he just slowly shakes his head, still staring.

Mike continues, "Dude, I love you like a brother. You know that, right? I'm always going to have your back. But I gotta say, aren't you being a little rough on her? I mean, things aren't always what they seem, and even if they are, people fuck up. And people learn. I'm just sayin, don't you think she deserves a little bit of grace here?"

"NO." Trick replies.

Sara interjects, "It's pretty raw, Trick. We understand.

I'm certainly not going to tell you how to feel. You spent the last year and a half wanting to blame someone, but there wasn't anyone. Now there is. If that's what you need to move on, then you do what you have to do, but I hope, at some point, you realize what's most important to you."

"I can't tell you what to do, Trick," Mike adds. "All I know is how she's made you feel these past few months, and that was pretty special. It's the happiest I've seen you in a long time. You'll have some tough choices to make. What I *will* suggest is that you don't make a decision on anything until you have a chance to take this all in."

Right then, Trick's phone chimes, notifying him of a text message received.

Rose's heart sinks as she hears the voicemail message picked up from Trick's phone. Not leaving a message, she just hangs up and sinks to the floor in the tiny cottage. She waits for several minutes and types a message, and waits to send.

"Can we please talk?"

After another few minutes of staring at the message, she hits send and watches as it dangles in the air, knowing Trick is receiving the message and not knowing how he will respond or what the outcome will be. It's like watching a half-court shot go off at the buzzer, knowing the entire season comes down to this last act of desperation. There is nothing she can do but wait and hope for the best.

Her phone dings as it notifies her of his response.

"LEAVE ME ALONE!"

At that moment, Rose's heart broke. She sinks back and rolls to the floor, curls her legs into the fetal position, and weeps. What she truly believed in—the only things she's ever truly believed in—the person who would be in her life forever, wanted nothing to do with her, and she ached.

This wasn't Rose's first loss. Her father. Her grandfather. She's even had boyfriends in the past, she thought she loved. This was different. This was crushing, like a cannonball dropping from the sky, crippling her, paralyzing her, and leaving her for dead.

Rose lay on the floor through the sun setting and didn't move until light once again filtered through the blinds on the front window; the parallel shadows resembling a cattle guard on the floor of the cottage. She lifted her head and felt the sharp pain in her neck muscles that weren't at all happy about her choice of resting places. The rest of her body felt numb with the exception of the dull pressure she felt behind her eyes from crying the entire night. Chase lay by her side.

Rose noticed the smell of the carpet on the cottage floor, a mix of dog dander, leftover beer stains from previous tenants, and dirt. She crawled to the couch and lifted herself into a sitting position. She began to relive the conversation with Trick—so many things she wanted to say to him, but didn't get the chance to explain herself. She could see the pain in his eyes as he made up his own reality for what happened that morning in April of last year. It wasn't fair. Or maybe it was.

The tears on Rose's face had long dried up in the night, like the many seasonal tributaries to the Missouri River. In the spring, they flowed freely, without obstruction, and often cut channels through muddy embankments, but eventually ran out to a trickle and then dried up to nothing but dusty stones. That's what Rose felt on her face—crusty salt from the many tears that ran down and dried on her face over the last 18 hours. And now, there's nothing left to give.

Picking herself up off the ragged couch that has seen much abuse from dozens of guides over the years, Rose stumbles into the bedroom and rifles through the closet. She pushes through the guide shirts and pants hanging from plastic hangers and sees a Remington 870 12-gauge shotgun, a Ruger .270 bolt action rifle, and on the floor, her dad's .41 magnum Ruger Blackhawk. Rose reaches for the Blackhawk, turns back through the cottage, and out onto the yard. Chase follows.

"You're going to stay here, buddy," she commands.

Rose opens the gate of the chain link fence and walks through, and then turns back to Chase. He usually won't let her leave in the morning without a fair amount of opposition. This morning, he sits on his haunches and cocks his head. His tongue hangs long past his chin as he pants. She walks back to him, kisses him on the nose, and tells him goodbye.

Rose closes the gate on Chase and runs through the yard, sneaks out the gate of the picket fence, making sure not to let it slam, and jumps into her Jeep. She tosses the Blackhawk on the passenger side seat and turns the key in the ignition. Careful not to spin her tires in the gravel, she lets the Jeep roll a few yards before stepping on the gas. Once on the asphalt, she accelerates and drives west towards the intersection of Hwy 434.

Driving up 434, the sun crests the horizon, illuminating the giant cliff walls of the Rocky Mountain Front. The grass is still a brilliant green from the rain that has graced the land for the past couple of months, and snow still caps the peaks of the Scapegoat Mountains in the distance. It's a postcard that every tourist sends to their friends and family when visiting the Northern Rocky Mountains. The scene typifies everything that Montana is and what thousands of people are now trading their urban skylines for as they move to Montana in the hopes of a simpler life. Rose travels the dirt road along the Front, glancing from time to time at the mountains as she gets closer to The High Bridge.

Crossing the bridge, Rose parks, nose in, towards the fence she has crossed dozens of times in the last few years. She grabs her backpack, already loaded with her favorite freestone flies, puts together her four-weight rod, threads the line through the guides, and ties on a yellow stimulator. She then reaches for the Blackhawk, wraps the holster around her waist, and cinches the buckle tight enough not to slide off her hips. Opening the make-shift gate made from barbed wire and lodgepoles, she slides through, then turns back to close the gate and traverses down to the Dearborn River.

The air temperature is still in the 50s, and the water is running clear and still very cold. Rose skirts along the bank of the river, heading upstream to have a conversation with the Old Woodsman and the trout he watches over.

Realizing she left her can of bear spray in the Jeep, Rose thinks to herself, "It's not like I'm going to need it."

The canyon is nearly silent with the exception of the gurgling of the river and aspen leaves fluttering in the breeze that is just now waking up. There are no cattle in the bottom of the drainage as ranchers have moved them into the high country, taking advantage of the thick, sweet grass that has been growing in abundance all spring. Rose has the canyon and the world to herself.

This isn't the first time Rose has felt this way—like the world would be better off without her. She often felt like this as a teenager. She and her father had a very complicated relationship. Rose remembered those times; those fights she had with him when she thought she was getting cheated. She remembered being the one called on to help her father make dinner and pick weeds in the garden, and even help him do valve jobs and replace starters and alternators on his '73 Monte Carlo because he couldn't make use of his right arm after his stroke. She remembered the guilt and rage she would feel after screaming at him and, once, even pushing him back against the washing machine as he tried to grab her wrist and twist her arm when she refused to fold the laundry. The stroke took away his voice, making it impossible to find the words to express himself, so violence was his only means of controlling her. She hated him. And when he passed away while she was in grad school, she cried for days, wishing she had told him more that she loved him.

"This fucking world is not for me," she thought. "Today it will get its wish."

A straight hike to the Old Woodsman, without stopping to fish pools along the way, only took her 20 minutes. She looked up at the cliff wall and nodded her head. She plucked the fly from the guide on her fly rod, ripped off some line, and began working the pool the Woodsman protected for one last time. A small rainbow aggressively smacked Rose's stimi, and as she set the hook, the trout came flying out of the water, landed on the bank, and flopped around in the rocks. The trout fought for his life, and as he flung the hook from his mouth before Rose could reach him, he made it back to the water and darted out of sight.

Rose admired the little trout and respected its resilience and its fight she wished that she still had. But she didn't. Not anymore. She had failed so many times and hurt so many people along the way, starting with her old man and ending with Trick. Taking another cast, another trout ate her fly.

Rose released the second trout back into the water and watched as it, too, darted off and disappeared in the clear water. She thought about how pristine and pure the water was, and how perfectly a trout disappeared when it left her hand. She thought about the food chain she was part of and how she broke that chain by releasing the trout back to the water, and if she was educating these trout, how that would impact other predators, as they actually relied on these fish for sustenance. Another cast, and another trout came to the surface and ate her stimi.

"Three fish on three casts," Rose thought to herself as she looked up at the Old Woodsman.

"You might want to let these fish know they should be a little more discerning in their choice of food," she said out loud.

Curious about the notion that these fish are not very particular on this day, Rose pulled

the stimulator to her, clipped it from her leader, and searched through her fly box for something different to show these fish. She found a size 12 parachute, Adams, and tied it on.

Recalling the day she had fished her way up to this pool after guiding James, the 17-year-old here, Rose remembered the turmoil she had been feeling and how sad she had been. She remembered watching the trout she was after show itself, and she remembered pulling the hopper from its mouth. Rose also remembered changing her fly to the Adams and accidentally catching the trout as the fly dragged under the riffle. She also remembered the peace she felt as she fished for that trout.

Turning to the rocks on the bank, Rose thought

about the fly she had buried after catching the trout. She wondered if it was still there as she kicked a few rocks over and then realized how ridiculous it was to think she might find it. She remembered that fly, however, and she remembered the symbolism of turning that fly back to the earth. She remembered thinking about it as not dying and being forgotten, but rather, being reborn—being redefined. She remembered she thought of herself at that time, following a similar path of self-examination and redefining who she was.

Rose stripped off more line from her reel and took another cast into the pool with the Adams, and just like the stimi, a 12-inch trout rose to it, closed its mouth on it, and Rose's line tightened as she lifted her rod tip.

After letting this trout go, she looked up to the Old Woodsman and asked, "What are you trying to say, old man?"

A cottonwood tree had lost its battle with the high water of the Dearborn earlier that spring and was lying on the ground along the bank. Rose walked over to the downed tree and used it for a seat to relax and reflect. She set her rod down and took off her pack. Then she pulled the Blackhawk from its holster and felt the cold, blued steel in her hands. Flipping the loading gate and spinning the cylinder, Rose noted five rounds, with one empty chamber, which is always in the firing position when carrying the gun for safety.

Rose thought about the last time she spoke with her mother, Ginny. She always admired her mother because of her strength. For most of Rose's life, her mom had to work two jobs to support her kids and her husband, and would never give up or give in to *real* problems. Rose thought about how hurt and how disappointed her mother would be. Rose also thought about how disappointed her father would be if he were still alive. She thought about how Trick would blame himself, and about the trips she had booked with the outfitters that had supported her in her first couple of years as a guide, and the obligation she feels. She thought about her nieces and nephews and the message she would be sending them. Drawing in an extended breath of clean, fresh air, she slowly let it escape her body through pursed lips, and she feels calm.

Rotating the empty chamber of the cylinder back to the firing position, she re-holsters the Blackhawk, stands up, slings her backpack over her shoulder, and picks up her rod. Looking up at the Old Woodsman, Rose gives him another nod and then turns back toward the High Bridge and back to her Jeep.

A PROTECTIVE MAMA

By noon, the sun had crested the rim of the Dearborn Canyon and was quickly intensifying as the rays penetrated Rose's fleece jacket. The wind, which had started as gentle updrafts, was now funneling through the canyon, making its presence known by spinning dust devils and swaying cottonwood branches. Rose's pain was pervasive and clung like hound's-tongue, but she was at least able to breathe. While walking back to the Jeep, she tries hard to take in the clean air and just be present in the midday sun, but her mind inevitably goes back to Trick and the sadness of knowing he never wants to see her again.

Rose looks up and notices a dark brown cloud rising above the canyon walls. She thinks it's apropos with how she is feeling, and she looks back down to the gravel and rocks along the river she was navigating. And then the significance of the cloud struck her.

"Shit," she thinks and looks back up at the cloud. "Fire."

Lightning from the storm the day before had struck a dead Ponderosa Pine on the ridge above the river. Embers from the strike can smolder for days before the right conditions blow the dry tinder from the dead tree up into a massive bonfire. High winds and plenty of fuel from dead lodgepoles can cause a fire to crown and spread through dense forests at highway speeds. With the winds now picking up in intensity, this fire was building a plume of smoke resembling a mushroom cloud looming over the Dearborn.

Rose stands in awe of the growing plume of smoke that is only a quarter mile from where she stood. Soon, provided someone has seen the fire blowing up and had access to a cell signal, there will be hot-shot trucks racing up the gravel road, towards the High Bridge to fight the fire before it gets out of control. With the Dearborn Ranch and plenty of cabins in the path of this fire, smoke jumpers and firefighting aircraft will most likely be deployed as well.

A ravine ran down from the ridge where the fire was spreading to the riverbed. A group of mule deer does and three fawns make their way down the ravine towards Rose. She watches as they bound back and forth in a zig-zagging path, avoiding thick elder patches and boulders. They had been spooked by the fire and were creating distance from the blaze in a hurry. They crossed the Dearborn about a hundred yards in front of Rose and continued up the other side of the canyon through an opposite draw until they were out of sight. Rose wonders how many other animals were in the path of the fire.

As Rose continued along the riverbank, making her way back to her Jeep, the fire distracted her thoughts. Soon, however, her mind snapped back to Trick. Her head dropped as she focused on the washed-out stream-bed and the sadness of losing the one person she believed, as sure as the sandhill cranes come back to Montana in the spring, was her soul mate. She slowly walks, kicking river stones along the way.

Approaching the path where the deer crossed in front of her, she notices their tracks in the sand. She analyzes them, noting the depth and size of the doe's tracks compared to those of the fawns. She also recognizes one set that is a bit larger than the others, with its toes splayed, thinking it must have been a small buck hanging out with the family of does. A mature buck would have been hanging out with other mature bucks, and she would have seen the stubs of antler growth already. A smaller buck with only spikes would have been less noticeable. These were things her dad had taught her when she was very young. She misses him now, too.

Studying the tracks, Rose reflects on the lessons and the longing and then the self-loathing for her many mistakes throughout her life. A few seconds pass before she registers the sounds that are coming down the draw along a similar path that the mule deer had taken. Rocks click together and branches snap, and before Rose recognizes the sound of something heavy and a lot less discerning for avoiding things in their path, it is too late. The first of three bodies crosses the river, passing by her only a few feet away. The second body, similar in shape and size, and color, was only a few paces behind.

"Oh, shit!" Rose lets out as adrenaline shoots through her veins.

She watches the two grizzly bear cubs bulldoze their way through the elders on their way up the opposite draw from where they came. Her head snaps back to the direction of where they had come as the "whoof, whoof," sound of a concerned mother grizzly grabs her attention like she had accidentally brushed up against a high-voltage electric cattle fence.

Rose reaches for her bear spray she always kept in the front compartment of her pack, and immediately realizes she has left the spray in the Jeep. The sow, weighing at least three hundred pounds, rises on her back legs, lifting her front paws, and then slams them down in the river. Her muscles rippled throughout her lean body as she had yet to put on the fat she had lost over the winter of hibernating and feeding her cubs. Her jaws snap shut, smacking her teeth together as if she were telling Rose to get the hell out of her way. Rose is now directly between this protective mother and her cubs. She whoofs and pops her teeth and again, rears up on her back legs and slams her front paws in the river, sending droplets of water spraying right up to Rose's feet.

For the guides that do wade fishing trips in bear country, it's a common discussion of what to do when encountering a bear. If it's a black bear, go big. If you present yourself as a pain in the ass to the bear, they usually just run off. If it's a griz, good luck. Their fight response is much stronger than the flight response of black bears, and if you are seen as a threat, they are going to fight you. If a griz charges, most often, they are going to bluff you to get you to move. However, they are also unpredictable, and there isn't a person alive that is going to trust 300 pounds of grizzled muscle charging them at 30mph with teeth baring and 3-inch claws protruding from open palms looking like heavyweight boxing gloves the like of which would put George Foreman to shame.

If they do charge, bluff or for real, Rose always said she would choose bear spray over a handgun because she knew how bad a shot she was on the range. She also knew, without ever encountering a grizzly up close, she didn't have a clue of how she would react and her best odds were going to be with a can of spray that sent a five to ten foot circular pattern of debilitating pepper spray with pressurized oil as the catalyst versus a single 210 grain projectile that would have to hit the bear almost perfectly to stop it. Unfortunately, for this first real encounter, she didn't have a choice.

Rose remembers she has the Blackhawk on her side and reaches for the wood grip. As she pulls, the bear charges across the river as if the water and current of the Dearborn didn't exist. The revolver was stuck in the holster. She forgot to unsnap the hammer throng, releasing the weapon. She pulls harder, jerking the belt off her hip, and then realizes it wasn't going to release until she unsnapped the throng.

The very second the sow meets her, Rose pulls the Blackhawk from the holster. The bear throws her shoulder into Rose, knocking her to the ground and taking the wind from her. Gasping, she tries to roll over to gain her feet. The bear swings her paw, catching Rose on her hip, rolling her back over onto her back. Rose still has the Blackhawk in her hand and lifts it to the bear's chest, but before she can cock the hammer and fire, the bear swings her paw again and sends the gun flying to the sandy beach a few feet from the scuffle.

Rose digs her heels into the sand and pushes her body backwards away from the bear, pleading with the bear to stop. She fights desperately to put distance between them.

"NO, NO, NO!" She screams, now fighting as hard as she can for her life. "Please! NO!"

The bear rushes her, grabbing Rose by the hip with her jaws. Her top incisors penetrate Rose's glutes, and her bottom jaw rips through her flexors along the inside of her groin. The sow picks Rose up off the ground and throws her with a single flip of her massive head and neck. As Rose tumbles to the ground, the bear is on her again within a fraction of a second. This time, she closes her jaws over Rose's head, and she hears the scraping of the bear's teeth against her skull.

The mother bear drops Rose back to the earth. Not yet satisfied she has ridden herself and her cubs of any threat, the bear stands up on her haunches and drops her paws, slamming down on Rose's side and back. Rose feels her ribs breaking like dried timbers. The pain is excruciating, and she cries out and then falls limp.

The attack only lasted a few seconds. Rose was left lifeless and bleeding on the bank of the Dearborn River as the mother grizzly loped after her cubs.

Trick's phone buzzed and chimed at about 8:30 am Sunday morning. The number showed as a Montana number, but he did not recognize it. He let it go to voicemail, and when the message alert chimed, he dialed the voicemail.

"Hey, Trick," came the voice. "This is Keith. I work with Rose on the river. We met last week. She didn't show up for her trip this morning, and I'm just wondering if you have seen her. Could you give me a call when you get this? Thanks."

Trick pulls up Keith's number on his received calls, hits the call button, and waits for Keith to answer.

"Hey, Trick," Keith answers. "Thanks for calling back so soon. Have you seen Rose?"

"No," Trick replies. "I haven't seen her since Friday night."

"Well," Keith explains. "I don't think she worked yesterday, but she was supposed to be on the river today working for the shop, and no one has seen her. She's never missed a day of work as far as I know. I have the day off, so I told the shop I would look for her. I'm at her cottage right now. Chase is in the yard, Ross hasn't seen her, and her Jeep is gone."

Trick's chest tightens, "Yeah, I don't know, Keith. Like I said, I haven't heard from her."

"So, you haven't heard anything?" Keith presses. "Did you guys get into a fight or anything. I'll be honest with you, Trick. She told me about what she did to you. She was pretty torn up. I asked for your number so I might be able to talk to you, but now I'm worried. Do you have any idea where she might go?"

"I think I do," Trick admits. "You're in Wolf Creek?"

"Yeah."

"Can you meet me at the 434, 200 crossing in an hour and twenty minutes?" Trick asks. "It will save us forty minutes."

"I'll be there, Trick," Keith responds.

"Bring Chase," Trick instructs.

Keith was already at the crossing as Trick pulled up in his 4Runner. Trick barely had a chance to stop the rig, and Keith was opening up the passenger rear door for Chase to jump in, and then he jumped into the front seat.

"Where are we headed?" Keith asks.

"The High Bridge." Trick responds as he steps on the gas aggressively, causing the rear-end of the 4Runner to break free.

He rights the truck, and as they drive up the gravel road, they look off to the northwest along the Front and watch pillars of smoke billowing up from burning lodgepoles. A helicopter with a bucket dangling underneath its carriage flies over just a few hundred feet above them. The helicopter is taking a straight path from the Missouri River to the burn. Another helicopter has dumped its water on the target and is circling back to the Missouri.

"When did that blow up?" Trick asks.

"Yesterday," Keith answers. "Must have been a lightning strike from the storm on Friday. Yesterday, the winds were nuking through here, so it must have blown up then. They got on it quick, but with all this dead timber and that wind, there's no getting ahead of it. This one might get big."

"It looks pretty close to where we're heading," Trick reveals.

"Look, Trick," Keith starts. "I know it's really not the time for this, but there's something you gotta know."

"How 'bout we find her first?" Trick asks.

"You gotta hear this," Keith continues. "I was there that night. The night before your accident. You have no idea how hard it is for a chick to get in with these guys—the guides. We're a territorial bunch, and these guys can be a bit misogynistic, and Rose took more than her fair share of shit. The only way she could compete was to show she could hang. Things got out of control, and we told her not to drive home, so we put her up in the Sutton Place in Craig. I left her there with one of the outfitters, thinking he was putting her to bed and then leaving. The stupid fucker took advantage of her. I'll never forgive him for that. I'll never forgive myself for that."

"We all have choices," Trick replies unsympathetically.

"Trick," Keith retorts. "Come on, dude. That girl loves you. She didn't mean for any of that to happen."

Trick goes silent, staring through the windshield as he drives along the Front.

Before the road drops down into the canyon of the Dearborn, a crew of Hotshot firefighters was staged in a field off the road. A windsock dangled from a pole and stretched out, showing the strength and direction of the wind that was pushing the fire to the northeast. One of the crew members standing along the road held out his hand to stop Trick and Keith from going further.

"Hey, guys," the firefighter addressed them. "Where you headed?"

He was a younger man with a yellow hard hat, green wool pants, and a yellow flannel shirt. His face was covered in soot. He wore a radio on his belt with a corded receiver clipped to the loops on his shoulders.

"Trying to find a friend," Trick responds. "She might be fishing at the High Bridge."

"We've had this area closed off since last night," he explains. "Everyone was evacuated along the Dearborn all the way up to the Bible School. What was she driving?"

"A red Jeep," Trick responds.

"Hold on," the crew member says and reaches for the radio receiver as he turns away from them.

The firefighter talks to another crew member and, after 30 seconds, walks back to the side of Trick's 4Runner.

"Yeah," he tells Trick. "Her Jeep is parked at the High Bridge just a little way up. Do you know where she might have gone? They tried looking for her, but then all the attention had been either on evacuation or fighting the fire. If you know where she is, let's go. I'll grab a truck and be right behind you."

Trick heads up the gravel road and follows it down into the canyon. The firefighter follows close behind, driving a green F-250 with storage compartments mounted on the bed rails and shovels and Pulaskis hanging from brackets for ease of access. As they wind down the road towards the bridge, Rose's Jeep comes into sight. A streak of panic runs through Trick's veins.

"There," Keith says and points. "That's her rig."

Chase stands up in the back seat of the 4Runner and whines.

The two rigs pull in side by side next to Rose's Jeep. They all pile out, including Chase. The firefighter reaches out a hand and introduces himself.

"I'm Jarrid," as he shakes Trick's hand first and then Keith's.

"I'm Trick, and this is Keith."

"Alright, well, let's hurry," Jarrid suggests. "No telling what this fire is gonna do."

"She always heads upstream," Trick tells them. "Chase will find her if something's happened and she can't respond. You have the only source of communication with the radio, so I say we all head up."

"Sounds good." Keith agrees.

Chase barks and doesn't wait for the three men as he pushes his way under the fence and works his way down to the river, turning upstream with his nose to the ground. Trick calls to him, but he doesn't even slow down.

"Let's go, boys," Jarrid calls out.

The three traverse their way down to the river and head upstream. Chase has disappeared from their sight. Half jogging, half stumbling over river rock and boulders, they push through elders and willows and try to keep pace. They hear Chase bark and then let out a yip and a painful howl, as if he was bitten by another dog or hit by something with force.

As the three take a bend in the river, Chase meets them, his tongue hanging out and panting. His tail waves nervously as he whines and yips. He turns back upstream and darts off.

As they push through the elders into a clearing, Trick's heart sinks. There, lying on the ground, limp and unresponsive to their approaching, is Rose. Chase stands over her, licking her face and nudging her shoulder. He's whimpering, shoving his nose into her. He's trying desperately to get her to move, but she does not.

The three pause for a brief moment to take inventory of the situation. Rose is curled into a ball on the ground. Her blond hair is matted with dried, dark red blood. Her back is facing them, and they can see her pants torn in the seat. Her backpack is still draped over her shoulder and has flipped over her head. The Blackhawk lies on the ground a few feet from her.

Trick takes a hurried step towards her. Keith grabs his arm and stops him.

"Hold on, Trick." He demands. "I'm not sure you want to see this."

Jarrid cautiously moves in. He scans the tree line and the ridge and then sees the sow's tracks in the sand.

"Looks like a griz," Jarrid says. "Keith, grab that gun and keep your eyes open. Trick, just hold on."

"Fuck you," Trick answers, and he runs towards Rose as Jarrid reaches down to check her carotid for a pulse.

Trick kneels next to her and asks, "Is she alive?"

"Barely," Jarrid reveals. "We gotta move though cuz she doesn't have much left."

"Fuck, fuck, fuck!" Trick cries out as he slams the palm of his hand repeatedly against his forehead.

"Hey!" Jarrid stops him and grabs his arm. "That's not gonna fucking help. Keith, you watch for that fucking bear. Trick, we're going to roll her over gently and make sure she's not bleeding out somewhere. These puncture wounds on her backside don't look like much, but she's gonna have other bites and wounds. Be gentle and on three, we roll and then ease her over."

They roll Rose over onto her back and slide the pack under her head. She lets out a whimper as they roll her, and Jarrid notes that it's a good sign.

"If she feels pain, she's still with us," he says. "It doesn't look like she's bleeding out. Everything is dry and looks like the wounds have clotted. Keep her company, Trick. I'm going to call in a chopper."

"Will they come off the fire?" Trick asks desperately.

"They have to," Jarrid explains. "Life first, then property, and then the forest. We can't wait for the flight for life. We don't have time. Our birds are only a couple of minutes away."

Trick hears Jarrid on the radio, "We found her. It's not good. Looks like a bear attack. We need one of our choppers stat! Have them pick up the medic from base, a backboard, and a litter. There's a landing spot on a gravel bar a couple of klicks upstream from the bridge, and make it quick. We don't have a lot of time."

Trick strokes Rose's cheek and tells her, "Babe, don't fucking die. I'm sorry. I'm so fucking sorry."

He sees one eye partially open, and she whispers, "Trick…" She labors for a shallow breath. "Please… help…"

Fifteen minutes pass as Trick comforts Rose, trying hard not to alarm her any more than she already is. Silent tears stream down his face as he holds her hand and promises to never let her go. Jarrid continually monitors her breathing and circulation. They both hear the gurgling sounds as she tries to breathe. There's nothing they can do but comfort her and wait.

The thumping of helicopter blades gradually replaces the sound of whipping wind through the canyon. Jarrid races towards the gravel bar and waves them in. They pull the litter from the hull of the chopper, and the medic and Jarrid run it back to where Rose is lying on the ground.

"Easy, easy, boys," the medic cautions as they load Rose onto the litter. "Alright, the four of us will bring her to the chopper. On three, lift."

The medic counts them in, and the four of them lift Rose off the ground and shuffle their way towards the helicopter. As they set her down on the floor of the chopper's hull, Trick begins to pull himself up and into the craft.

"You can't come," the medic tells Trick.

"I'm coming," he demands.

"We're picking up a doctor in Choteau, sir. We won't have room for you."

"I'm fucking coming with," Trick yells.

"Listen, sir!" The medic runs out of patience. "If you want this gal to live, you will fucking stand down!"

Keith grabs Trick and pulls him away from the helicopter, and as it lifts off, Trick collapses to the ground as if his skeleton has left his body. As the adrenaline dissipates, his muscles tense and he feels his back tightening and burning as if he had just narrowly missed a head-on collision with an oncoming semi-truck barreling down on him on the freeway. He buries his face in the crux of his right elbow and sobs uncontrollably.

EPILOGUE

Hellgate High School had just let out for the summer. Fourteen-year-old Rickie Patterson was standing in knee-deep water on the inside edge of a riffle along the Bitterroot River just outside of Hamilton. The sun had risen to its mid-day apex, and the riffle was becoming alive with noses poking up to munch down emerging PMD's before they go airborne.

Rickie, son of Trick, is a lanky 6'1" freshman at Hellgate, and unlike his father, his passion for sports is occupied with basketball. Like his father, however, he needed to put on a few pounds as he developed his game, and was an incredibly determined teenager with the work ethic to pursue sports beyond Hellgate. He also developed a passion for fly-fishing as his parents had been taking him on extended float trips since before he could remember, and taught him to throw a tight loop by the time he was four.

Rickie studied this riffle as he watched trout rising to the rhythm of the emerging mayflies. He was discerning the trout, wanting to pick out the biggest one before offering his "comparadun", which is a pattern Rickie loved because it sits low in the water, with a tuft of elk hair sticking up above the film just enough to visually follow as it drifts through the riffling water. Trout can be insanely selective while keyed in on emerging PMD's, but Rickie is confident in the pattern and his ability to present it as long as he can find the trout he wants to go after.

Commotion from the riffle fifty yards downstream grabs Rickie's attention, and as he wheels his head around, he sees his father hooked up on another 13-inch rainbow. Trick gives Rickie a head-nod and then drags the trout through the riffle to his hip, wedges his rod into his left armpit, and pops the fly from its mouth with his right hand. Rickie gives him the thumbs up and turns back to his riffle.

At fourteen, Rickie has already experienced the trajectory that a lot of fly-fishers realize throughout their journey of mastering the sport. First, the objective every day on the water is not to get skunked. Then an angler feels like they need to catch every fish. However, at some point, it becomes less about the number of fish and more about technique. Instead of nymph fishing, which is often considered a less technical form of fly-fishing, matching hatches and throwing dry flies to spooky fish is the mark of true mastery. And then, recognizing a single trout worthy of throwing a cast to and catching that fish becomes the pinnacle of one's development. The only thing left is bringing this knowledge to others and mentoring them through their journey.

At the far edge of the riffle, Rickie sees his target. As the riffle dumps over the gravel bar, the current pushes to the outside of the bend, cutting along a sandy bank that has been eroded from years of fluctuating run-off. Roots from cottonwoods standing along the bank are exposed as they extend into the water. At the top of the run, an eddy forms in the corner between the gravel bar and the cutbank. Rickie's target is on the seam of the eddy just as the riffle dumps down off the ledge to run along the bank.

Rickie studies the fish. Every six seconds, the trout rises to the surface, slowly opens its mouth, sucks down a bug, and submerges back to the shadow of the bank. With every rise, Rickie notices the width of his back and the amount of water he displaces as he takes in another bug. He can also see the yellow hues and reddish halos illuminating along the trout's head and lateral line as he travels through a ray of sunlight sneaking through a gap in the bank. The other trout in the riffle go unnoticed now as he trains all his attention on this fish.

Stripping line off his reel, Rickie whips the tip of his rod downstream, shooting line out away from the rising brown trout. Wading a few feet further into the riffle, he turns towards the eddy and the seam that is just a little sharper than forty-five degrees upstream and about twenty feet away. He takes several false casts while ripping a few more feet off his reel until he is sure he has enough line to cover the seam with his fly. The first cast lands 2 inches from the target, and Rickie watches as the big brown gulps down a natural bug next to his comparadun.

The fly drifts well downstream from the trout, and Rickie picks up his cast again, being careful to slowly release the surface tension of the fly before lifting it into his back cast, so he doesn't spook the fish by popping the fly off the water. False casting until he sees the trout rise again, he then lays the fly back onto the water; this time, directly on the seam three feet above the spot the brown came up the last time.

The timing is perfect, and Rickie's cast is perfect, and his fly is convincing enough to trick the brown into rising, and without hesitating, take the fly into his mouth like every other natural he had eaten on that seam for the past hour. Rickie lets the brown disappear and lifts his rod tip, and his line tightens.

Trick watched in awe while his son studied the fish and then efficiently took only two casts to get him to eat. He was now watching as the brown trout rolled and thrashed his head as his son was calmly putting just enough pressure on him to keep him out of the cottonwood roots along the cutbank. It was perfection. It reminded him of Rose.

Trick quickly pushed through thigh-deep water to help his son land the two-foot brown trout. As it curled around the insufficient net they used for wade fishing the smaller streams, Trick knelt down with the fish, making sure to keep his head in the water, facing into the current.

"Son," Trick congratulates him. "That's a monster. Nice work. Do you want to get a pic?"

"I'm good," Rickie answers.

"How about we get one for your old man?" Trick insists.

Rickie held the fish up with the sun glistening off its haloed spots and kyped jaw remnant of last fall's spawn. He smiled while his father took the photo, not with pride for catching the trout, but because of the pride and admiration he knew his father had for him. Facing the brown back into the current, Ricky supported it from getting swept downstream, and when the trout was ready, let him swim out of his hands and back to the cutbank.

"On that note, Rickie," Trick tells him. "We should get back. Mom's waiting."

"Sounds good," Rickie replies with absolute contentment. "I got what I came for."

Trick and Rickie pull into their driveway that winds through old-growth spruce trees. With the popping and crackling of tires rolling over pinecones that sound like corn popping, they park in front of the outside bay of the two-car garage that connects to a modest ranch-style house. The house is perched above the Bitterroot River between Lolo and Missoula and was the only home Rickie has known.

They enter the house to the sounds of a two-year-old

who is obviously late for his nap and the directions of a mother to her seven-year-old, explaining the importance of making sure all the chocolate chips get mixed thoroughly into the cookie batter before dishing them onto the sheet to bake.

"Hey, babe," Trick greets her and pecks her on the cheek.

"Hey, Beth," Rickie greets his mom.

"Beth?" She asks with a look that causes Rickie to shrink. "It's Mom to you."

"Hey, birthday girl," Trick grabs his seven-year-old daughter around the waist, picking her up to kiss her on the cheek. "How's seven feel?"

"So old," Trick's daughter, Emma, replies with her red hair and dimpled cheeks glowing in the sun.

"What do you need from me before the party?" Trick asks Beth.

"How about you get that little monster to take a nap," Beth replies.

"I'm on it," Trick agrees as he chases his youngest son, Russell, from the kitchen into the living room.

It was sixteen years ago, Trick watched the helicopter take Rose from the streambed of the Dearborn, up over the canyon walls, heading north to Choteau. They picked up an ER doctor from the clinic and then flew to Missoula, where a team was waiting for them at St. Patrick Hospital. The team worked on Rose to re-inflate her left lung and stabilize her before inducing her into a coma. She had multiple puncture wounds that would have to be treated for infection, a fractured hip, a collapsed lung, broken ribs, and extensive traumatic brain injuries, including a fractured skull from the bite of the grizzly.

She stayed in Missoula for eight days before her

mother had her transported to Minnesota for subsequent surgeries and treatments. Rose's mother felt it was in her best interest, both medically and for support from her family. Trick stayed by her side for those eight days before she was transported.

During one of the surgeries at the Hennepin Trauma Center in Minneapolis, Rose suffered a perioperative stroke, causing even more damage to her brain. It was unclear at the time what the long-term effects were going to be; however, loss of speech and motor functions was likely. Recovery was also unknown.

It was just after the Montana State High School football tournament in late November when Trick could travel to Minnesota. Rose's mother, Ginny, offered to let Trick stay with them at her house in Baxter, MN, while visiting. Rose was recovering in a St. Cloud rehab center, which was an hour from Ginny's house.

Initially, Trick had called Ginny every day for updates on Rose's condition. Those calls became less frequent as Trick could sense Ginny growing a bit tired of not being able to offer new information or encouraging news. Rose was discharged from the hospital in August; however, her rehab was painstakingly slow, and it was heartbreaking to not be able to offer the news Trick wanted to hear.

Trick flew into Minneapolis, rented a car, and drove directly to the rehab center to meet with Ginny before seeing Rose. He still talked with Ginny at least once a week, getting updates. Ginny had been incredibly honest about her progress, wanting Trick to be prepared for what to expect. Even with that, Trick remained optimistic and assumed she was being a bit pessimistic in an effort to protect Rose and prevent Trick from getting his hopes up for a future that might not be possible; one foiled by an accident, a bear, and an act of forgiveness that might have come a day too late.

Trick and Ginny had formed a relationship over the past few months of talking on the phone. She felt for Trick, for the pain her daughter had brought to him. But she also was a mother to a daughter she loved dearly, and knew what was in her daughter's heart and through the story Trick told, which was an accurate story describing the love they share but also pain and confusion, Ginny developed a smoldering resentment for Trick she hid from him as she knew it would serve no purpose.

She often thought, "Had he shown more compassion or understanding for what Rose had gone through, she wouldn't have been on the Dearborn that day, by herself, and none of this would have happened."

Ginny spent many mornings talking with the priest at her church, trying her best to resolve her pain and resentment, but not yet to the point of giving it up. The best she could do was suppress it and, hopefully, someday, find the capacity to forgive him as well.

She hugged Trick as he walked into the rehab center. They made their way to Rose's room, where she was napping after a physical therapy session. Her day was filled with physical therapy in the morning. A nap. Then lunch, and then speech therapy and other cognitive exercises. Then another nap and dinner, and then she had free time to watch a controlled amount of TV or play games that would work on fine motor skills. Eventually, she was able to spend time with other residents of the clinic for socialization once she was back to being able to carry on conversations without becoming too frustrated with not finding the words she wanted to express herself.

As Trick and Ginny entered Rose's room, her eyes

opened. It was the first time she had seen Trick since the Dearborn. Her face lit up, and she reached out to him. She tried to speak but couldn't formulate the words. He walked over to the side of the bed and placed his hand on her cheek, and kissed her.

"It's ok, babe," he assured her. "We have time. You don't need to talk right now."

It was the fourth morning while Trick was eating breakfast that Ginny's anxiety became too much to hold back. Trick had been with Rose at the rehab center for the better part of the first three days during his visit. He was showing her daughter the hope and promise of someone she believed refused to see the inevitable. Ginny had watched her daughter over the past few months, not showing the progress she had prayed for. She fought with Rose. She advocated for her. She cried for her. She felt the pain her daughter felt physically and emotionally. As much as she wanted to believe in Trick and believe in a love they may have once had, she couldn't stand to watch her daughter hurt any more than necessary.

Lacking the grace of a mother who hasn't seen what Ginny had, she asked, "What's your plan, Trick?"

A little stunned by the tone, Trick replied, "I just…I just want to be there for her."

"You don't owe her anything, Trick," she contested. "I know you mean well, and I bet you feel responsible. We all do, Trick. But we don't know what's going to happen. We don't know how long it will take for her to recover or even if she will. Trick, you have a life in front of you. She can't give you anything. Not right now. Maybe not ever."

"She saved my life, Mrs. Davidson," Trick pleaded. "What I did, after finding out she was the one in the accident, what I told her…I'll never let that go. She saved my life when I met her. I'd never known love before her. I thought football was everything, but she showed me I could live without it and be happy—be happy even like this."

Trick nodded toward his prosthetic.

A wave of humility and compassion flooded over Ginny, and she reached out to hold Trick's hand and said, "I know, honey. I know. Maybe that's what she was here to do. Maybe it was her purpose. But Trick, this isn't yours."

Beth met Trick for the first time in Missoula at the hospital before Rose was transported to Minnesota. Beth had been Rose's best friend since they worked together at AYA. She was living in Missoula while finishing her graduate degree in Social Work at the University of Montana. When the attack happened, she was one of the first people to show up at the hospital and the one person in communication with Ginny before she was able to get to Missoula to help with Rose. She advocated for Rose and made sure she was getting the best care. She was also someone Ginny could lean on.

Those first few days in the hospital, Beth was also there for Trick as she felt horrible for him. She held him while he told the story of what happened, all the way from the accident to him telling Rose to leave him alone. He cried with her for hours sometimes.

When Trick arrived back in Missoula, he reached out to Beth. He needed her, and she felt compelled to be there for him. They spent many evenings talking about the blame he felt for hurting Rose and for causing her to be up on the Dearborn that day. Trick couldn't rid himself of the "what-ifs" and the shame he felt after sending that text message he could never take back. The pain he felt from finding out about his accident was real, but why couldn't he see that it wasn't Rose's desire to hurt him, and why couldn't he have just shown more understanding? Trick struggled with all of these emotions, and now, the thought that he would inevitably have to say goodbye was sending him sinking lower and lower into a wallow of self-pity that only Beth seemed to know how to pull him from.

Beth also kept in contact with Rose and sent letters, and eventually spoke to her on the phone when she was able to carry on sustained conversations. A liaison between Trick and Rose's family, Beth shared Rose's progress with him. Rose knew of the fight she was in and was grateful for the friendship she had with Beth. She was someone she knew was out there in the Universe who would always be there for her and was also the one person she could trust to take care of those things she loved most in her life. One of those things was Chase, and when Rose's mother asked, Beth was happy to foster him.

Through all the pain Trick had shared with Beth and the comfort she was giving him, they grew closer and before long, fell in love. Beth knew it was going to be a difficult conversation, but asked Trick if she could be the one to tell Rose. Trick protested but gave in to Beth, knowing she could break the news in a way that would preserve Rose's dignity.

Rose was aware of her condition. Her mother didn't hide it from her. When Trick was there with her in November, she felt like telling him he needed to move on without her, but she couldn't, even if she could find the words; her condition smothered. When Beth told her she and Trick had fallen in love, Rose felt relieved. She loved Trick more than any person she had ever met, and because of that, she needed to let him go. Trick was the other being she would only trust with Beth, and was happy they fell into each other's lives.

Beth, Rose, and Trick kept in contact throughout Rose's rehab and beyond. Although Rose was not able to attend their wedding, she gave her blessing and was genuinely happy for them. They often spoke of a time when Rose could travel, and that they would have her come back to Montana and stay for a while.

Now, sixteen years after the bear attack and after Trick watched as the helicopter took Rose away, a knock on the door sent a rush of adrenaline through Trick's body. He looked toward Beth and was relieved and proud of his wife as he saw that she was just as excited and just as nervous to hear the knocking, too.

Beth runs to the door before Emma can cut her off. Standing there on the porch is Rose and holding her hand, standing next to her is her daughter, Tricia.

"Oh my," Beth kneels to embrace Tricia. "You are one beautiful little girl."

Tricia leans into her mother's thigh for protection.

Beth stands and wraps her arms around Rose. "You look amazing, Rose. And she's so beautiful."

"Thank you," Rose says humbly. "It's been a long road, but I think the doctors got it all back in place. Is this the birthday girl?"

Emma takes cover behind Trick's frame.

"You do look great," Trick adds as he slings his arm around Rose and kisses her cheek. "Almost as if you got the best of that bear instead of the other way around. It's too bad Jim couldn't make it out."

"Yeah," Rose sighs. "Someone has to pay the bills."

Rose met Jim eight years ago while continuing her rehab. He was a traveling physical therapist who was filling in for her regular therapist, who was on sabbatical and volunteering at a hospital in Cameroon. Jim decided to stay on with the clinic when a permanent position became available. There was a slightly ulterior motive for taking the position, as he had become quite fond of Rose. He couldn't act on his impulses until after the permanent therapist was back in his role with Rose, but once they had established they were no longer professionally engaged, Jim made his feelings known, and a year and a half later, they were married.

"All right, girls," Beth cuts in. "You all gotta get over your shyness. We don't have time for that. Life is way too short. Let's have a damn party!"

Rose stayed in Missoula for three more nights in Mike and Sara's apartment above their garage. It brought back so many memories, but not memories that stirred regret or sorrow. She could love Trick and Beth and her husband, Jim. She was at peace.

The day she left, she met Trick and Beth at the airport to say goodbye. They all hugged and cried and promised they would see each other within the year.

As Rose gathered her bag and scooped Tricia into her arms to make her way to the gate, Trick called out to her, "Hey Rose, tight lines."

"Tight lines, Trick," she replied. "Tight lines."

As she looked out the window of the plane, she remembered the last time anyone called her "Fly." It was Keith, the night before she went up to the Dearborn to end her life. But she didn't end her life. In fact, she fought to live, and although Fly, the sassy female guide, might now only live in the memories of her fishing buddies in that little town of Craig, MT, she has traded that name for another. She is now Mom, and she is happy.

www.ingramcontent.com/pod-product-compliance
Lightning Source LLC
Chambersburg PA
CBHW061117100726

47911CB00013B/577